Barriers

Anderson Special Ops, Book Three

Melody Anne

With
John Henley

Copyright © 2021 Melody Anne

All rights reserved. Except for use in any review, the reproduction or utilization of this work in whole or in part in any form by any electronic, mechanical or other means, now known or hereafter invented, including xerography, photocopying and recording, or in any information storage or retrieval system, is forbidden without the written permission of the author.

This is a work of fiction. Names, characters, places and incidents are either the product of the author's imagination or are used fictitiously and any resemblance to actual persons, living or dead, business establishments, events or locales is entirely coincidental.

Printed and published in the United States of America
Published by Falling Star Publications
Editing by Karen Lawson, Janet Hitchcock

NOTE FROM JOHN HENLEY

This book, focusing on the character Green, is inspired by a person I know who's similar in nature, doing more than ever anticipated or expected at early stages in his life. My prayer is that many of us can take pieces of this story and learn to treat those young of life and respect their desire to learn, achieve and succeed — and for us to not hold back in treating them respectfully when they yearn to do more. People rise to the occasion, especially when given the tools to succeed as well as receive words of encouragement during times of doubt. Be a great ambassador for them and they are all but guaranteed to pass it on.

I'm ever thankful for all of the reviews that The Anderson: Special Ops books have received. We continually learn from each other, and your words push me to think of the way my portion of these stories are being told.

To my wife and children, thank you. The sacrifices each of you made while I was away for training, working overseas, and transitioning back into civilian life, are always appreciated and never taken for granted. None of this would have been remotely feasible, or possible, without your strength and endless encouragement. Your love of family, God, and country are wonderful pillars to build the foundation of life on. Go, be great!

Last, and in no way least, thank you to the men and women serving and protecting the freedoms we enjoy. From the front-line warriors, to the supply chain gurus, to the cooks in the galley, to the decision makers, and everyone in between, all of you together make the mission work, and when it works well it's a thing of beauty. From my family to you and yours, thank you for letting us stand on your shoulders. Continue to be the giants you are.

PROLOGUE

"Sleigh bells ring, are you listening? In the lane, snow is glistening..."

"What in the actual hell are you singing?" Green asked as he looked over at Smoke, who was gazing through a pair of Pulsar Accolade 2 LRF XP50 Thermal Binoculars, the best of the best with built-in laser rangefinders, recorders, and video sharing. Of course, Brackish had upped the technology inside them even more. Every tool they used was the best, and this was no exception.

"A Christmas song. It felt appropriate," Smoke answered, smiling as he continued his song. *"A beautiful sight... we're happy tonight..."*

"Stop, just stop!" Green said. "It's the Fourth of July in case you were wondering. Were you dropped on your head a lot as a child?"

"There's nothing wrong with feeling the holiday spirit," Smoke said before chuckling in his rich, deep timbre.

"There's a lot wrong when you're singing Christmas carols on Independence Day," Green told him with a roll of his eyes. But there was a smirk on his lips that said he was enjoying the Christmas carol even if he didn't want to admit it.

"I'm bored. I despise these babysitting missions," Smoke said. "Why do Sleep and Eyes get to have all of the fun while we're in the middle of the hills instead of in the action?"

"Because they drew the long straws, so they get to have good food and fun. *You* drew the short straw. Besides that, you stand out too much in a crowd, and *I* like to keep a low profile," Green told him.

"And I have to listen to both of you whine," Brackish said through the comms.

"Quit inserting yourself into the conversation," Smoke told their tech genius. "That's a sign of narcissism."

"Oh, little boys, there's no denying I'm a narcissist. It's hard not to be when I'm the best of the best and everything I touch turns to gold," Brackish said with a chuckle.

"You might be good with the tech stuff, but we all know I'm the best at everything else," Smoke said, cockiness radiating off of him in droves.

"I'm the youngest and can run circles around all of you," Green piped in.

"Neither of you have survived walking close to one hundred miles while your body is loaded with bullets," Sleep piped up.

"Fake news," Smoke said, making all of the men laugh.

"Hey, I was there," Eyes said. Sleep groaned, knowing what was coming next. "Of course, it *was* Sleep who shot me all to hell . . . not the enemy."

"Maybe you shouldn't have been sneaking around like a stalker beneath a MILF's window," Sleep countered.

"Really, Eyes? Really?" Green asked, bursting into laughter.

"Hey, don't knock hot mamas," Smoke said. "I've had a few of them in my days."

"There's only one future mom I'm interested in," Sleep said, his voice going mushy.

The entire team went silent for about three seconds, which was unheard of. Chad was the one to break it.

"Are you pregnant?" Chad asked.

"Yep, it's been killing me not to say anything, but Avery's through the first trimester so I can officially announce I'm gonna be a dad," Sleep said with pride.

All of the men piped in with congratulations and enthusiasm. They weren't only tough and the best, they were loyal, and they knew what family meant.

"I guess since it's not my kid, I get to spoil the hell out of it," Smoke said. "And she'll never complain about me singing Christmas songs in July."

"Are you saying you won't spoil your own kid?" Green asked.

Smoke laughed then held his hands up in surrender. "I'm never, ever, ever, *ever* having kids. No way. No how. I'd have to get married to do that, and this fine piece of machinery isn't falling into the marriage trap."

"I have a feeling you're *very* wrong about that," Brackish said. "I thought the same thing, but when that woman comes along who takes the breath straight out of your lungs, and nearly sends you into cardiac arrest because she makes your heart pound so hard, there's no turning back."

"Nope. I'm the love-'em-and-leave-'em type," Smoke assured the team.

"The biggest men fall the hardest," Chad said. "Trust me, I know."

"Just cause you losers like falling for the *marriage flu* as Hudson Anderson is so famous for saying, doesn't mean all of us are so prone to the illness."

"I like to think of it as Cupid shooting a nice fat arrow into your ass," Eyes said. "Those arrows can even penetrate *your* thick skin."

"I think you're far more likely to fall than I am," Smoke told Eyes.

"Nope. Not gonna happen. I'm just a broken old man who needs a lot of attention and care," Eyes said.

"Broken my ass," Brackish countered.

In reality both Eyes and Sleep had nearly lost their lives on their last mission with their SEAL team. It was a miracle they'd survived. But even saying that, none of them considered themselves weak or less than who they were before bullets had ripped into their bodies.

"I'm broken," Eyes insisted. "That means I need a lot of medical care and sponge baths . . . from multiple nurses."

"You need help," Chad said with a chuckle. "*All* of you. The kind where they put you in straitjackets."

That made them all laugh again. "Don't forget that *you're* the one who hired us," Green said. "So, who needs more help? Us? Or You?"

Chad's sigh came through the comms loud and clear. "Checkmate," he said after a few seconds.

"Sleigh bells ring, are you listening . . ." Smoke began singing yet another Christmas song. Then the air shifted.

"Hold up," Green said, all humor dropping from his voice. The team was instantly on alert. No one asked questions, no one said a word. They waited. They knew that tone, and they knew things had gotten serious . . .

CHAPTER ONE

Two weeks ago, Senator Miller had called Green, aka Hendrick Meeks, since he was only known to her by his real name. She'd requested a meeting with him . . . again.

Hendrick had been at the wedding reception for one of his best friends, Brackish, known to the world as Steve Bregon. The senator had made her first call to him then. He'd been putting her off for weeks, and he had her exactly where he wanted her — panting at his feet.

The Anderson Special Ops team, founded by Joseph Anderson, and run by Chad Remington, had been busy since they'd been organized the year before. From the beginning of their operation they'd been going a thousand miles per hour, things speeding up even more since Brackish and Erin had eloped.

Though this connection with the senator was essential to their ultimate goal of eliminating the huge drug ring that plagued Seattle and the surrounding cities, the consensus among the team was to make the senator wait to meet with Green.

She was eager, which put the power in their hands. It was quite fun for Green as he knew beyond a shadow of a doubt that Senator Miller was used to getting what she wanted — and she *wanted* Green. The fact that she wasn't getting exactly what she wanted *when* she wanted it was humorous to them all. She might talk a big game, but she was about as useful as a cotton ball in a rock fight.

Green waited . . . and then waited a bit more as call after call went unanswered.

After the fourth day of waiting, the senator had one of her lackies call Green to check on the status of their meeting. He ignored that call too.

After a solid week passed, a new lackey called, this one leaving a stern message stating that a meeting needed to be solidified. He ignored this call too, all the while grinning.

When ten days had passed since her first call, Green got a call from the president of the political action committee, saying there were issues needing to be addressed immediately. He didn't answer that call either.

"Well, guys, I just got a call from the chief operations officer for the shipyard. He's the father of the idiot kid who thinks he's my boss there." He paused and grinned. "You know the senator has called, then had two lackies call, then the president of the political action committee was unleashed on me. They're all eating out of the palms of my hands, and none of them can stand the fact I'm not responding — especially the senator."

"What did the COO have to say?" Chad asked.

They were all sitting around their table in their operations center, food getting consumed, Brackish typing away on his computer, and Eyes and Sleep cracking jokes. Smoke seemed bored, and Chad was rolling his eyes as he tried to rein in the unruly group. Although they might be unruly, they knew exactly when it was time to get serious.

Green looked smug. "The chief said there's nothing on my schedule to prevent me from meeting with the senator. He didn't threaten, but he made it clear I *would* meet with her."

"Interesting," Brackish said, looking up from his computer.

"Yep, he said I could take the time off work whenever, day or night, since she is a VIP," Green said.

"Day *or* night?" Eyes said with a laugh.

"Yep, looks like someone's gonna take one for the team," Sleep injected as he leaned back and smiled.

"Whatever, Sleep," Green said. "I'm not taking *anything anywhere* for the team." They all busted up.

"Is it putting out, or putting up?" Smoke asked between breaths of air as he held his stomach.

"How am *I* the mature one here?" Green asked, refusing to crack a smile, though it was difficult to hold back.

"None of us are the gigolo in this situation," Sleep said.

"I do have to say the pressure for us to meet is insane," Green said.

"That's because she wants your hot bod," Eyes told him.

"It *is* an incredible body," Green said as he flexed.

"It's nothing like this one," Smoke said, standing up and doing a full spin for them before he flexed and kissed his massive bicep.

"Oh, Smoke, how I want you," Sleep said in a girlie voice as he fluttered his lashes.

Eyes stopped laughing long enough to get serious. "Okay, okay, enough of Green's bedroom tangles. We've made Senator Miller wait long enough. Go ahead and schedule the meeting."

"You got it," Green replied. He pulled out his phone and sent a message to the two lackies who'd been repeatedly dinging him; *Friday between five and eight will work.* He smiled. Senator Miller would be ticked that he was dictating the time as if he was busier than she was.

Brackish looked up, his face now serious as well. "They'll pat you down and wand you before you're allowed to meet the senator. I have the perfect undetectable devices they can't possibly find with their shitty equipment." His total disdain of anybody else's technology was amusing.

"Perfect," Green replied as his phone dinged. He looked up with a satisfied smirk. "They are hot to meet. I already have a reply from both of them. We're confirmed for Friday at 1900 hours at The Pink Door downtown."

"Mmm, isn't that next to a nice cozy hotel?" Smoke asked.

"Yep, he's *definitely* taking one for the team," Sleep replied, putting his hands behind his head and leaning back.

"Bite me," Green said.

"Nope, I think that's the *senator's* job," Smoke said. "I have much more sophisticated tastes than your leathery skin."

Before Green could reply, Brackish piped in. "What if your boss makes you work late?" His mock serious tone made the men chuckle and Green growl. He hated that kid. "Has there been a weekend yet that he hasn't tried to get you to work? I think he might also have a crush on you. Maybe he, the senator, and you can all go out together."

"I'll hook you up with that if you want," Green said, turning it right back on his teammate. "I'm pretty sure I'm getting a promotion. Now that the word's out that I'm being courted by a US senator, it seems my talents are being requested in other areas of the company. I think this goes even deeper than we imagined."

"Yeah, this is going to be fun to bring down. I like leaving nothing more than a pile of ashes," Eyes said, the glint of combat in his eyes. They'd all served a lot of missions but doing this one without their hands tied was their favorite.

"My lovely *boss,* Andrew, told me the other day that he didn't think I was ready for a move as there was so much more for me to learn," Green scoffed. "As if there's an art to stacking boxes."

"Hey, don't knock a good job," Sleep said. "I stacked many boxes in my younger days and a paycheck is a paycheck." He was still smiling but there was truth to his words. They'd all done their share of less than desirable jobs. They were all grateful to have had employment.

Chad chimed in next. "You *do* have a lot to learn about this business," he said, smiling.

"What?" Green asked, confused. Chad knew this was a fake job. Chad knew what Green's bank account was — and it was large.

"Yep, if you work hard and put your nose to the grindstone, you might just make it from assistant management into senior assistant management. There are rungs on the ladder you can't skip so take your time and don't do everything at once."

The room went utterly silent for a moment as Chad's words processed. He normally didn't joke with the team. He let them blow off steam but when he spoke it was almost always with a purpose, so they were stunned into silence before they erupted.

"Good one, Chug," Smoke said. "I didn't think you had a sense of humor."

"I could school all of you," Chad told them.

"That's because you're ancient," Sleep said. "Unlike us young, strapping studs."

"I'll take you on any day of the week," Chad said with a laugh.

After they got their laughter out of the way, the meeting continued with a review of the different operations they'd been working, the breakdown of players they were following, and the boring stuff Brackish could go on and on and on about for hours if they didn't rein him in.

When they were finished it was just Eyes and Chad left in the room to go over the next missions. Luckily the rest of them didn't have to stay for the even more boring items on the agenda.

What scared all of them — and they didn't often get scared — was Damien Whitfield was still at the top of their list of suspects. Damning information continued piling up on his movements, and his financial gains, tucked away in hidden accounts the last few months, had been staggering. None of them wanted to find him guilty — none of them wanted to take that evidence back to Joseph. They had no doubt it would break the man's heart.

Joseph was known as a powerhouse around the world, but he was a family man through and through. There was nothing he wouldn't do for his family, nothing he wouldn't sacrifice for them. If he found out one of his nephews was a big player in a bad game, it would crush him. But no matter how much they tried finding a way to prove Damien innocent, they couldn't clear him.

Sometimes their job really sucked.

And sometimes the bad guys weren't who you thought they'd be. They might be masking themselves as a doctor, a lawyer, a paramedic, a schoolteacher, or even a businessman in the light of day. But what they did in the veil of darkness was sick and twisted and ruined lives. They prayed that wouldn't be Damien. They prayed they wouldn't have to break their benefactor's heart.

They'd soon find out . . .

CHAPTER TWO

Green walked into the shipping yard on Friday morning, knowing he wouldn't be returning to his current position after this day. Human Resources had called him the night before to schedule a meeting, telling him to report to them at 0700 hours sharp. He could imagine his little bossman was seething at losing some of the power he'd been trying to lord over the big man since Green had taken this assignment. The kid truly loved to hold his position over others.

As Green moved forward, stopping to talk to a few of the men he'd worked with over the last few months, he was surprised to learn he liked several of them. He laughed to himself at having any sentimental thoughts at all about the warehouse and his fake job there. It was also amusing that he was going to become a so-called corporate paper pusher.

He stopped when he came up to his young boss, Andrew. He wasn't disappointed this would be his last time seeing the young punk. Some people were born to be leaders while others were pretenders who thought if they puffed out their chests enough and talked down to others it would make them into what they wanted to be — but it never worked.

Pasting on his famous smile, he held out a hand to shake "Thanks for all you've done for me, Andrew. It's truly been an . . . interesting experience," Green told him.

The kid acted as if he hadn't seen Green's hand. "Yep. No problem. Just give me a ring when you get lost up in the big offices. You know I can bail you out." He paused, probably giving Green time to jump in and tell the kid how wonderful he was. It didn't happen. Green waited him out.

"Well, get out of here before I call HR and take back my recommendation for your promotion," he finished. Green was very aware that was a bald-faced lie; no way he'd recommended him to management. If the kid had anything to do with it, it would be him sitting in that office upstairs. That was the epitome of success for the punk while it was a serious demotion for Green who'd already developed and sold a multimillion-dollar corporation.

"You got it, Bud," Green said. He didn't add more before he walked away from the kid, letting out a sigh of relief that it was over. He didn't have to pretend the jackass was his boss any longer. He'd love to tell him who he truly was. The kid would probably crap his pants. But then again, he was so forgettable he wouldn't cross Green's mind ever again after this day.

Green made his way to the HR suite and was immediately directed to a woman's office who was on the phone as he appeared in her doorway. She sent him an apologetic look, waved him inside, then pointed to a chair at a large round table overlooking the shipyard and the beautiful Puget Sound. It was an incredibly impressive view, especially for an industrial work site.

He sat quietly while the woman finished her conversation. When she was done, she hung up, stood, and moved over to Green. He rose as well and took her hand when she offered it.

"Good morning, Mr. Meeks. Thank you for arriving on time. I'm Sue Bailey, the director of the Human Resources department."

"It's a pleasure to meet you, Ms. Bailey," Green easily replied. He could certainly hold his own in a board room, so an HR department was like walking on a soft bed of grass.

"Please call me Sue. I insist," she replied, her smile genuine, reaching her eyes. He wondered how she worked for this company. He wondered how many people were crooked in it. She certainly wasn't — he'd make a wager on that.

"That's a difficult one for me, but if you insist," Green said with manners instilled in him. "And please call me Hendrick. Mr. Meeks was my gramps, and I always look around when I hear it," he added with a chuckle.

"I was my gramps's favorite from the start so I understand those little pangs at hearing something familiar," she told him. Then she shook her head. "Sorry about that. It's so easy to get off track and there's a lot to do today."

"Never apologize for sharing a memory," Green told her. "I love a good gramps tale."

"Me too," she said. Then she sat, and he joined her. "Let's get started."

They easily chatted as she laid out Green's new transition with the company. He was shocked at how pleased she seemed for him. He was once again convinced she was a truly good person. She walked him through the new pay structure and gave him papers on his added benefits. The conversation and signatures took about half an hour by the time it was all said and done.

"Are you ready to see your office?" she asked when his last paper was signed.

He had to fake enthusiasm as he replied. "I can't wait."

Her smile turned up. "I know I was beyond excited the first time I stepped inside this room. I started on the floor years and years ago, then pushed my way through college while working full-time and taking care of two kids. But the long days and sleepless nights paid off in the end," she said.

"I love hearing a success story," Green said, meaning it.

"Me too. I knew I wanted to do more in life but wasn't sure how I'd get there. I finally decided with hard work and iron-willed determination I could get it done. And now here I am."

They moved down the hallway, stopping a few times so she could introduce him to people he categorized for later. Brackish already had all of their names, but it was good for Green to see them in person and look into their eyes. You could read a lot about a person in their eyes.

"Here you go," she said as she walked through an open door.

He followed her inside the small office that was outfitted with a desk, chair, file cabinet, and empty walls. "It doesn't look like much now, but you'll be able to make it your own. Bring in some photos, certificates, posters, anything to make you feel comfortable. Sometimes clients come up here though, so make sure you follow the company guidelines of what is and isn't appropriate."

"Of course," Green said.

They chatted another couple of minutes then she was gone, and he was left in the nearly empty room, wondering how long he'd survive in his fake position. He couldn't stand being locked inside. He hadn't minded the shipping yard so much because he'd gotten to move and get outside as much as possible. But this room was a nightmare come to life.

His new position was basically a split of working for the COO as well as following the orders of the company's political action committee and essentially being their gofer. He didn't like being anyone's gofer.

Who in their right mind woke up one day and said I want to be a US senator? In Green's jaded mind, it was someone who wanted something. Some of the team members disagreed with him, saying there truly were those out there who felt a need to serve the people and the country they loved. When Green met one of them he'd admit to being wrong — not a second before then, though.

One thing Green knew for sure was the high players in this company were definitely crooked, because what company in their right mind would allow an employee to come and go at the whim of a political action committee? Green wouldn't have made the tens of millions he'd made if he'd allowed his staff to come and go as they pleased — or worse yet, influenced by political figures.

Green's new boss was Andrew Senior, the punk's father. Unlike the kid, the father knew his stuff and had a very old-school work ethic. There weren't a lot of rough edges in the way Andrew Sr. spoke.

The man was above average intellectually and worked hard and long hours. It was easy to see why people were willing to follow him. That was something worth paying attention to. Green couldn't see how the man had such a lazy, power-hungry son. Maybe Andrew Sr. had just worked so many hours he hadn't taken the time to instill the same values in his child. Or maybe his morals and ethics hadn't passed down to his son.

It didn't take long for his new boss to appear at his door.

"I hope you're settling into your new position," Andrew Sr. said.

"I think it'll take a while to get comfortable, but I've never failed to conquer something I've put my mind to," Green replied.

"Very good," Andrew said. "That's the kind of attitude that builds up a company."

"I agree with you there," Green said.

Then Andrew got to the real point of his visit. "I hear you're meeting with Senator Miller this evening."

"Yes, it appears so," Green said, watching for a reaction, trying to figure out how much Andrew had to do with the politician.

"Make sure you're a positive ambassador for yourself as well as this company. I don't know a whole lot about you, but the people I've talked to have all said the same things — you're a straight shooter, hard worker, and do what you say you'll do. You might be a bit of a late bloomer in the business world, but if you want to make a go at this with a real career, working here will give you the resources you need to make that happen." The man seemed to mean exactly what he was saying. No wonder Sue loved her job so much.

"Thank you, sir. I appreciate the opportunity to prove myself," Green said. "As far as tonight goes, I don't exactly know what they want to meet me about, but I'm excited to find out." He gave a genuine smile as he forced himself not to laugh. It was a joke how many people wanted to rub elbows with those they deemed important.

It was also a good thing the company he'd sold had kept his name and face out of it. If this man before him knew of that sale, he'd know it was a joke for Green to be working for him. He was nearly a billionaire, and men like him didn't work for another corporation.

The reality of humanity was that everyone came into the world the same way, and they all exited the same way too. Just because a person rose to celebrity status of some kind didn't make them any better or any worse than the next person. Reputation was also a way to lift a person onto a pedestal. It was odd how politicians, outside of the President, had become so coveted — and it had begun when the internet had made its appearance in the world.

Before the internet the average American didn't have a clue who the congressmen or senators were for the US. They might know who they were in their own state, but even that was doubtable. The internet had changed all of that. Now politicians flashed across screens on a daily basis, and recognition of those faces raised their status.

In Green's opinion that was the biggest fail of society as a whole. The politicians and people alike had all seemed to have forgotten that the whole point of *serving* in the government was the word *serving*. They didn't *own* the people, they *represented* them — and somewhere along the way everyone had forgotten that one very important fact.

Those thoughts all flashed through his mind in a matter of seconds. Andrew smiled as he patted Green on the back.

"Enjoy this ride while you're on it," Andrew told him. "If the senator sees something in you, you must be special. I want to hear all about your meeting on Monday morning. Why don't you take the rest of today off so you can get ready for your big night?"

Green cringed as he almost expected the man to tell him to *take one for the team*. Luckily that didn't happen. He internally rolled his eyes.

"Thank you, sir. I appreciate it. It's also great to meet you. I hope you don't regret it," Green said.

They shook hands and the COO took off. Green was quickly behind him. He might not be excited to meet with the senator, but he was ecstatic to move forward with his true mission. The senator was crooked. He had no doubt about it — now he just had to find the evidence to put a nail in her coffin.

CHAPTER THREE

Brackish leaned back, bored as he hacked into the server of the restaurant where the senator was meeting Green later that night. He loved a challenge and hacking a ridiculously unsecure server didn't ring any of his bells. He took control of the program used for seating diners. He found that Senator Miller and Green were at a table for two in a quiet corner — she wasn't playing around in her quest for romance. That made him smile. He enjoyed the torture Green was going to be put through acting humbled by her attention while also giving off an air of indifference.

Once he mapped the tables at the restaurant, he sent Smoke to discretely place a few of his top-of-the-line undetectable listening devices in the lobby, bathrooms, and dining area. He watched as Smoke did his job smoothly without a single eye seeing what he was doing — and the man still had time to flirt with the pretty young hostess, making her blush and swoon. The man truly was good.

Brackish laughed when Smoke placed devices beneath the lip of the table Green and Senator Miller were sitting at all with the breathless hostess at his side, not seeing his sleight of hand. Brackish and the rest of the team would hear everything from their conversation right down to the sound of pants rubbing together.

"How's it going?" Chad asked as he looked over Brackish's shoulder.

"We have such good sound, we're going to hear the friction of Green's pants when he gets a boner for the pretty senator," Brackish said smugly.

Chad groaned. "TMI, Brackish, TMI."

"Well, we can also read their body temps, so we'll know when either one of them gets all hot and bothered and be able to detect their heart rates. Thermal dynamics can see how much the senator actually wants our little Green."

"Little? Who in the hell are you calling little?" Green asked as he stepped into the room.

Brackish spun around and grinned at Green. "We're just getting the sensors placed in the restaurant so we know when you're smoldering for the senator," he told him, while clicking a button and shifting the image on the screen.

"The senator is hot, but I don't go for the power-hungry types," Green said with a shrug as he sat across from Brackish. He wasn't interested in looking at the computer. He trusted his team. They all trusted each other.

"I like a powerful woman," Smoke said through a microphone that came through loud and clear. He'd just exited the restaurant and was on his way back to headquarters. "It makes it so much more fun to tame them."

"I'm going to replay you saying that at your wedding," Brackish promised.

Smoke laughed. "I'm not worried about that as I'll never get married," he assured them.

"That's what I said too," Brackish said with a laugh. "Stupidest vow I ever made for myself. Now that I have Erin in my life, I realize what a blessing she is. Besides, can you imagine how lonely it would be to go home to an empty house for the rest of your life? Why would anyone choose that?" For once there was no teasing in his voice.

"I have to admit it sucks sometimes," Eyes said as he entered the room. "But it doesn't suck so much that I want to give up my freedom of coming and going as I please."

"I thought the same thing," Sleep said. "And sometimes the marriage isn't perfect, but that's when we grow the most. I'm a better person with Avery in my life than without her, so I'll take marriage any day of the week over my bachelor life before her."

"I'll drink to that," Chad said as he lifted his coffee cup and took a long swallow.

"I'm going to work out. The waiting is driving me crazy," Green said. The team went back to what they were doing as Green headed to the state-of-the-art gym they'd insisted on having at the facility. They worked hard, and they needed to not only keep fit but burn off energy on a daily basis. They all spent a lot of time in the gym.

When he finished pushing himself to the limit and headed to the showers, his phone pinged. He pulled it from his pocket and found a message from one of the senator's lackies stating she needed Green's address so he could be picked up. A pang of irritation filled him. He didn't like being fetched, and he didn't like being under their control. He would've much rather driven there himself. But he'd play their game for now. His team would be nearby with a car if and when he wanted to leave.

He'd been staying at the ops center since he'd come there, not because he couldn't afford a place, but because it had everything he wanted, and he wasn't seeing anyone, so he hadn't needed an undercover house. Now he did. The day before Chad had figured out they'd want to know where he lived, so they'd found a place and hired a host of movers and decorators who were nearly finished installing everything a bachelor would have in his home.

I can get there on my own, Green texted the lackey back, just wanting to show the entire team working for the senator that he wasn't a lapdog. There was a fine line between acting starstruck and being a puppy dog.

I must insist, sir. I've been given direct orders to drive you myself. MB.

Green looked at his phone having no idea what the MB was about.

What is MB? He texted back.

Mallory Black. I'm the chief of staff for Senator Miller. Please send your address and I'll be there to pick you up at 5:30.

Green knew Mallory's type instantly. Male or female, this type of person was a go-getter without the experience or that *thing* to be the boss, however always wanting to be *next* to the boss, hoping some of the praise and accolades would spill over on them. Some assistants, which is what they really were, were okay people. But throwing out their titles said a lot about them.

Green didn't argue with Mallory, but sent his address, knowing his alter ego — the man they thought he was — would be excited about getting picked up. He threw his phone on the bed as he stripped and headed for the shower, getting ready quicker than he wanted so he could get to the house before MB arrived.

He barely beat her there.

With no surprise, at exactly 5:30PM on the dot, a blacked-out SUV pulled into his driveway. Before the text came that his ride was there, he bound from the house with a smile and a wave to the driver.

Green couldn't stand the fakeness of it all. Through every adventure he'd taken in life, he'd made sure to be himself. It didn't matter if it was while he held a long gun in the freezing cold, the scorching heat, or the melting humidity of a location he was at, or if he was sitting in a board room where he was in command as the youngest person in the room by at least twenty years and making decisions that moved millions and millions of dollars — he was always himself. There were many sides to Green, but fakeness and insincerities weren't a part of him at all. Being fake made his skin crawl.

He moved down his sidewalk, opened the passenger door, and climbed inside. He immediately shifted as he turned and held out a hand. "You must be Mallory. Great to meet you," he said. "Love the ride." He was putting as much enthusiasm in his voice as he could.

Mallory, dressed exactly as he'd expected, was already backing from his driveway. She ignored his hand and gave him a brief look of disdain as if he were a bug on her expensive heels, and she was far too important to be playing taxi driver to a punk like him. He was instantly intrigued. She might be dressed the way he'd expected in a sleek, fitted business suit with thin wire-framed glasses, little makeup, and no fragrance to speak of, but there was fire in her eyes that had his body stirring in a way that shocked him.

Once they were on the street, she took a breath and seemed to remember to act civilized. His hand was still in the air as a challenge. She sighed, reached out, and clasped his fingers briefly in hers. "Mallory Black. It's good to meet you," she finally said. Then she faced forward and focused on driving.

The zing of electricity that shot through him at their very brief touch surprised the hell out of him. He hadn't felt that enticing jolt of electricity in a long time. It was too bad she wasn't the senator, that she wasn't the mission.

He decided to observe her while they made the long drive to the restaurant. She didn't talk, and neither did he. Instead, their drive was met with a mixture of talk radio, PBS, and a ten-second phone call from the other lackey who'd texted Green, confirming the retrieval of Green and that they were on their way. If Mallory had the ability to make small talk, Green couldn't find it.

The vehicle pulled up to the entrance of The Pink Door, and a valet opened Green's door. He stepped out, and before he could say *thanks for the ride,* the SUV pulled away. Mallory had been a strange woman indeed. Very attractive in a nerdy way, but wound way too tight for him. He liked a secure woman who let go and went wild in the bedroom.

Even though there'd been a spark between them, he knew it would sizzle real fast. She most certainly didn't have a kissing game, let alone a kinky bone in her body that he was curious about. The top of her suit had fitted quite close to her. He wanted to know about the bottom half.

The other lackey who'd called while they were on their way stood at the entrance to the restaurant, waiting to pull Green to his table. It appeared they didn't like making the senator wait for anyone. That's why they'd insisted on getting him there early. Just as Brackish had stated, they did a security sweep on him, searching for weapons or bugs. He came up clear with their amateur equipment.

"The senator will be with you shortly," lackey number two informed him.

"I'm here pretty early," Green said. He was having a difficult time staying in his role of star-struck lapdog.

"Senator Miller's a busy woman. It's better for you to wait for her than for her to wait for you," lackey boy said with a cool look, indicating he didn't see why the senator was taking anytime at all with Green. Green smiled at him, seeming to fluster the man. He turned and Green followed him inside.

"Please send an affirmative text I'm coming through," Green whispered as he walked a few feet behind the lackey. He felt his phone instantly vibrate. He pulled it from his interior jacket pocket to see a childish response — *You're coming through . . . by taking one for the team.*

No one is taking anything for the team, Green replied.

"Have a seat. Order an appetizer and a drink. The senator will be here shortly," lackey number two said, then turned and walked away.

This is gonna take a while, Brackish texted. *She's nowhere near the place yet.*

I figure this is all a part of the game, he replied.

And it did take a while — forty-five minutes, in fact. Maybe that was his punishment. He'd made her wait too long to have a meeting and now she was attempting to gain her power back. She'd never met a man quite like Green before, he was sure of that.

There was s stir in the restaurant as a few people buzzed at the sight of the senator walking inside. She moved with purpose to his table. He stood to shake hands with her, they exchanged greetings, and then sat in unison.

She was a well-polished politician. An easy smile stayed on her face throughout their opening lines, giving any onlookers the appearance that she was as happy as could be to be in the restaurant as simply one of the normal people she lorded over. Everything about her was put together perfectly, and Green surmised it took a team of four or five people to get every piece put into place.

While she wasn't the stunning model type, she was an attractive woman, and it was evident her curvy figure was the result of more than simple genetics. She obviously worked out and seemingly had had work done. He could spot fake lips and boobs any day of the week. He wasn't knocking it, either. If mother-nature didn't give a person the gifts they wanted, why not go out and buy them for yourself? What a person did with their own body was their own business and he'd sure appreciated a good surgeon a time or two in his life when his hands had been roaming over the work of those doctors.

"I'm glad our schedules finally aligned, and we have time to meet," Senator Miller said with a Cheshire cat smile and a glint in her eyes that told him she knew how to play games just as well as he did. She was far more his type than the prickly woman who'd chauffeured him to the place.

"Sorry about the delays, but I appreciate you taking me out for dinner. I have to admit, I'm confused about why," Green said, trying to keep the character of a barely educated man who'd gotten lucky in life and was now able to intrigue a senator.

She didn't hesitate. "I don't beat around the bush, Hendrick. It isn't my style — in work *or* play," she said. The waiter stopped her from speaking for a moment as he offered a bottle of wine she'd preordered and poured their first glasses. Green was very aware she hadn't asked his opinion on their drinks. He didn't say anything about it as he waited for the waiter to leave so the senator could continue speaking, which she did as if they hadn't been interrupted.

"First, please, call me Anna. Second, I find you attractive. When we met at the announcement party there was no way to talk to you privately and, unfortunately for me, the dating scene in my world has a very limited pool," she finished before taking a sip of her three-hundred-dollar bottle of wine. He knew the brand and how pricy it was. She didn't blush at her bold words, and it was apparent she hadn't anticipated being rejected. She'd been at the top of the totem pole for a long time and probably hadn't been turned down for anything since she was a child.

Green felt his phone buzz and knew there was a text from the team that would piss him off right about then. He smiled as he held his hand out beside the table where the senator couldn't see it and flipped up his middle finger. He was sure his team saw it loud and clear. His phone buzzed again, and he ignored it, again.

Creating a false sense of embarrassment and eager excitement, Green squirmed in his seat while not making eye contact with the senator when he said, "Well, I, um, are you . . .?" timing his response to be perfect. Green knew he'd nailed it when he looked up and locked eyes with Anna Miller. "Are you saying you want to date me, Senator Miller?"

She reached over and gently put her hand on top of his, keeping her eyes locked on his. "I said to call me Anna. I insist," she told him. Then she softened her tone. "I don't know if I'm ready for dating, but I'd like to see where things can go between us. Let's have dinner and find out where the night might take us."

His phone buzzed again, and he didn't even have to read it to know what was being sent to him. He was going to kick all of their asses when this night was over. He reached in and turned off his phone with a quick flick of his thumb.

"I think that sounds good," Green said, then held up his glass. "To where the night might take us," he finished. The senator gladly met his glass with hers as she gave him a flirty smile. It was so fake it made his teeth ache, but he gave it right back to her.

The night went in the direction Green had figured it would go — in the direction his team had figured it would go. They talked politics, sports, family, and everything in between. Green knew what he was telling her was a bunch of crap, and he had no doubt it was the same from her. But it's what people who just wanted to get laid without having a commitment did — they talked to impress.

Green was normally very adept at adjusting to a conversation and then moving it in the direction he wanted it to go. But with the senator it wasn't as easy for him — she was a great match to his wit. There was something about her he hadn't expected, and he found it actually interested him.

As the meal came to an end and the obvious point of sitting and socializing in that setting passed its time, the senator looked over to Green and stated, "I'd like to continue this evening. There's a private wine bar not far from here that I'm a member of. Would you like to join me?"

It might've been formed as a question, but Green knew if he didn't go, there'd never be another invitation of any kind from her. This evening had to go a very specific way and he needed to walk a razor thin tightrope. He agreed — taking one for the damn team.

They were driven to a wine bar, a member-only establishment and those members were paying a high price for that exclusivity. A bar made of African blackwood with sandalwood inlays, surrounded by deep leather high-backed barstools, was the centerpiece of the place. The Brazilian rosewood flooring was polished to a high shine. High-top tables had two to four seats surrounding them with candle centerpieces and low-hung crystal chandeliers. The atmosphere screamed money, and the members wore clothes that likely cost more than most people's mortgage payments with jewelry that cost as much as the house.

They were in the center of the room when a voice called out to Senator Miller, making an audible hush throughout the room as people turned to look at the could-be President of the United States walk inside as if she owned the place, her arm in Green's. They wanted to know who he was — and it was more than obvious she loved making them wait.

"Madam President," another voice said, obvious enthusiasm in her voice. Senator Miller had a loyal following, that was for sure, and a lot of people who were willing to buy her stories.

"Hello everyone. Thank you for the warm greetings," the senator said. "But I don't want a fuss. I'm just here with my friend to have a quiet drink or two." She was smooth with her words, letting them know they were important to her, but she wanted time alone. She did it without offending anyone in the room.

"This is my friend, Hendrick, and we're going to take the Mariner room as I need to talk shop for a bit. After that I'll join you at the bar to tell some stories about who caught the biggest fish." She finished her sentence with a fake laugh, causing the patrons in the room to chuckle along with her.

"You enjoy yourself, Senator," someone said.

"Yep, looks like it's you who caught the biggest fish tonight," another piped in.

"I just might have," Senator Miller whispered in Green's ear. A shudder rippled through him. He wasn't sure if it was one of desire or revulsion. Maybe a few more drinks would let him know.

The Mariner room had a couch running along the back wall with an oversized chair on each side of it. Well-placed shelves were filled with leather-bound books, and multiple small tables were around each seat with a coffee table on top of the silk Persian rug.

"Please, have a seat on the couch. I'm going to grab a couple bottles of wine and some glasses. Do you prefer red or white?" she asked plainly. After the restaurant he was surprised she was asking.

"I don't drink much wine, but I liked what we had at the restaurant," Green said. It was an outright lie. He drank plenty of wine to know exactly what he did and didn't like.

"I'll be right back," she replied, then walked away.

Green had to admit her curves from the backside were just as flattering as those from the front. Maybe there was more to this woman that he'd given her credit for. She was definitely power-hungry, which had always excited him. Beyond that, he wouldn't mind bragging to the boys he'd bedded the, possibly, first female president. A little skip in his normally steady heart rate made him realize it had been far too long since he'd last had sex.

He remembered he'd turned off his phone and pulled it from his pocket while he had a minute alone. There were a couple of dozen messages, but the last one popped up; *Lost comms, please confirm all is well. Smoke is trailing you, but not inside.*

All is good. Don't wait up.

He turned off the sound again and placed his phone in his pocket before he could get a response. It was tucked away just as the senator entered the room, carrying two bottles of wine and four glasses, and sporting a big smile.

"Is someone joining us?" Green asked innocently, already knowing the answer.

"What?"

"There are four glasses. Are you expecting anyone else?"

The senator gave a quick laugh at the obvious lack of Green's experience in fine wine drinking. "No, these are two different types of wine. We don't want to mix them when drinking. It changes the flavor profile."

Green knew the custom and also knew if anyone had drunk an entire bottle of wine themselves their taste buds wouldn't care if a different type of wine was poured into the same glass. He might be worth millions but his pragmatic ways from growing up poor had never left him.

Senator Miller slid the heavy curtain closed, encasing them, the low murmur of voices all but disappearing. The senator walked over, sat next to him, poured two glasses of wine, then gave a long exhale as she leaned back, kicked off her shoes, ruffled her hair out, and pulled four well-placed clips from hidden parts of her locks. "This is more like it. Let's truly get the evening started."

"That sounds great." Green said with laughter as he loosened his tie and undid the top button of his shirt as well as his cuffs. He mirrored her body position and leaned back against the couch, making himself comfortable.

"That won't do. Stand up," ordered the senator as she stood.

Green gave her a quizzical look, not understanding what she wanted, but he stood in front of her, easily feeling the tension in her body. She reached out, finished untying his tie, then threw it on the seat next to them. He raised a brow but didn't say a word. He liked a confident woman who wasn't afraid to go after what she wanted. She slid off his jacket, threw it onto the same spot, all while looking into his eyes. Green was very aware he could have anything he wanted from her right then and there. She was his in that moment — did he want what she was offering?

"What do you want from me, Anna?" Green whispered, as if he was confused. She obviously was turned on by weak men. It was difficult for him to play that part. The senator playfully bit at the corner of her bottom lip. He wondered how far he would allow this to go. But the senator wasn't ready to quit playing games. She stepped back from him, sat back down with a sigh, picked up her glass, and took a long draw of bright red wine.

"What I *want* is to be able to do what I want when I want without thinking of the four hundred things that might, or might not, happen with each choice I make. What I *want* is to have you strip me down right here and now and ravage my body until I cry out in ecstasy over and over again. I haven't had a good fuck in almost two years and men who look like you do *not* come around very often," she said, taking another large gulp of wine. "But I can't have sex behind a curtain because of those four hundred things that might, or might not, happen if I let go for even a moment . . . and the dozen people in the other room. My life is public, and I'm never allowed to forget that."

"So . . ." Green started, exaggerating his look over both shoulders as he stood directly in front of her. "you do, or don't, want me to ravish you?" Was he going to do just that? He still hadn't made the decision. He was playing a game with her, and he wasn't sure who'd be the winner that night.

The senator looked at him with want in her eyes, then looked at the curtain blocking them from the other room, before turning back and locking her eyes on the bulge in the front of his pants that instantly made her eyes catch fire. Holding up one of her hands in a non-verbal command, the senator rose, standing only inches from Green. Then she seemed to make a decision and turned, lifting her hair above her shoulders.

He glanced down at a dainty zipper at the top of her back and decided he could play. He took hold of it and slowly pulled down, exposing her bare back. She had a smooth, flawless olive complexion. He didn't have to be forced to take a taste as he leaned down and kissed each new inch of skin he revealed. The zipper stopped at the dimple in the small of her back and he dropped to his knees as she shrugged her arms from the dress, allowing it to drop to the ground, showing him a lace thong dividing two amazingly toned cheeks. Green continued his downward motion, his hands now clasping her hips as he nipped at one of her cheeks, causing a feminine cry to rip from her.

With no resistance he turned her so the front of her panties was directly in his face. He looked up and wasn't shocked to see how perfectly round her breasts were. They locked eyes, both of them smiling as he kneeled in a submissive position in front of her. Oh, how the men would love to have video of this moment. This wasn't where Green ever resided. But his alter ego might, he assured himself — the man the senator thought he was would certainly kneel.

Without breaking their locked gaze, Green slid his fingers up and took control of her panties, slowly sliding them down her toned legs. He felt a modicum of desire stir inside him but was surprised it wasn't greater with a naked woman before him.

He pulled her the last few inches closer to him and kissed her toned stomach, her hands circling his head, her fingernails scratching their way from the back of his neck up to his ears, her control nearly gone. He reached up and took hold of her breast, sliding her hardened nipple between his fingers as his palm gently massaged the area.

He kissed her stomach again, his head moving lower, her legs shaking as he held tight to her hips. "Yes, Hendrick, yes," she said, tangling her fingers in his hair as she began to push him lower, guiding him to where she wanted him to be.

"Senator Miller, are you in here?" a woman's voice called from the other side of the curtain. The wine bar had a very strict policy that this room wasn't to be entered if the curtain was closed. That made Hendrick wonder how many times the senator or other patrons had gotten lucky in the cozy, dim space. Would he have if they hadn't been interrupted? He wasn't sure.

"*Do not* come in," the senator barked, irritation clear in her throat. She stood as if she had all of the time in the world, then leaned against him, not at all embarrassed in her nudity. Her hand slid down his body and squeezed his semi-erect arousal. He gave a moan, knowing it was what she wanted to hear.

"We'll finish this later. It'll be your turn to strip next," she demanded. They hadn't even kissed, he suddenly realized.

Green hurriedly put his clothes back in order while it seemed the senator was in no hurry to redress. She'd told the person to not come in and she wasn't worried about them disobeying. She bent over to gather her clothes, the slow, calculated movement allowing him to take one last look at her naked body. She did have an incredible one. Maybe they'd finish later, maybe they wouldn't.

Once they were both put back together and properly seated on the couch with a glass of wine in hand, the senator called out to the interloper. Green's driver from earlier opened the curtain, gave zero indication of being aware of what had been transpiring only moments before, and asked to speak to the senator alone for a few moments.

Green nodded and rose. He discretely hit the record button Brackish had installed on his phone, then left it sitting on the table. He wanted to know what was so urgent the driver had to interrupt when Green was sure she'd been told not to. Neither he nor the senator said a word to each other as he left the room.

CHAPTER FOUR

Mallory Black waited for Hendrick to walk from the room and be out of earshot before she spoke to the senator. She was used to this — used to the men the senator used like toys. None of them stuck around for long. But none of them had alarmed Mallory like Hendrick did.

She wasn't sure what in the hell had happened in the SUV when his hand had slipped into hers. The heat that had coursed through her had shocked her to the core. And though the man was acting like a nitwit, she wasn't buying it. He was much smarter than he let on. She could read it in his eyes. She didn't know who he was, and she was more than a bit worried he'd compromise her job — her *real* job.

"What's so important that you needed to interrupt my night when I specifically told you I didn't want to be disturbed?" Senator Miller asked with an air of arrogance that had gotten her far in life in a short amount of time.

"Ma'am, when I came onboard you asked me to highlight any and all landmines you might be stepping on. You told me to get my point across even if you were being stubborn," Mallory reminded her boss. "I promised to do just that and assured you I'm not easily intimidated. Well, that man you were alone with you is definitely a landmine."

The senator looked at Mallory with unapologetic eyes as she tried to assess whether she was going to take her warning or not. Mallory had been her right-hand woman for almost three years, and she was doing a fine job. Mallory could tell the senator believed her. Now that the moment had been broken, Senator Miller would be thinking of the four hundred other tasks she needed to finish before the day ended.

"Mallory, I'm running for President of the United States. I'm a forty-five-year-old single woman who knows what I want and how I want it. I also love sex — and lots of it. None of that is a good combination to win what I'm after. It's a must that I have, at minimum, a partner on my arm as I start going through all of the press traps that will be laid out for me. You know I must always have a propitious mindset. More than that, I need to feel a man touch me, to make love to me. What you interrupted just now was something I've needed for the past year as I've tried to clean up my image," the senator said calmly.

Mallory didn't try to correct the senator, but she knew she'd had at minimum two lovers in that time. Maybe they hadn't satisfied her. Mallory was pretty sure Hendrick wouldn't leave a woman wanting for anything when he was done with her.

"I understand, but not *this* man, there's something that doesn't feel right about him," Mallory said with a chill in her voice.

"Is it because he isn't *quality* stock?"

"Sure, that might be a part of it, but he doesn't carry himself like someone who just came into money. There's a way that he sits, walks, and acts that doesn't fit," Mallory insisted.

"I can tell you something of his that would most definitely fit," the senator smiled greedily as she brought the wine glass to her lips, taking in the aroma of the drink for a moment while her imagination went back to what could've been.

"Seriously, Anna!" Mallory said, rolling her eyes at the never-ending ways her boss shocked her with what came out of her mouth.

For several beats the only sound came from the noise of other patrons, too far away to hear any part of the conversation between the two in the Mariner room.

"Well ladies," Green said as he stepped inside the suddenly smaller space, a large smile on his lips as he broke the silence that had been hanging in the air. "Is everything good?"

The senator dropped her shoulders in a defeated manner. Mallory nearly sighed with relief as the senator made her decision. She could read it in the woman's eyes — utter disappointment.

"Hendrick, I apologize, something's come up and we have to cut the evening short. I'll have Mallory drive you home and we'll talk soon."

The senator stood, walked over, and gave Green a quick hug. He went to give her a kiss on the cheek, but she stepped back before he could. The look of confusion his fake persona gave wasn't met with a response of any kind, other than the senator stepping back to the couch.

"Let's go," Mallory said as she moved between Green and the senator. To the untrained individual it would've seemed as if she was turning in a natural way toward the exit, but Green knew it was a well-trained box out move to keep him from having any additional interaction with the senator. This lady was good.

He was impressed.

He was absolutely certain in that moment that Mallory wasn't who she said she was. But his team was better than anyone she'd been trained with. They'd know all about her soon enough. For someone who'd sparked a brief interest in him earlier, she'd just become his main focus. He wanted to know more. He grabbed his phone without saying another word.

They walked in silence to the SUV parked around the corner from the wine bar, and Green wondered where Smoke was. He didn't see the man anywhere, but he was well aware his friend and running partner was out there. He wondered what he was thinking about the change in plans. They climbed into the SUV and Hendrick quickly sent the audio to Brackish. He wanted to know what the two women had been talking about while he was out of the room.

The beginning of the ride from the interior of Seattle toward Green's house started the same way it had earlier that evening. Mallory wanted to drive in utter silence. This time Green had a million questions he wanted to ask her. He waited though. If nothing else Green was a very patient man. There'd been times he'd remained still for countless hours, his eye on the scope of his gun, his breathing steady, and not a sound emanating from him. This drive was nothing.

Green watched Mallory as they drove and concluded she was either former military or she'd lived under a parent who was. He decided to test his hypothesis. He could slip his earpiece in and turn on his mic and include Brackish in this conversation, but he didn't want to do that quite yet, unsure why.

He looked directly at her to see her reaction. "What branch were you in?" he calmly asked.

Mallory visibly jolted from whatever she'd been thinking about. "What?" she asked.

"What branch were you in?"

She didn't answer, so he decided to give her a story and see if that opened her up.

"My brother was a Navy officer, and you act just like him," Green said, making him laugh internally at how opposite that sentence was, as his own brother lived with his dad, both of them drunks who'd never done anything with their lives.

The stoic and hardened features of her face made an instant change.

"I was a Navy officer too," she said eventually. She finally turned his way the slightest bit and gave him the semblance of a smile. Noticing her actions seemed to have thrown her off kilter, but she recovered quickly, and maybe, just maybe, he'd earned a little respect from her. That was soon to be determined.

"Thank you for your service, Mallory. I respect all who serve our country," he said, seeing her soften.

She turned to look at him for a moment, a transformation in her energy obvious. He was starting to gain her trust, and he had no doubt he needed that in order to get close to the senator again. He shut down the pang of guilt he felt at the thought of using

Mallory to get what he wanted. It was for the mission he assured himself, which could save a lot of lives. He wouldn't be hurting Mallory by lying to her. She was just a small fish in a very large pond. She was also in the wrong place at the wrong time. He didn't think she was involved with the senator's profiteering, but he'd never know if he didn't look into it. He had a feeling about her.

"Did you go to the military school in Washington D.C. or did you go to college first? My brother went via ROTC and has been in forever," Green said, knowing that Annapolis, Maryland was the home of the Naval Academy, but it was good to continue to play the part of an uneducated simpleton.

A completely different woman sat before him. She was relaxed, calm, and easy to talk to. She responded to his question and started giving more than he asked for, "Yes, I went to the academy and served seven years after graduation. I met Senator Miller my last year in, and she promised me a job if I ever got out. Obviously, I took her up on the offer almost three years ago."

A quick calculation led Green to suspect there was a gap between her serving seven years in the military and then the three years she'd been working with the senator. He didn't want to open up that line of questioning quite yet. Instead, he kept going with the natural flow of the conversation.

"I'm impressed. I wish I would've been more focused in my youth. I don't know if I would've been a good officer or not, but it definitely would've been good to try," Green said as if he knew what it was like to not conquer every obstacle ever put in front of him. He was adapting to his inferior role far too easily. He didn't like that at all. Could a person lose their brain function if they stopped using it? He'd better not find out.

"You're in a great position now so past choices don't have to define who you are. It's good to move forward and know who you are, where you're going, and what you're becoming," Mallory said, truth in her words. She was one of those people who saw the best in everyone. He didn't want to like this woman, but it was hard not to once she let her guard down.

She was highly educated and an obvious protector, but she wasn't nearly as adept at leading people down conversational roads as Green was. Without her realizing it, the two of them spoke fairly openly all the way to his house.

As Green exited the vehicle Mallory asked, "Hey, Hendrick, I don't mean to impose, but do you mind if I use the bathroom?"

"By the way you've been drinking water I'm surprised we didn't stop three times on the way here." Green laughed while waving her in with a nod of his head.

The problem for Green was that he'd only been in the house for a few minutes before being picked up that night, and he hadn't used the bathroom yet. He remembered it was on the left side of the hall but couldn't fully recall if it was the first or second door.

"Please, come in, the bathroom's down the hall on the left," he said, better to keep it vague and let her open the wrong door than for him to send her in the wrong one.

While Mallory was in the bathroom Green took a quick inventory of his living arrangements. Chad's people had done a great job of making it look good. The ambience was of a guy who was transitioning from no money to one who'd just gotten handed a check with a hell of a lot of zeroes in it. The profile Brackish had given him was a rich relative had died, leaving him a ton of money suddenly. He couldn't be a nobody and have the attention of a senator. It was a good thing Brackish was great at his job. If they knew who he really was, and the amount of money he had, they'd know he'd never be a warehouse employee.

There was new furniture and a huge television with an exaggerated surround sound system. There was also old artwork of beer signs that had cheap framing, a rather ragged dining room table that had one chair that didn't match the other three, and a bookshelf containing collectables, mostly encased baseballs, and a few books that had obviously never been read.

As he was reviewing the signatures on the baseballs, he heard his guest leaving the bathroom and turned around, momentarily taken aback. The stuck-up, uber self-controlled, former military officer was actually a beautiful woman.

In the past few minutes she hadn't done anything to change her appearance, but this was the first time Green was seeing her in normal lighting, away from any other distractions. He looked her over from head to toe, and by the way she looked back at him she was *very* aware of it.

Mallory had thick hair, pulled back in a tight bun at the moment, but he could tell that when it came out of its binding it would cascade over her back in thick full waterfalls of brown. He'd love to see how that would look against her naked skin while she was riding on top of him.

That thought shocked him. He'd just been with another woman trying to decide if he was going to have sex with her or not, and now that woman was completely out of his mind and this one had overtaken his thoughts and hormones.

What in the hell was wrong with him? Sure, he liked women, but he didn't court two of them at the same time — and he was straight forward when he went into an affair with one. Would he be with this woman if things moved in that direction? He was more than a little confused with what was going on inside him.

Green's eyes stroked Mallory's body in a way that he felt as if he were touching her. And he found he *wanted* to touch her. She was trying to hide her silver-grey eyes that had a beautiful light green color around them. He barely caught a glimpse of them before she looked down. The business suit she was wearing somewhat hid her body, but he could tell she was curvy yet toned. The senator held nothing on her. He wasn't ready to let Mallory go, so he quickly devised a plan to keep her right where she was.

"Hey, I hate to put you out but since you're here, I have a favor to ask," he said. "My new TV was delivered today, and I have no clue how to set it up. Do you know anything about electronics?" He was playing dumb again. When she met his gaze this time he saw doubt in her eyes. He really tried to sell the idiot act — he was sort of glad she wasn't immediately buying it. That would say a lot more about him than her.

After a long moment holding his breath, he let out a sigh of relief when she laughed.

"What do you need done?" she asked.

"Everything. I know to hit the source button to change it to the DVD-player," he said purposely since he was aware few people still had a DVD player. He'd made sure and told Chad to have one at his place. He actually had a bit of nostalgia for the old technology. "But how do I turn on the surround sound? How do I get Netflix, Amazon, and that new one . . . what's it called?" He paused as he thought for a moment. "Oh yeah, that Disney Plus. My favorite movie is The Lion King." He stopped and then belted out, "Oh, I just can't wait to be king."

This time Mallory really laughed, completely comfortable. He had her hooked. It had to be the DVD comment. Or maybe it was his singing. He'd been told he didn't have a bad voice.

"My last TV didn't have any of these streaming services. The world keeps moving forward and I keep trying to shift into reverse," he shared. There was a lot about that statement that was actually true for him. He was still a fan of Redbox when he could find them.

"I think I can help you," she said after her laughter stopped. "Let me have the remote."

Green handed it over, thankful it still had the protective plastic cover on the back side of it, confirming it was new and unused. He then turned to face the massive screen, standing shoulder to shoulder with Mallory. She had a mild sweet scent about her that drifted over him, stirring up his hormones again.

After a few minutes she had the surround sound going, but she was stuck getting the internet to connect. While she fiddled around, Green excused himself and hoped the people who'd set up his kitchen had stocked some wine.

Thankfully, he'd been taken care of and there were a few different bottles to choose from. Quickly opening and pouring two glasses, he appeared next to Mallory and offered her a glass without saying a word. She absently took it while staring at the setting options on the TV then took a drink after a distracted thank you. Once the internet issue was resolved she made quick work of getting a few different apps set up on the home screen.

"Okay, you have Netflix, Prime, Hulu, Disney Plus, and YouTube set on this screen," she said while highlighting each respective application. "Are there any other apps you'd like?"

"What are my options? Are there sports apps?"

"What kind of sports? ESPN, NFL, MLB, NBA, NHL . . . anything you can think of I'm sure it's here."

"Really? Please help me find ESPN for sure, but if there are apps for each individual sport, I'll take those as well. Do I just click them, and it changes the channel for me automatically?" Green innocently asked.

"Yeah. And this is a great remote with voice command, so you don't even have to select, you can just push this button and say which channel you want, and it will go to it. If you want to watch a specific team, you can say that team's name into the remote. I'm sure you're all about the Seattle teams, so we can get those for you, but if it was up to me, we'd delete them all," Mallory said with a smirk. He was entranced with the speaking remote. He truly hadn't known that technology existed. He'd been in the dark ages long enough. He decided not to focus on that, though, instead wanting to taunt her on teams.

"Do you have a favorite team that Seattle beats up all the time? I can see why that might pain you."

"Well, the Mariners don't beat anyone, so that isn't an issue, and the Seahawks only started winning a couple years ago, so there isn't any history there either. Heck, your basketball team left you. I'd say you'd be okay supporting the Sounders, but you probably don't know anything about soccer," she chided.

"I played for fifteen years, was left striker or center midfielder. And, you still haven't answered, what terrible teams do *you* support?" Green asked with a big smile while he took a drink of wine.

Mallory looked at him with surprise in her eyes. She matched his drink of wine.

"I'm a Denver girl. Through and through," she said with pride.

"Oh . . . my . . . gosh," Green said with as much disgusted enthusiasm as a Seattle fan hearing this information would show.

Knowing she was hooked, Green sat down in the recliner to the side of the couch, gave her an open arm invitation to sit on the couch so they could argue over who had the best hometown sports teams.

At one point Green rose, continued his dialogue as he walked into, then back from, the kitchen with the bottle of wine. He offered her the first refill and, again, she absently took the offer during her own retort to which team had the best player in the history of each team.

Over the next hour and a half, the two mock-raged over rivalries that became both wonderful and terrible family memories that followed wins and losses.

Green pulled out another bottle of wine and it proved to be the undoing of their ongoing conversation. She realized the time, acknowledged she had a little buzz, and realized she'd been talking for far too long with Green. She was clearly irritated at her lapse in professionalism.

"Can I have a glass of water please? I shouldn't have stayed so long," she said with open frustration.

"Sure, though it's not an issue. I enjoyed talking you into becoming a Seahawks fan," he joked while filling a glass of water. He only left the living room for about thirty seconds but came back to find that Mallory had stood and was putting herself together, an obvious stage of leaving.

"Thanks," she told him, taking the glass and guzzling the entire thing before she handed it back and began moving to the front door. Green didn't try to stop her, but found he was oddly disappointed she was leaving. She wasn't his assignment, and he wasn't sure why he wanted to keep talking with her. Before she exited though, he did call out to her.

"Before you leave, can I have a two-minute talk with you on a serious note?" Green asked.

The transformation back to the cold, steel-eyed, politician's aide was quickly returning. If he was going to get through to her, he had to do it now. If she left, he probably wouldn't get her to open back up for some time, if at all.

"Two minutes," she said flatly.

"I don't know what, or why, Senator Miller asked to meet with me. It's cool, and I don't mind the attention, and tonight was, well . . . interesting," he started, giving his best to look small and meek, before starting again.

"I've always been a shadow. To my brother, to society, to my own life. So, to be invited to go to dinner with a senator, to drink wine at a wine bar like the one we were at, made me feel as if I couldn't say no to any of it. My work found out about it, as you know, and they told me to leave work early just to make sure I was ready to meet with her. I'm not sure what comes next." He left it hanging in the air, not quite posing it as a question.

The wall that had started going up instantly came back down. She obviously knew exactly the scenario he was speaking of. He was sure that many times in her life she'd felt as if she had no option but to say yes to someone who was in a much higher position than she was. It wasn't a great feeling. Her empathy was on full tilt.

"I know I'm an attractive man, but I don't flaunt it, and I don't use it to gain any advantages, but I do know that's all I seem to be to the senator. What exactly am I to her? A distraction? Candy on her arm? Was tonight it?"

Mallory stood still, contemplating how to answer the raw question. She was obviously surprised by his openness. He saw the wheels turning as he looked into her eyes. He watched as suspicion rattled through her. She knew something didn't fit with him, but he was sure she was lost on knowing why she was feeling that way. That's why he hated lies so damn much.

"What would you like me to say?" she asked

"I'm asking for your advice in this situation. Do you think I should meet her again?"

"You should make that decision for yourself. I know she wants to meet again on Sunday for a brunch. That being said, your awareness of the situation is fairly accurate. As a grown man you don't need advice from me," Mallory said, though there was no weight or feeling of honesty to the words.

"I might not need it, but I'm asking you for it," Green said.

"I'll answer you, if you can answer my question," she said with defiance.

Green cocked his head sideways, thrown off by the inquisition request.

"Who are you? I've done a background check on you, read the file, and did a scrub on your life. It all looks legit, but it doesn't fit. I've told the senator I don't think she should have you around. So, *who* are you?" Mallory asked. Her eyes were curious but not completely cold. She was confused and Green could tell she didn't like the feeling.

Green's phone started ringing at the same moment she finished her question. He wanted to ignore it but had the feeling of needing a moment to find his way out of this conversation. Thankfully it was the restricted caller he knew to be the control room at the operation base.

"Hey, brother," Green said in an overly exaggerated voice. "Do you know what time it is here? What's going on? Is everything okay?"

Brackish was on the other end, "Tell her the truth of our investigation. I found info. She's former military intelligence, has hidden in plain sight. On our side. Trust me."

Brackish saying *trust me* was all Green needed. He looked at Mallory, and gave a fake smile, as if the conversation on the other end of the phone was humorous.

"You should be really sure about that," he said in a sweet voice.

Brackish laughed. "Don't want her to know it's me on the line?" he taunted. "That means I could pretty much get away with saying anything I want right now." Green had to fight not to roll his eyes.

"That's correct," he answered. "I'm unsure if I should do that." Mallory looked at him with clear suspicion.

"You truly have to trust me. You can bring her in on this op. She's as close as it gets to the senator. Make her a part of the team."

Green paused for a moment as he made a decision. "Okay, kiddo, will do. I love you and miss you, but I need to go to bed. Yeah, it's late here. Bye, bye." He hung up and looked at Mallory.

"My five-year-old nephew. Can't wait to get back at my brother for that one," Green said while putting his phone away.

"Kids have a way of reminding us that any problem has a solution. Look at what they work through on a daily basis," Mallory said. Green nodded. It was now or never.

"You asked a question, and I'm going to answer. Before I do, I'm going to get another glass of wine and pour you one. You don't have to take it, but you might want it by the time I'm finished talking," Green said while walking back to his chair. His manner had changed. There was no need to keep up the act now. His gait, his voice inflection, everything about who he was, was in that room, and Mallory noted the difference.

"It's late and I don't need any games. Can you please just tell me?" she asked, her irritation clear.

"Trust me, you'll want to sit," he replied.

Exasperated, Mallory gave a huff of breath and plopped down on the couch. Looking over at him with raised eyebrows showing her impatience, she lifted her palms up in front of her and said, "Okay, here I am, let's have it."

"Mallory Black, former military intelligence, age thirty-one, never married, daughter of Dennis and Laurie Black, birthday October thirteenth, two older brothers, and one younger sister, and an avid Denver sports fan," Green said, hoping the last part of this reveal would ease some of the shock.

Her impatience turned into surprise and confusion.

He continued after taking a drink of wine, "The only thing you know about me is my name. Your *spidey senses* were on point. I'm part of an investigative team looking into the world of drugs in Seattle. The senator's name came across my desk and while she specifically isn't a person of interest in the drug world, people closely connected to her are. Being invited into her circle happened in a different manner than we expected, but we aren't going to pass up this opportunity."

"How . . . am I . . . What . . ." Mallory stuttered. Her mind was obviously jumping in a multitude of directions, and she couldn't get it to settle on one line of questioning.

"You're not a part of that investigation. And I'm not at liberty to share who is at this time. The phone call I just received wasn't my brother, it was my command base telling me to trust in sharing this information with you. Why would that be? You might as well tell me. My team would never tell me to share with you unless they have unequivocal evidence that you haven't been fully transparent with me," Green said.

A sly smile took over her face as she bent forward, grabbed the glass of wine and took in a large mouthful of the liquid. She eyed him, trying to figure out if she could share with him or not. It was a strange feeling. His phone buzzed.

He lifted the receiver. "Is my house bugged?" he gasped, just realizing his team might be listening to their entire conversation. Dammit. Brackish *would* wire his house, the guy couldn't help himself.

"Of course, it is," Brackish said as if he was stupid to think anything else. "You can tell her everything about operations . . . except for our benefactor. The team, the mission, it's all a go."

"Can you also read minds?" Green asked as he glared toward the walls. If they were wired, there had to be a camera somewhere.

"Don't worry, we'll shut the cameras off if it looks like things are going to get frisky," Brackish said.

Green held up his hand and flipped the middle finger up, then waved it all around not knowing where the cameras were.

"That's not very nice, Green," Brackish said with a laugh. Green hung up.

"Let me make a call," Mallory said as she stood up and walked from the room. When she came back, she seemed to be better. "Okay, if you show me yours, I'll show you mine," she told him, making him laugh hard.

And then they began talking . . .

CHAPTER FIVE

Mallory was a confident woman. She knew who she was and where she was going in life. She'd warned her team before her latest mission that she wouldn't pull off the act of a simmering assistant. So, she'd told them if they wanted her to hold the position of aide to the senator, she'd have to be herself . . . to a point. They'd agreed. And that attitude had gotten her foot in the door. This was the longest mission she'd ever held in her distinguished career.

"Who are you? Your name checks out with no flags on it, but other than that it's very difficult to find anything at all about you," Mallory told Hendrick.

"Why would you be checking me out?" he asked.

They were dancing around each other, and neither one wanted to allow the other to lead. Mallory had a feeling that's what it would be like to be in a relationship with this man. Not that she wanted that. But she did have a weakness for strong, confident men who weren't intimidated by her. She'd thought that wouldn't be so hard to find, but the minimal relationships she'd attempted over the past ten years had fizzled faster than Rice Krispies in milk.

"The senator's interested in you. Of course, we've checked you out," Mallory told him. She wanted him to tell her the truth of who he was before she shared anything with him.

Even though she'd told the senator she didn't trust the man, she felt the opposite. She knew he wasn't who he said he was, but she also had a feeling about people, and there was something deep inside that said he could be a confidant. But how far could she take that?

Hendrick lifted his glass and took a long swallow before she saw the switch in his eyes. He was ready to talk. She didn't say a word as she waited.

"I work for a team that's trying to break the huge drug cartel that's slowly taking over the entire western states. They seem to be growing stronger in Seattle, and we need to put an end to it. The senator's name came up on our radar." He stopped and waited for her reaction. She let his words process. He'd already said as much, but now they were actually listening to each other.

She knew a lot about him, or what he wanted people to know about him, but not enough. It had been insane when they'd done the checks on him and his profile had popped up. It was too good, but there were no holes. Everything he'd told them had rung true . . . but she still hadn't bought it. She wasn't sure if that was from her years in the FBI or if someone a whole lot smarter than she and her team had painted him an identity.

"I knew you weren't a blubbering idiot," she finally told him, then her lips turned up in a mocking smile. "But you play one so well I had my doubts."

Hendrick didn't take offense at her words. Instead, he laughed hard for several seconds. "My teammates might agree with you on that. It's the baby face I've been both blessed and cursed with from the time I was in high school. It gets people to trust me a hell of a lot faster and makes acting like a stupid kid a bit too easy."

"Or maybe it's your lack of wit and charm," she said, testing what the man was made of. His chest puffed out.

"Baby, I guarantee you there's nothing kid-friendly about me," he said. "Want me to prove it to you?"

She felt desire clench in her gut and had to squeeze her thighs together to try to alleviate the ache a few well-spoken words had produced in her body. The man might have a youthful appearance, but his body was delicious and the gleam in his eyes was all male. She could picture the animal he'd be in the bedroom — just the way she needed it. Some people liked soft lovemaking, and some people wanted to break the furniture — she was the latter.

"What's the team you're on?" she asked a bit breathlessly.

He gave her a knowing look and she knew he was very aware of every little action he took and how his words affected her. He could think he knew, but she'd stab her own foot before admitting it to him. It was rare when Mallory felt inferior with a person, but she feared she'd judged Hendrick wrong — he might be smarter than she was. That was saying a lot, considering she'd always been at the top of her classes and her career.

"We're an off-the-books team, but we keep fully legal. We just don't have to jump through the bureaucratic BS agencies have to go through," he said.

"Do you have a name?" she pushed, wincing a bit at his words. She was well aware of that red tape and it infuriated her.

"No," he said. She knew he was lying, but she didn't push that. If she were on a secret team she'd only divulge what was absolutely necessary as well. They didn't know each other very well at this point, and it would take time to earn trust. She didn't need to hide her position from him anymore, though. He'd make a far better asset than enemy.

"I work for the FBI," she finally told him. He didn't even blink. She could tell by his expression he was slightly surprised, but he'd also been aware she wasn't just a senator's aide. Someone had shared something with him. She suspected it was from the earlier call. He hadn't been on it long enough for a full rundown, but long enough to allow him to talk to her.

"So, you're working undercover." He didn't say it as a question, but a statement.

"Yes, I'm working undercover. We've been following the senator for quite some time as there are financial inequities in the money entering her multiple bank accounts. As a matter of fact, we believe the entire political thing started out as a scheme, but as soon as she had the power of a high-ranking political figure, she ran with it. We think in the beginning of her campaign she was simply trying to justify handfuls of money running through her.

Now, we think she's truly going to run for president. We're just not sure we can nail her down. I've been on this case for three years and she never slips." Mallory let out a breath of frustration.

"She's good," Hendrick said as he leaned back comfortably. "We have a tech god who works for us and he hasn't cracked her yet. He can see everything coming and going, but she hides her tracks incredibly well."

Mallory laughed without humor. "Yes, she does, from the government, from her growing fanbase, and from every investigative group who's been on her trail. She's unbelievably good."

"No one's perfect," Henrick said. "They always get a little too greedy, and they *always* make a mistake. This is just one hell of a long stakeout, and as long as we drink plenty of coffee and stay awake twenty-four/seven, we're going to be there when she trips."

"That's the problem with the FBI," she said. "We have a hell of a lot of red tape and we can't do anything without approval, so she could've easily messed up in the last three years and we could've missed it."

"So, if we work together, we're bound to get her," Henrick said reasonably.

"I won't get permission to work with a special ops team," she told him.

"We won't do it officially," he said with a wink. "You're the senator's aide, and I'm her newest piece of candy. There's nothing wrong with us . . . communicating."

She had a feeling he wanted to do a lot more than communicate. Her body again clenched, but she locked down that feeling when she remembered he'd been about to have sex with the senator in the wine bar. Of course she was attracted to a man who could easily sleep with two women in one night; it seemed to be her curse to fall for the wrong man. Hell, she wouldn't be surprised if he was a man who had a different woman every night of the week. She might have to remind her body she didn't like men like him. She wanted a bad boy, but one with a heart of gold who believed in monogamy and midnight dates. She wasn't what a man expected. She was tough and mushy at the same time.

Mallory might not be the roses, sonnets, and chocolates kind of female, but she did need honesty and love in a relationship, whether it lasted a week, a month, or a year. She stopped that last thought. The longest relationship she'd been in had lasted five months and four days. And she had a pretty good idea it had only lasted that long because they'd both been so busy they'd normally only met up once a week, sometimes three times a month to scratch their itches and then be on their way.

"I guess at this point both of our covers are blown so we really don't have a choice other than to work together," Mallory told him.

"Nope, it appears as if we're stuck together," he said, looking far too pleased with himself. She shifted on the couch next to him.

"So, what comes next?" she asked, realizing she was far too tipsy to drive anywhere. Knowing that, she lifted her glass and took another drink. She had a feeling she'd need it to get through the rest of their conversation that didn't seem as if it would end anytime soon.

"We catch the bad guy," he said with a simplicity that made her laugh.

"If only we could snap our fingers and all the bad men and women of the world would magically appear in handcuffs in a cell," she told him.

"Why not? If we are determined, we can bring evil into the light," he said as if solving the world's problems was truly that simple.

"How can you work in this dark underworld and stay so light?" she asked.

"I work with great people. When we start falling, we lift each other back up. It's that simple. If you surround yourself with trash, you get thrown out with trash. But if you wrap yourself in truth, nothing can get to you. The people I work and hang with are all suited up. Maybe you just need to be in a different circle."

His words hit her hard, *really* hard. Was she in the middle of a dumpster unable to climb out, or was she simply not finished arming herself? She didn't know.

"I guess it's time to take out the trash. I have some ideas . . ." she said. And then they began taking notes. They kept on talking until nearly dawn. When exhaustion overtook them, Hendrick convinced Mallory to sleep over . . . in his spare room. She agreed with reluctance.

There was no doubt in Mallory's mind that she desired Hendrick, but she also knew better than to sleep with him. There was so much sexual tension between the two of them, they could ignite a nuclear power plant, but Hendrick didn't attempt to push her. It was almost as if he was taking his time before he pounced. Then again, maybe that was wishful thinking on her part. When he talked her into staying, there was zero sexual innuendo to the invitation.

He showed her his spare room and extra unopened and unexplained toiletries, and then he walked away and closed his bedroom door. Did the man have guests at his home so often he kept spare items there? The thought depressed her a bit.

Mallory used the toothbrush, floss, and facewash to ready herself for sleep. When she came out, a navy T-shirt and pair of boxers were on her bed. She ran her fingers over them, wondering if she could wear them or not. They were obviously his clothes, and ones that had been pressed against his bare skin. Would she be able to get any sleep at all wearing his shirt and knowing he was only a room away? She was exhausted, but thought of him naked, sweating, and panting over the top of her was enough to keep her up all night.

Realizing she couldn't drive determined her final answer. She changed into his clothes, loving the smell of the detergent he used to wash them and practically feeling his arms around her as she lay down on the unbelievably comfortable bed.

She fell asleep rather quickly with more images of the two of them pressed up close and naked flashing in her mind, which she knew would lead to some hot and sweaty dreams . . .

CHAPTER SIX

There was one thing emphatically known about Joseph Anderson, the head of a vast fortune and basically royalty in Seattle, Washington, if not the entire world — he was a family man, through and through. And the most important person in Joseph's life was his wife, Katherine. She was the sun that rose on a new day, and the moon that gave light in a dark wilderness. She was his reason for staying fit, and the reason he was the man he was today.

After she'd been attacked, Joseph learned she had a cancerous tumor in her head, and his world had spun off of its axis. He couldn't lose her, couldn't imagine facing a single day on this planet without her. Everyone who knew Joseph was highly aware of that simple fact.

Because his Katherine had been attacked, he'd formed the Special Ops team that had become just as important to him as his own family. He'd always been of the mindset that family didn't have to be blood but love bonded people together. He'd believe that even past the day he took in his last earthly breath.

People also knew Joseph Anderson was overprotective and wanted to put a giant bubble around his wife. He wanted to fight off the evils of the world for her, wrap her in his tight embrace, and never allow any harm to come to her. What people knew about Katherine was how much she loved her husband in spite of this fact. She loved how much he loved her, and she loved him just as much — that didn't mean she didn't put her foot down quite often when there was something she was determined to do. They were currently at a stalemate as they walked through the giant building in downtown Seattle.

"Joseph Anderson, I'm *going* to do this my way. If you cannot keep your mouth shut while we're in there, then stay out. Either support me or don't. I'm not asking for your permission in this," Katherine said in a firm voice she rarely used.

Their footsteps, in perfect cadence, were the only sound echoing off the walls as they made their way through the corridors of the courthouse, leading them to a room Joseph never wanted to take his wife into. He knew there was nothing he could do to prevent Katherine from moving forward with her plan.

"You know how I feel about this, darling," he said, unable to keep completely silent.

She was *refusing* to press charges against the man who'd attacked her.

Joseph not only wanted to personally wring the man's neck, but he also wanted the book thrown at him. Joseph had to remind himself he loved Katherine *because* of her heart, not in spite of it. He couldn't choose who and when she was kind to someone, even if he disagreed with how she chose to proceed with something. And he certainly wasn't standing by while she faced this person alone.

Besides that, he had to begrudgingly admit that what she was doing was a kind, honorable, and gentle plan. Nonetheless, he wanted her to show her forgiving heart to anyone other than the man who'd put his wife in the hospital.

It would be easy to count the times there had been a legitimate dispute between Joseph and Katherine over their many decades of marriage. They'd learned very early on how much they cherished one another, and their love allowed them to not just be honest with each other, but to allow the other to grow in their own way and support that growth, even when it meant going against their own natural inclinations.

This time though, it wasn't about being correct or incorrect, or even growing as a person. Not to Joseph. His anger was still alive and brewing. The idea of forgiving a man who laid his hands on the most important and precious thing in Joseph's life was beyond comprehension. It was an open wound to his very soul.

Katherine had discussed it with him three times to try to make him understand why she was doing what she was doing. Unlike the angst and vile thoughts consuming Joseph, she was relaxed and showed absolute peace in her decision. The last-minute attempts to change her mind started only moments before reaching the courthouse steps and were futile.

Once she put the ultimatum out, Joseph knew if he chose to say another word about it, the tongue-lashing Katherine would give him in front of everyone would be talked about for years. Heck, the courthouse security might show the closed caption TV recording to their children's children.

"Good morning, Franklin," Katherine said as she walked up to her lawyer.

"Good morning, Mrs. Anderson," the lawyer replied, reaching out his hand as they approached. He'd been told to call her by her first name at least a hundred times, but he always said that when they were working he preferred to be professional. He hadn't budged from the rule he'd made for himself a long time ago.

Joseph was a full step behind Katherine, receiving the second handshake.

"How are Lisa and the boys?" Katherine questioned her legal counsel, who'd worked with the Anderson family for at least twenty years.

"All are good, thank you," Franklin stated. "And I don't even have to ask you as your family is all over the internet in their different pursuits. They truly are beautiful."

"Yes, we've been fortunate with our amazing family," Joseph said, only a slight pout in his voice at having been shut down by his petite wife.

"Is everything ready to go?" Katherine asked.

"Yes, ma'am. I have all the documents here. Mr. Kotzen's in the office as well as Sheriff McCormack." Franklin said.

Katherine looked over at her husband, gave him a look showing how at ease she was, and the rise of her brows told him she expected the same behavior from him. All he could give was a glance down at his shoes and a rumple in his forehead.

"Well then, let's do this," Katherine said as she opened the door without hesitation, not allowing Joseph to open it for her, which she knew drove him absolutely crazy. He felt a man should always open the door for the woman he loved as a sign of respect. He quickly stepped up beside her to walk hand in hand.

Katherine moved with grace as she walked forward with her back straight, her chin held high, and an energy that shouted confidence. Joseph loved this look on her. It wasn't even close to the first time he'd seen it and he knew when she held her body like this, she could walk into any situation and not have a hint of a stumble.

Mr. Kotzen, also known as *that piece of trash* to Joseph, shot out of his chair, looking at Katherine, then Joseph and their attorney, then the sheriff, and then back to Katherine. If there was a sorrier looking human than Kotzen looked right then, none of those in the room had ever seen it before.

"Good morning," Katherine said across the table.

"Mornin'," replied the attacker, no louder than a whisper.

He was told this meeting was going to happen, that his response would determine if he was going to spend a very long time in jail, and possibly prison, or next to no jail time at all. It was confusing to the drug pusher to be given an opportunity like this. There was no precedence for him to follow, so he didn't know how to act — that was more than clear in his demeanor.

For a beat Katherine and her attacker locked eyes and her look of comfort and sincerity obviously disarmed the man. Joseph was sure the man hadn't had someone look at him like that for a very long time, possibly since he was a child. It was possible that he'd never had someone look at him the way Katherine did — with kindness and forgiveness.

Sheriff McCormack broke the silence by asking the attacker, "Kotzen, is there anything you'd like to say to Mrs. Anderson?"

Running a hand through his greasy black hair, the man stopped his hand at the back of his neck, keeping it there, then barely tilted his face up and squeaked out a simple, "I'm sorry."

"I accept your apology, Mr. Kotzen," Katherine said quickly.

Joseph rolled his eyes, the sheriff clenched his jaw, and the attorney sat there stone-faced, as any good attorney would.

"There are a couple of things I'd like to offer you, Mr. Kotzen," Katherine stated.

He looked up at her, confusion written all over his face.

"You see, I don't know your story. I don't know why you've led the life you lead now. It doesn't make sense to me, but I believe people can make it through their personal darkness and find a light they can share with others. What you've chosen to become is sad to me and I can't believe it's what you dreamed of being as a young man. Somewhere along your path something went terribly wrong for you, and I'm offering you a way to start a new path," Katherine shared.

Giving an almost frantic look to the sheriff, Mr. Kotzen squirmed in his chair, trying to gain an understanding of what Katherine was saying to him.

"I . . . I . . . I don't . . ." stuttered the man, unable to get a sentence out of his shocked lips.

Katherine didn't interrupt. She wanted him to work through whatever his brain was trying to process.

Finding his words, the man said, "I don't understand what you mean, lady."

"Mrs. Anderson!" Joseph harshly barked out.

Katherine snapped her head and stared Joseph down while he refused to look at her. He also refused to feel any guilt for correcting the way this *man* had addressed his wife.

"Sorry. I don't understand, Mrs. Anderson," said the criminal.

Katherine wanted to snap a slew of profanities at her husband for his outburst, but she knew where he was coming from and why he jumped down this guy's throat. She collected herself and focused her thoughts.

"What I'm trying to say is, I don't know why you deal drugs, make poor decisions, and live a life that isn't fulfilling for you or those around you. Somewhere along the way you made a choice that wasn't beneficial for you or other people in your path, and then you followed that choice with more poor choices, which led you to hitting an innocent woman out for a stroll at a place that should be safe. This life has you in and out of jail, and it's hurting others around you because you're giving them drugs that they become dependent on, which puts them on the same bad path as you've taken," Katherine said.

Kotzen started to get defensive, but with one firm look from Katherine he settled down. He looked away and stared at his hands. Katherine was sure the man had been through a lot this past week, probably the past dozen years, but she hoped her forgiveness could lead him on a new path.

"Yeah, I've made some bad choices," Kotzen finally admitted.

"I've been given a choice in our situation, Mr. Kotzen. You see, I'm with my husband, my lawyer, and the sheriff, and each of them have their own thoughts and ideas on what my choice should be.

Each of these men have made choices that set them up to be successful in their personal and professional lives, but more than that, they're each worthy of respect in our society because they perform some sort of function that has a positive impact on those around them." She paused as she took a breath. He didn't interrupt her before she continued.

"It's been a blessing to have all of these people in my life, and I pray I've been a blessing for them as well. In all of this, we make choices, and today I'm here in front of you asking you to make a choice that will change your life for the better. You don't have to accept my offer, and as much as that will hurt me, it's your decision, but I won't force it upon you. I'm also not making my choice conditional to you accepting my offer. I'm here with an irenic proposal," Katherine finished.

Kotzen looked at her blankly and more than a little confessed, "I'm sorry, Mrs. Anderson, I don't know what you mean by that. Don't know what *irenic* is."

An understanding smile showed on her face and she said, "It means peaceful, or to promote peace."

"Oh," said Kotzen, obviously still not understanding.

"My irenic proposal to you, sir, is this. You come back to the veteran's center and stay for twelve months. You go to every class we set up, you go to every meeting, and you only leave the center with a chaperone. That's it. You won't have to pay for any of it. Your food and shelter is included with your therapy and the resources to train for a real career path." His eyes widened as he waited for her to finish. "That doesn't mean you won't be expected to work at the center. I've learned long ago that anything that's handed to you for free isn't nearly as appreciated as something that's worked for." She paused and looked his way before continuing.

"Before you ask, I'll tell you why. It's simply because I know beyond a shadow of doubt that once you see the positive changes in your life, and you see the type of company you keep become positive, it'll change your life," Katherine said.

Kotzen sat there, face turning and scrunching up while trying to process the words he'd just heard. Katherine knew the man's mind had been foggy for many years from drugs. It would take him longer than someone who'd been free of the parasitic substances to comprehend the offer on the table.

"What happens when I screw up? I ain't been too good at followin' rules," he shared.

It surprised no one when his response was negative instead of positive. As with anyone's mind, the output was equal to the input, and his had been trained to lean toward the negative after years and years of poor decisions, which ended up in a bucket filled with poor outcomes.

"What happens when you don't?" Katherine countered, then continued, "There are no strings attached to this offer, Mr. Kotzen. While I don't have the power to remove any charges that have been brought by the police, I won't be pressing personal charges against you. Once we conclude this meeting you can either take a chance to change your life and work toward something greater, or we go our separate ways. I'm sure you've seen enough of the path you've been on that choosing the option of going to the center can lead to nothing but good."

Deep lines creased over Kotzen's forehead. The struggle to break free from the grip his foundation of brokenness had on him was painfully obvious. An internal battle raged within. The small sliver of wanting out of the life he was in was easily losing to the comfort of the normalcy of what the last twenty years had given him. Then, something happened that shocked every person in the room at the courthouse.

Katherine stood, walked around the table to where the man who'd violently attacked her was sitting, pulled out the chair next to him, sat down, and proceeded to give him a hug. A conversation started between the two of them as she whispered in his ear.

"Whatever pain you've suffered, whoever has hurt you, and why you're in this position doesn't matter right now. You might not believe in yourself, but there are people who do believe in you, and I'm one of them. I'm a mother and have three boys of my own, and I can't imagine how hurt I'd be if they were given an opportunity to better themselves, and they passed it up. Let us work through this together and help you create a life you can be proud of. I know you can do it," Katherine said, making all of the stiffness from his rigid body melt away.

Kotzen went from a hardened lowlife to a broken young man in those few sentences. Silent tears fell from his hidden eyes. He admitted to Katherine that his mother had died when he was a young boy, and his father had drunk himself into an early grave, leaving him and a brother to fend for themselves as teenagers. She gently placed a hand on his cheek, bringing their faces close, and told him that his mother would never have wanted him to go through that heartache or to live the life he was living now.

Joseph watched in shock as Katherine's gentleness brought the walls of the career criminal crashing down. It was more than obvious that this man had never been treated so kindly.

"Okay, I'll do it. I'll go. What do I need to do?" he asked as he wiped his eyes with the sleeve of his shirt.

"First, you need to stand up and give me a hug and promise me you're going to do everything asked of you," Katherine said as she stood next to him.

The emotions continued to roll through Kotzen. He stood as requested and as his body felt her secure hug, he started crying again.

"I'm so sorry, Mrs. Anderson. Please . . . I . . . please . . . forgive me," he stammered.

"It's okay, dear. I accepted your apology and don't need you to do it again. You're forgiven. I don't say that lightly. Now, dry your eyes and let us finish this. There are a few papers you need to read and sign. Franklin will talk you through each of them. It's nothing more than you agreeing to stay at the veterans center and understanding the rules there," Katherine said as she initiated a look between her and the lawyer to get all of the paperwork out.

"When will I go?" Kotzen asked through a deep sniff to catch the run in his nose.

"I've talked to Sheriff McCormack, and an agreement is already in place. If you choose to go to the veteran's center, there will be no jail time and no charges brought up. They didn't want to give you that information until you made your choice. We have a vehicle waiting for you outside the courthouse that will take you there once we're done. I have a doctor's appointment after this, but I'll come by later today to see you," Katherine replied.

"Okay," was all Kotzen could say.

Katherine grabbed his hand as a final gesture. "I know there are layers of complicated feelings in this, layers of anger and frustration and mistrust and heartache from years of despair. Get through this one day at a time. Soon, those layers will be broken and when you shake them off new ones will take their place. You'll have help, but you have to walk through those hard days and not give up."

Again, the broken man could only say, "Okay."

Katherine looked across the table at her husband and smiled. She could see the emotion in his face had changed, and his own eyes had welled up during the last few exchanges.

After the attorney read word for word and went line by line through each of the documents, Kotzen signed his copies and everyone stood in unison.

Once in the hallway of the courthouse the bustle of people overtook the silence of their group. Handshakes were exchanged between the Andersons, their attorney, and the sheriff. Franklin and another officer escorted Kotzen to the waiting vehicle while Joseph and Katherine slowly made their way down the corridor.

"Katherine Anderson, you're beyond remarkable. I stand in awe of you and the angel of a soul inside you," Joseph said, smiling while weaving his fingers into hers.

"What? Why do you say that?" Katherine asked.

"For what you've done with Kotzen. I was completely against it, and after seeing what you did and how you're changing his life, I have to admit I was completely wrong," Joseph replied.

After a few more steps Katherine halted their walk. She pulled her hand from Joseph's, turned around, looked down the hall they'd just come from, then turned back again and looked up at her husband with confusion, "Where did we just come from?"

"What?" Joseph asked, confused by the question.

Katherine shook her head, as if she was trying to break loose from a bad dream, then she sat herself down on a bench along the wall.

Joseph's internal alarms started ringing, alerting him that something most definitely needed attention. Kneeling in front of Katherine, he took her hands in his, investigated her face, and asked what was wrong.

After a few extended inhales of air Katherine composed herself. She looked at Joseph and asked him to excuse her behavior, that she'd just felt a little off but was feeling fine now.

"Stop fretting, Joseph," Katherine commanded.

"You scared me, my love. Of course, I'm going to fret," Joseph replied.

Katherine stood and started their walk from the courthouse. She reached down and took his hand again, making him feel better at the connection.

"Oh, stop looking at me like that. Even without having to look at you I can feel the stare," Katherine said with a sigh. Then she gave Joseph a playful smile. "And if you don't, I'm going to get my new best friend to beat you up."

It was way too early in all of this for Joseph to handle a joke about Kotzen, but he did smile, thinking of how *his* friends already had beat up the lowlife once before and would gladly do it again. The thought brought a different kind of smile to his face. He'd keep an eye on Kotzen — and on his wife — whether she liked it or not.

CHAPTER SEVEN

Ten Years Earlier

Green was sitting as still as a rock with Jim O'Bryan, known to him and the men as Maps, who was currently his spotter — and the best damn man for the job. Maps had a seemingly photographic memory of every map he'd ever studied, and Green had a feeling there wasn't a land he hadn't felt the need to map out.

His love of geography and his photographic memory made him pretty damn coveted as a spotter for every sniper in the military. Maps had been teamed up with Green for nearly twelve straight months, the last five in Syria. Green had been bummed when he'd gone on another assignment and Maps had been called elsewhere.

"Green," Maps said in nothing more than a whisper. The voice of Green's spotter wouldn't travel much sitting inside of the room they'd occupied for the last six hours, but they never took unnecessary chances. They always assumed someone, somewhere, was listening.

"Yeah?" Green responded. His focus hadn't altered since he'd taken his position, shifting his left eye to the scope that was zoomed out to its fullest power, giving the right one a break but still maintaining situational awareness downrange.

"We're active. Ten minutes out. Confirmed target in second vehicle. They're traveling at forty miles per hour, but they'll drop down to approximately thirty-four when making the turn, and then slow even more at the small incline just after the corner. My estimation is they'll drop to twenty-nine. The target vehicle consistently rides twenty yards behind the lead vehicle. They'll be stopped by cross traffic for ten seconds. Current temperature's eighty-one degrees, forty-eight percent humidity, wind is at four miles per hour from two hundred thirty-three degrees, distance is two thousand, six hundred eighteen yards. Target's sitting in rear seat, passenger side," Maps said, reaffirming the information they'd gone over at least half a dozen times.

"Copy," Green said.

The next nine minutes and fifty seconds went by at the same rate the first six hours had. Then the first vehicle in the train Green and Maps had been waiting for came into view and the plan unfolded exactly as planned. Due to the distance, the front of the lead vehicle was lost behind a building, but the second vehicle sat in perfect position.

"Going hot," Green spoke against his rifle, right eye set on the target. A simple click of the safety was the only sound heard. No response from Maps was needed or expected.

Green took in a slow, deep breath, let it all out and then waited to shoot between heartbeats. Many didn't believe men like Green could fire between heartbeats, but Green didn't care what men did or didn't believe. He was so in tune with his body he could easily know when his heart relaxed between beats at any time of day.

The MK 15 Mod 0 rifle was as still as a brick, the trigger set at 2.3 pounds, weighing almost 30 pounds with all of the attachments but still had a considerable jump to it when the bullet exploded from the barrel. Ripping through the air at 2,700 feet per second, it would take almost five seconds to reach the target. The spotter would watch the round split the air, making a vapor trail all the way to the target.

As expected, the round found its mark. Upon Maps confirming a positive hit, the two of them quickly put their gear away and began exiting from the dilapidated two-story house, doing their best to remove themselves without being seen.

Before they got out, a volley of machine gun rounds ripped through the air. Green looked out a window and saw the train of vehicles following a small band of Canadian troops working through the town. Expecting the Canadians of being at fault for the attack the insurgents took out their anger on the US allies.

"Call this in, we need to engage," Green said to Maps as he pulled his rifle out and set up to start to range out the targets. After a few seconds Green demanded an answer to what was taking so long.

"No engagement confirmed yet," Maps said with a high level of irritation in his voice. It was the same anywhere and everywhere a military member went. Wait for permission to do anything and then wait to receive confirmation on that confirmation.

"I'm not watching our brothers be mowed down," Green said as he started the process of engaging enemies with one of the most accurate rifles in the world.

Maps was cut from the same cloth as Green, and when hearing the decision Green made, Maps went to work on setting up his own gear. It took no time to get his eyes downrange and onto the insurgents who had the Canadians pinned down. With a quick count Green estimated there were about 20 Canadians and 40 terrorists. The odds wouldn't be much of an issue if the conflict was expected, but this was a surprise for both sides, and it was a mess.

Two Canadians went down, then another, filling Green with rage. These criminal masterminds didn't care who they shot, didn't care if they were innocent or not. They'd mow down a child, a grandmother, and a family pet without batting an eye. They didn't just go after soldiers; they went after anyone in their way. Those remaining alive were doing their best to form up and get out of the box they'd found themselves in when the gunfire had begun. Groups of insurgents splintered off, surrounding the Canadians. This was going to go terribly if Green and Maps didn't engage quickly.

Thankfully the firefight had come much closer to them. The range was now 1000 to 1500 yards. All but potshots for Green.

"Let's try to work an opening for them at the section where the mosque on Al-Amarah is, get them going north. There are only seven insurgents there.

See them? You have range?" Green and Maps combined sentences as if their minds were melding.

"Yep. The one at the corner of the building is at one-zero-eight-eight." Maps spoke out the yards between them and the terrorists.

Green started turning the dial on the top of his scope, found the first target and went through his steps of taking a shot, breathe in, breathe out, wait on heartbeat, pull trigger, watch target until hit is confirmed while simultaneously racking the spent round, inserting a new one, and readying the rifle for another shot.

"Good hit," Maps said.

Four more shots were taken, and four more terrorists' lives were extinguished. Green quickly dropped his magazine, inserted another one, racked in a round, and found the next target. The insurgents became wise to a sniper and stopped filing from the same corner. It didn't matter, though, because these men had managed to find themselves on the wrong end of a US Navy SEAL sniper round at the next turn as well.

It was a unique situation for Green and Maps to remain in the same place, firing over and over again. That was never done. The reason became evident when a couple of rounds from an AK-47 hit the building they were in. Time was up for the spot they were shooting from. Instead of calling it good and getting out of there, though, they decided to stay in the fight and help as much as they could.

The two quickly got up and repositioned to a new firing spot. Three more shots, three more targets connected. Then another volley of rounds hit their building.

"We have to get out of here, Green," Maps said. He wasn't looking to quit, but he knew they were going to become sitting ducks if they stayed any longer.

"Yep," Green agreed, immediately packing his gun away.

"There are two options. Another two-story house about a block from us to the south or an apartment building to the north about three blocks, which is unconfirmed abandoned," Maps shared, showing why he deserved the call sign he had.

Thinking for a few moments, Green didn't like the idea of something not confirmed, but to go south of their current location was asking for a more difficult situation in getting out.

Before a decision could be made a barrage of rounds started hammering the outside wall of the room. Pieces of broken brick showered the room Green and Maps were in. The two of them got out of the room and down the stairs, and then decided to go toward their original escape route, which was near the apartment building.

Maps took a look around the corner to see two insurgents coming at him. Before the insurgents could register an enemy was on the ground in front of them, Maps used his long gun, which had a silencer attached to the end of the barrel, to dispose of them.

The SEALs worked together carefully to serpentine their way to the apartment building. It took all of a few seconds for them to agree going into the dilapidated building wouldn't work. They set their direction for another building that was still within sight of the firefight.

Before they could make it around the next building a group of five insurgents turned the corner in front of them. The opposing groups of men were surprised to see the other. Unfortunately for the terrorists the US military men were running in the ready position — armed for anything that might come at them. Maps had his long gun aimed and kicking out rounds into three men before they could bring their weapons up to return fire. Green used his sidearm to put one down and was pulling the trigger on the last remaining terrorist, but the enemy was able to get a single round off. It hit Maps in his left shoulder.

"Maps!" Green yelled as his partner spun like a top, falling on his face.

"I'm good, I'm good!" Maps replied, scurrying to his feet as quickly as possible.

"Damn . . . it burns!" Maps yelled out in rage that he'd been hit.

"We need to get off this street," Green said, looking at his partner's arm and seeing that it was, at minimum, structurally sound.

"There." Maps gave a nod to an old roughly built building.

Taking up position on top of the building, and knowing they weren't seen by anyone below, Green took a moment to give aid to Maps's shoulder, which was bleeding at a good clip, but the round had gone in clean through the muscle. Patched up and given a clean bill of health, or as much of a clean bill as could be given on the field, the duo went to work helping their brothers-in-arms.

It wasn't only the terrorists who had taken notice of the sniper, the Canadians had as well. There was no way for Green and Maps to know, but outside of the first few men who'd gone down it appeared as if the rest of their squad was alive and had gotten themselves set and working in a good tactical manner.

"Get our guys on that damn phone, Maps; we're going to need help carrying that team out of here," Green commanded.

"Already on it, brother, have confirmation, they'll be here in fifteen minutes," Maps replied.

Green made an out-of-character decision. He stepped to the edge of the roof, looked over, saw no one coming toward them, and yelled out as loud as he could the beginning of the Canadian national anthem, *"Ohhh, Canada, our home and native land, true patriot, love in all of us command."* He gave a pause then finished. "Come to us boys, we're getting you out of here."

Green knew there was no way the terrorists would know what was yelled out — just that someone was yelling in English.

His decision worked; in small groups of three and four the Canadian men started closing in on their location. The insurgents followed without discipline.

"We're at six five three," Maps said. He knew Green didn't need any additional information. Shooting from 653 yards was a no contest for Green. Shoot he did. In the course of three minutes, he put down five attackers. Maps took up a position on another railing and kept lookout for Green, in position beside him.

With a whistle, Maps got the attention of the first wave of friendlies who arrived at the intersection in front of them. After a brief showdown to ensure they weren't getting hammered from above, the Canadians quickly made their way into the building and then up to the top, taking position in an offensive manner.

"Hey! Get your man over there next to mine — he's been hit and will need an assist if insurgents come," Green commanded to the closest Canadian military man.

"How many more do you have?" Green questioned while eyeing another insurgent.

"At most thirteen but I think it'll be ten. There were sixteen total before we were ambushed," said the warrior.

Soon, the building was a beehive of activity. As the man thought, ten more arrived and it was confirmed that three wouldn't be joining them.

"Who's your CO?" Green yelled out between taking two more enemy forces down.

"Here!" A middle-aged man came over. He'd obviously seen more than his fair share of battles. He wasn't hardened, but he was far from soft. When he wasn't in the throes of battle, it was obvious he smiled a lot, those wrinkles around his eyes weren't made by a sad man.

"Name's Green, over there is Maps. This is going to be our hard point until transportation arrives. You take over setting your team to keep this place ours until the ride arrives. I don't care who gets here first, we're all going with first on scene. Understand?" Green asked while looking through his scope. It wasn't a moment of who had the superior military experience or rank, it was a simple matter of getting off the X.

"Name's Iron Fist, and . . . agree with all of it. Thanks for the assist, we were up shit creek, still are, but at least we have a paddle now," the Canadian officer said while turning back to look at the team he'd left. He went back to barking out strategic orders to his team.

A large round blew through the concrete five feet from Green. He instantly swung his large rifle to the direction of the other sniper, looking hard through his scope to find him.

"MAPS! Get over here! Stay low!" Green yelled. He kept searching at each opening of every building in the direction the round had come from. Nothing caught his attention.

A solid *thwomp* hit the closest man to Green. A head shot ended the Canadian's fight. Green was pissed, he missed the second shot, which meant the enemy would be able to put down another shot soon. Green looked at the head wound, studied the information it gave, calculating distance, bullet type, angle, velocity of round and other pieces that only snipers would ever think of.

"Here," Maps said, pulling out his spotting scope without being asked. They'd been in fights before and they knew how to work with each other.

"He's higher than our location. The entry wound is at a slight downward angle. I have yet to locate him. Looking at less than one thousand," Green informed his partner.

"Copy," Maps answered as he was already looking downrange for the enemy sniper.

A shot from the sniper rang out and confirmation from below came quickly that another military man had been critically hit.

This time he'd given his location away with the shot. Maps located the barrel flash, gave the location to Green and the two worked together to range the shooter.

"I don't have the shot," Green said calmly. For SEALs, there was no notion of quitting in them, or that they couldn't get the job done. It was just information.

"I'm going to go through the wall," Green informed Maps.

"Copy," Maps said. Maps would question him if there was a need for it, but he knew what Green was doing and knew it would work.

Deep breath in, deep breath out, heartbeat, pause, trigger pull.

The concrete next to the sniper exploded and a massive splash of red covered the wall at the back of the room. It was a gruesome scene, but Green knew it was a quick death and that was the most honorable thing he could do for anything he shot. It was a life motto he carried with him ever since he'd started hunting rabbits and groundhogs as a kid. For Green, life wasn't easy as a kid, but he carried a respect for life and knew that death shouldn't be met with suffering. It was a personal promise he'd made to the world and he'd kept that promise when in war.

The team was taken away from the hell hole by a bunch of American troops, the Canadians were picked up in route to the American base. There were only a few handshakes and waves. The Canadian group had to get their fallen. They honored their men too much to leave them there.

Green and Maps were met with a rousing chorus of cheers and questions as soon as they exited the vehicle at their base. Maps went to medical; Green was requested to meet with the base CO and he told the runner he'd be there once he got a shower. The poor seaman apprentice in charge of gathering Green wasn't equipped with how to deal with a SEAL and stood there awkwardly and more than a little scared of the man who'd just walked past him.

It was only a few months later that Green learned he'd been submitted for a Medal of Honor as well as Canada's Victoria Cross. Both were massive accomplishments and an honor. No one could remember someone being put in for both of those medals. Green didn't think anything of it. He'd only been doing his job and protecting people to the best of his ability.

Later that year, he'd been awarded both medals, making him the first. He was the ripe age of twenty-two. Green took his meeting with the US president with his award-winning smile and drank a few beers at a random Canadian bar with a bunch of the guys he'd saved that fateful day, then he'd gone on to win more medals and citations over the next few years that he'd served. Lucky, good, whatever the word, he was able to get through all of it unscathed, both mentally and physically.

Maps received a Bronze Star and a Purple Heart. His wife had pleaded with him to leave after the injury. He'd completed the remainder of his contract and once out of the military had happily lived his life on the plains of Oklahoma.

The two SEALs never worked together again, but they'd talk on the phone at least once a month — they'd be brothers for life.

Green served a couple more years before moving on in the private sector, but the day of that battle, more so than any other, would stay with him for the rest of his life. He was one of the lucky ones who didn't struggle with the numerous demons that came with PTSD, and he found that he could talk about it easily and openly if in the mood, but a darkness would creep over him if someone else asked. One should wait to be invited into the darkness of someone's memories of war, never invite themselves in . . .

Green's mind was focused on that fateful battle as he slept and dreamt of that day exactly ten years ago. He shot up in his bed, sweat coating his naked body. He struggled to find his bearings, and after a few hard thumps in his chest he realized it was the new bedroom he'd slept in for the first time hours ago. He hadn't had a dream like that for years, and he chalked it up to drinking too much wine and being so tired.

Then again, he'd long ago stopped trying to analyze himself and why he did what he did. Maybe this new war he'd found himself in was reviving the past, or maybe it was the constant battle of life. Or maybe it was demons trying to break in. Whatever it was, he'd figure it out. He wouldn't dive into a hole and hide from his past. He'd face it head on, and he'd conquer it, just as he'd conquered every other battle he'd ever faced.

CHAPTER EIGHT

Green glanced at the clock on his nightstand and huffed in disappointment. He flopped back down, lying to himself that he'd be able to fall asleep again. After rolling around in multiple angles and positions he finally surrendered to consciousness, slowly lifted his torso, slung his legs off the side of the bed, and ruffled his hair and face — hoping there'd be some form of cognitive reality of what to do next.

He'd only gotten a few hours of sleep and those had been filled with reliving one of his missions; that always woke him up feeling unsure if he was back at war or a free civilian. He didn't suffer trauma from his time in the service, but he did remember every minute of it.

He went through a mental checklist of the things that had to happen for the day, most of which included getting back to the operations center and giving a full read-out of what had transpired the night before.

He thought about that for a moment and decided a full readout wouldn't be necessary, as the guys didn't need to know about that sixty-minute window of getting a little crazy with the senator. He wanted to erase that moment with the woman he'd been shocked to find any attraction to. He'd much rather focus on his time with Mallory that had been so much better. His body had been on fire the entire night. It had been far too long since he'd been with a woman, and even longer since he'd been with a woman who was willing to live dangerously.

There was no doubt in Green's mind that the senator would be good in bed, but boring and focused on only her own needs. She was the type of woman a man forgot about as soon as he was pulling up his pants. Crude? Yes. True? Also, yes.

Mallory on the other hand . . .

Before he could even begin to get a grasp on what he felt for the second woman he'd spent the night with, he heard Mallory enter the guest bathroom. The sound of her shuffling through his make-believe home had all thoughts of any other woman evaporating from his mind. She'd surprised him quite often during their multiple-hour conversation the night before.

She was confident, sexy, and had a passion burning inside her that pulled a man straight into her web. He had no doubt the woman got exactly what she wanted when she wanted it. The problem with a woman like Mallory was that most men couldn't handle her. They were either intimidated or felt smaller next to her. Green smiled. There was no fear of that happening with him. He'd searched for a woman like her his entire life — and he was certainly willing to see where this new adventure might lead them both.

He wasn't so sure Mallory was ready to take the leap. But would it be any fun for either of them if they simply fell into bed together? He laughed aloud. Hell yes, it would be fantastic, but Green knew he appreciated something so much more when it wasn't easily handed to him. He was a natural hunter, and he wanted to stalk his prey — and Mallory just might be his next target. With her closeness to the senator, it wasn't an easy task. But that made it much more fun.

Was he ready to run down that path without knowing where it would lead? No, he was once again getting ahead of himself. Before his mind could get caught in tomorrow, a month from now, or a year from now, he had to get to know this woman.

Mallory was smart. She could also weave in and out of a plethora of topics without missing a beat. He found intellect as sexy as a great body, which she also happened to have. Her clothes hid a lot of it, but Green's imagination filled in the blanks. He rose, threw on some sweats and a shirt, then opened his bedroom door.

The sound of the running shower gave him an instant thickness the loose sweats did nothing to hide. He'd better get himself under control quickly or Mallory would run from his home screaming. But the thought of her beneath that hot shower spray, soap trickling down her body, her head thrown back as she sighed with pleasure . . .

"No!" he snapped to himself as he moved to his kitchen sink and grabbed the coffee pot, filling it with water. "No, no, no! Guns, ammo, targets, snow, dirt, grime." He kept on muttering words that had nothing to do with sex, and thankfully, just as the shower turned off, he began softening. He'd do his best to keep his body under control. He heard her wet steps down the hall from him and turned as hard as a boulder again. "Dammit!"

He quicky moved down the hall to his room and threw his oversized university sweatshirt over his head. If he couldn't get the beast to settle, he'd have to cover it. He left his room, doing all he could for now. Other than meeting her in the doorway and pushing her back inside the shower to satisfy them both, oversized clothes was plan B.

Snapping himself back to the present reality that was far away from his fantasies, he dropped to the floor and did a quick fifty pushups and the same number of crunches, in less than three minutes. That helped tame the beast . . . a little.

The coffee was brewing so he opened cupboards and took stock of the groceries available to him. It was obvious Chad had told those who stocked his kitchen that he enjoyed cooking as his pots, pans, utensils, and accessories were all top of the line. He also had a huge amount of quality food in the refrigerator and pantry. It rivaled his personal collection he'd been missing.

After taking inventory of the produce, he quickly went to work making a few courses for breakfast. Green wasn't sure if Mallory was going to be staying to eat, or if she liked or disliked specific foods, or if she had any allergies, but he was going for it. He'd always had a knack for seeing foods work together with whatever he had to cook with. This morning he had enough to make a few things that would either impress her or weird her out. Some women were intimidated by a man who could cook better than they could. Green smiled because he had no doubt he could outcook her. He'd be willing to bet he could outcook most people. He was that damn good.

It didn't take long to hear Mallory's steps coming toward the kitchen.

"What's that smell?" she asked, her eyes frantically searching for the source, making Green puff out his chest in pride.

Green looked over, smiled, and said, "Good morning. I hope you aren't in too much of a hurry. I'm pulling together a couple of things for breakfast. Would you like coffee or tea?"

"Good morning," she said, as if unsure how to act. It technically was a morning after for the two of them since they'd slept in the same house. But they hadn't kissed, hadn't touched one another, so there was no reason to be awkward. "I'll have coffee, please. I can't decide what smells better, the coffee or the food."

"Both will be delicious," he assured her. He already had an assortment of creamers and sweeteners on the counter. She put in two sugars and a splash of creamer in her coffee and leaned against the counter while she watched him work.

"You've been making all this?" she asked. He was used to the shock when he cooked.

"Yep, I love to cook," he told her. She looked at the island that was already set with plates and silverware.

"What can I do? I normally have a piece of toast and yogurt for breakfast, so there's no way I'm turning down this treat, but I should do something as it appears you've made us a feast that's sending my growling stomach begging."

Green laughed. He enjoyed the shock and, if he wasn't mistaken, awe that was in her tone and eyes.

Normally Green didn't feel a need to impress anyone, but he *really* wanted to impress her.

"No need for you to do anything but tell me a story of your funniest moment while you served," Green said while mixing ingredients together.

"First off, thanks for not being a creep. Last night was very unusual for me and, while I was only a little buzzed from that wine, there are plenty of stories of men taking advantage of women in situations like that," Mallory said. "I truly appreciate you remaining a gentleman."

"Not my style at all," Green replied, pouring his blended egg mixture into his prepared potatoes, flour, and spices.

After giving Green an appreciative nod, she said, "Second, you need to send a big thank you to whoever selected the mattress in that room. It was one of the most comfortable I've ever been on."

"I can't take credit for any of the furniture in here," he admitted. "I'm a workaholic and taking time to shop isn't my idea of a good time, unless it's at the grocery store." She laughed at that.

"I've never heard of a man loving the grocery store, but from the smells emanating from this kitchen I'm gonna thank whoever gave you a love of cooking." She smiled as she sipped her coffee and sighed. "Delicious."

"They are great coffee grinds and I like to try new creamers. It gets boring to have the same thing over and over again. But we get so used to our routines we get into a rut and forget to break it if we're not careful."

"I so agree with you. I truly love my routine. I order the same food at restaurants and stick with the same movie genre. I like the same colors and the same styles of clothes. I'll hang out with friends and they'll try to shake things up for me. I always complain, but I know it's good for me in the end."

"Well let's break that routine this morning," he said. He had her sit at the island where he could finish and still talk to her. "Our first course is a fruit medley. I only have blueberries and strawberries, so it won't live up to its fullest potential, but it has a splash of raspberry vinegar, a spritz of lemon juice, a couple mint leaves, and a fine layer of caramelized sugar around the edge for an added layer of sweetness as well as texture," Green finished as he set a small bowl on top of Mallory's plate.

"First course?" Mallory questioned.

"You don't make a habit of having multiple-course breakfasts? Today's your lucky day then," he told her as he kept cooking. He was truly enjoying pleasing and surprising this woman who was more beautiful in the morning with no makeup and finger-brushed hair. He was going to enjoy their first real morning-after — and he knew that was going to happen.

"This sugar is normally a no-no for me, but dang it's perfect," she told him as he kept cooking and she ate her fruit, looking as if she was savoring every bite.

"For a second course we have a miniature Brie quiche. My normal quiche takes almost two and a half hours to complete, but with a little magic from the microwave and a tiny portion, it should be satisfactory," Green said as he set down a golden topped, fist-sized pie.

She sat there, her eyes a bit glazed as the smell from the dish wafted to her nose. She didn't pick up her fork as a courtesy to not eat before everyone had their meal in front of them. He laughed.

"Don't wait for me; I have a couple more pieces coming and don't have time to sit and eat yet. The best compliment a chef can receive is a satisfied customer," he told her. "You can entertain me while I cook, though. I'm still waiting for your story."

"I'm not a good storyteller," Mallory admitted.

"You're not a practiced storyteller?" Green asked, his question suggesting that anyone could be just about anything with enough practice.

Mallory caught on as well and raised a hand to note her error, corrected herself, took a drink of her coffee, and then spoke. "Give me a moment to think on this." She picked up her fork and took a bite of her quiche, a groan rumbling from her that instantly brought his hardness right back to life. He turned away so she didn't see anything.

"Oh my gosh, Hendrick," Mallory said after another erection-producing groan escaped her lips. "This is the best thing I've ever had in my mouth." The pure lust of her tone had him nearly dropping to his knees. Maybe cooking for her had been a bad idea after all. He might throw everything from the island onto the floor and eat *her* for breakfast instead if those moans of pleasure continued.

"I'm glad you're enjoying it," Green said, his voice husky. She was so in ecstasy over her food she didn't appear to notice his complete discomfort. He had a few other things he wanted to put into her mouth . . .

She took another bite and groaned again. He was going to die. Or he was going to ravish her. One or the other. "This is ridiculously delicious!" Mallory said again between her second and third bite.

"Thank you. Cooking's a stress release for me and cooking for people brings me a lot of joy," Green said. At the moment it wasn't a stress relief as her sounds sent his heart rate into the heart attack zone, but he wouldn't change this moment for all of the money in his bank account — and that was a lot. He had to get the moans to stop.

"Not another plate of food or another word from me until I get a story from you," Green demanded. If she'd have been looking at him she'd have seen the fire burning in his eyes, but she wasn't looking at anything other than her quickly diminishing food.

"Okay. I have one but let me finish this first. No way I'll be able to concentrate with any of this remaining in front of me."

"Fair enough," Green replied, going back to his latest concoction. He flinched a couple of times as she whimpered and moaned. It took her a solid minute to finish the food in front of her and he had beads of sweat dripping from his brow as if he'd just run a damn marathon . . . in an hour. At least she'd think it was from cooking over a hot stove and not the moans he wanted to hear while she was lying beneath him.

Mallory finished the food, then leaned forward and placed her elbows on the island, cupped both of her hands around the coffee mug, and took a long, slow sip before starting her story.

"My summer tour onboard a submarine between my junior and senior year in the Academy. There are actually a few funny moments during those months on the submarine, but I think the funniest for me was mail call," Mallory started.

Green had been aboard a couple different submarines on SEAL-in-training missions, and he recalled how crazy those crews could be. He continued with the last portion of his breakfast without interrupting her.

"I was on the USS Nevada with the gold crew, patrolling around Hawaii, when I heard some of the crew talking about a mail call. The setup was that it was a three-person job. The sub would surface just enough to get two of the people out of the sail with gaff hooks to pick up the mail in a floating bag. The third person would ensure they didn't fall, watch over the situation, and keep comms with the team downstairs."

Green looked over at her with a knowing smile at where this was going.

"Well . . . wanting to show that I was a leader, I volunteered to go with two young, enlisted guys. I still remember their names — Johnshoy and McCarthy. The three of us geared up with overboard safety suits, gloves, the whole nine yards of craziness to not only keep you safe but to make you look absolutely ridiculous. Of course, all of the gear wasn't in the same compartment as the sail, so we ended up doing a promenade through the missile compartment, past the galley, and then up two flights of stairs. By the time we got there I was sweating like a stuck pig. Johnshoy looked as if he was about to pass out, and McCarthy's gear weighed as much as he did. We were a sight to behold for sure," she said, starting to laugh at the memory.

Green brought over another dish, the sight and smell interrupting Mallory's story. She looked up at him in awe, a definite stroke to his ego.

"A fried egg adorned with hazelnuts, chanterelle mushrooms, garlic, and blackberries," Green said as he sat with a plate of the same.

"Please, keep going," Green encouraged as he started into his plate of quiche and fried egg.

Mallory took a quick bite of her egg, enjoyed the multitude of flavors for a moment, then started again.

"The three of us were standing there, looking like absolute idiots, Johnshoy and McCarthy had the gaff hooks, I had a small, laminated checklist with me, and we're ready to go. Everyone seemed to know what was going on besides us. Hearing different commands for depths to decrease and the specific target angle, I was solely focused on making sure I did a great job of getting this task done. Hearing someone say, *good morning captain*, my head turned to see the captain. He saw me, laughed hard, something he never did, and asked the officer on watch when mail call was. A sinking feeling started brewing in my gut. Something felt wrong when he laughed. Then a couple of chuckles started rolling through the control room, and I knew what had happened. We were being hazed. I was so embarrassed that I fell for it. Johnshoy and McCarthy started cracking up laughing at the entire situation. What could I do but give a chuckle with the captain standing there? The more they laughed the madder I got. The madder I got the more everyone laughed. It was a vicious cycle I was thankful finally stopped when the captain said to call off the mail call and for us to get out of the gear," she said, a full smile on her face.

"How long did that get talked about?" Green asked.

"Oh, for the entirety of my career," Mallory replied.

"Ha." Green let out a laugh as he stood and walked to the counter. "I think we all have those hazing stories. I love them. I love the ones that live on forever. Remind me to tell you the story of crossing the equator for shellback initiation."

"Oh, that sounds good!" she said. "Tell me now."

"Nope you have to keep eating. I have one last item for us," Green said as he pulled something from the oven. "And I need you to *have* to see me again, so the curiosity will bring you back."

"I'm only allowing you to get away with that because I want whatever it is you have cooking," she said, her mouth practically watering. "What is it? It smells like apple pie."

"Close. It's Apple-Cinnamon Bostock."

Green sat the single pastry down in the middle of the island, handed Mallory a new fork, then sat down. "Bon Appetit."

The next few minutes were more torture for Green as Mallory moaned, whimpered — and he'd swear in a court of law — purred, as she slowly ate her dessert. She took her time, slowly opening her mouth, gently setting the fork on her tongue, closing her lips and sucking the food from her fork, then chewing before swiping her tongue back out and running it over her lips. He couldn't finish his food as his throat had closed and his sweating increased. He'd never wanted a woman so bad; he'd cut off his own arm to have her.

"Mallory . . ." he began, about to beg her to come to bed with him. But she stopped him cold as the last crumbs were picked off her plate and she pushed it away. She didn't seem aware of the pain and suffering he was going through.

"I apologize ruining this gourmet meal with real life, but we need to hammer out what we're going to be doing with you and Anna," Mallory said.

Those words were the cold shower he'd needed. At the mention of the senator, he felt his throbbing erection release some pressure. He had nothing to feel guilty about, but knowing he'd been fooling around with that woman on the same day he'd met Mallory made his stomach ill.

"Agreed," Green said simply.

"At this time, I believe the best strategy is to continue to go at this as we've started. Tomorrow she wants to have brunch with you, and I think you should make that date. If you want me to look into the person or people you guys are investigating, I'm sure I can help," Mallory shared. She continued before he could say something.

"You know . . . I never thought I'd be in this weird undercover world. I never realized how much corruption and depravity there is in politics. There's so much the public never sees, and it wears me down at times. But don't worry, I don't give up and I won't quit. In fact, it never enters my mind, but in the rare instances I have quiet time to sit and think, I realize how depressing it all is."

"I agree. When the rainbow glasses come off, it hardens a lot of people. I refuse to let it harden me, though. I'm a lot more aware than I used to be," Green said.

"I'm glad to know there'll be someone I can trust inside that circus," Mallory told him. He felt his ego stroked again and he liked it. Mallory was strong and determined and she was leaning on him. Not much, but a little. He'd prove to her it was a smart move on her part.

As she finished her sentence her phone started ringing.

"It's the boss. I'll let it ring out, but I should be going. Please let me at least wash the dishes and clean up since you cooked all of this amazing food. Thank you, it was by far, hands down, the best breakfast I've ever had. You're a phenomenal cook," Mallory said.

Green waived her off. "No, I've got this. You have to run. Don't worry at all about it. Take off and deal with whatever the senator needs. Give me the best secured number to talk with you."

Mallory gave Green the correct phone number without hesitation, then gave him a quick, friendly hug, and practically ran from his house. He leaned against the counter and groaned, this time without restraint. His body was going to be on supercharge until he got to bed her. Hell, it might be on supercharge for a month or a year after that. There was no doubt that he was in total lust.

It had to end eventually. But he sure as hell hoped it wasn't anytime soon.

CHAPTER NINE

Eyes and Chad were sitting in Chad's office at the special ops command center discussing mundane matters the other team members had little care for. Expenses, paperwork, all of the stuff that had to be taken care of but had no romance to it.

"After we're done here, I'm going to call Damien and see about getting together. I figure it's time to take him up on his offer to meet up," Eyes told Chad.

"Sounds good," Chad said, obviously distracted. Eyes gave him a few seconds, knowing he needed time before he continued. Chad finally looked up.

"I was surprised you and Damien knew each other. I don't do well with surprises. And sometimes running this team is a challenge because I'm dealing with very self-sufficient men who've never done well with orders when they disagree with an action."

"Yeah, I have a hell of a time with that out in the field. I don't like giving orders to men I deem my equals." Eyes paused for a moment. "But if a person doesn't step up into the leadership role, especially when you're a pack of wolves, then chaos is bound to erupt."

"I want you to be aware of the family relationship with Damien, so it might be better for me to step away from this and let you lead. I don't want my past with Damien to affect how we're looking at him in the present. In the real world, I understand good people can go bad. It's very difficult for me to imagine Damien being on the wrong side of the law. He has a wife and a child. It's incomprehensible to me."

"I understand," Eyes said. "I've served with some men I'd lay down my life for and then watched them fall apart when they came back home, cheating, lying, breaking the law. In battle these men were the ones I counted on to keep me safe. Then we returned to the real world, and I wouldn't trust them to walk my dog. I don't see how people allow that to happen to themselves."

"I don't think it's something they willingly enter. I think they do one small thing wrong and get away with it, and then the crimes grow. Before too long, it's all so out of hand, they don't know how to turn back the clock," Chad said with sadness.

"And drugs play a bad role in the behavior too," Eyes said, his expression narrowing.

"That's why our team was formed. Someone has to draw a line in the sand and help eliminate this problem that's destroying so many lives."

"We're doing it. We just have to remember it's a marathon and not a sprint," Chad said.

"I want to snap my fingers and have the world right itself. Maybe I empathized with Thanos," Eyes said with a chuckle.

"I don't think mass extinction's the way to go, but yes, it would be nice to eliminate true evil at the snap of the fingers," Chad said, joining him in laughter.

"As fun as the Avenger world is, I'm going to bring it back to Damien," Eyes said. Their smiles both faded. "Now that we're getting more information on him, it's time for me to help dig into him on a personal level. Green's tracking him through the senator. Brackish is pulling all of the electronic files. It's time for me to get intimately involved in this case."

"Good. Beyond us wanting to get this done, Joseph wants to know if a member of his family is involved in this. I can't imagine what's going to happen if Damien is found guilty," Chad said.

The conversation dropped naturally as the two finished looking over paperwork and consolidating forms. Twenty minutes later they were finished. Chad filed out of the office and went to his car.

Once the taillights of Chad's vehicle had passed out of sight, Eyes powered on his phone, flipped down the list of names on his contact list, highlighted Damien's, then pressed the call button. A series of rings passed before the call was connected.

"Hello."

"D-Train, that you?" Eyes asked, using Damien's call sign that few people knew.

"Eyes? What's going on, brother? Are you still in the Seattle area?" Damien asked with what seemed genuine enthusiasm.

"Yeah, brother, it's me, and I'm still around. I know it's been a minute since we saw each other at the veterans center, but I'm wondering if you're still available to meet up," Eyes said.

"Hell yeah, I am. Anytime for you. Damn, man . . . what are you doing this afternoon? I'm surprisingly free and would love to have you over. You can meet my wife and kid, have a barbeque, and we can drink a couple of beers and talk about the good ole days," Damien said. His attitude and enthusiasm seemed real, but that made Eyes suspicious. Was it over the top? Why did Eyes have to question everything now? He hated that.

Eyes wasn't going to focus on that, though, as the invitation was the best possible outcome. The two agreed on a time. Eyes won the argument on bringing beer and a side dish, and they hung up; the first phase of his part of the operation was underway.

Brackish wanted to get all of the bells and whistles set up on Eyes, but the only thing Eyes would accept was the data collection device, ripping all of the information off of Damien's phone. There was a quick protest from Brackish, but he knew Eyes wasn't going to be talked into being a walking audio and video robot. Eyes had given the argument that if he couldn't judge the character of someone he'd gone into battle with then his time as a team leader should end. Brackish didn't push the issue after that.

Eyes used the next hour and a half to get in a hard workout. The release of endorphins, dopamine, norepinephrine, and serotonin from working out not only helped him feel better overall, but it had a direct impact on how focused he was the rest of the day. He'd worked out in some fashion almost every single day since Sleep and he had gone through rehab in Germany.

The continuous moving helped stave off the depression that would start to creep in during those quiet times. The reality of not being able to serve, or even move the way he had before the injuries set in, would be enough to make even the strongest eventually break down. If it wasn't for the workouts, Eyes knew he'd have had to battle an invisible enemy. He wouldn't allow the darkness to creep in — not ever.

Physically exhausted, but mentally rejuvenated, Eyes went to his room in the special ops building and started his process of getting ready for the afternoon. He knew he'd need to get his own place soon, especially if he planned on trying to get close to Damien. It wouldn't make sense to never invite his old war buddy to his place.

If Eyes was being honest with himself, there was a piece of him that didn't want to put down roots in this area, even if those roots were under a false pretense and couldn't be considered settling down. In this building, nothing was his, so there was no attachment to it other than the men he was working with. Having individual keys, a couch, and a bed was more than enough to make a man feel like a place was his home.

Eyes didn't want to get that feeling and he knew it wouldn't happen while he stayed in the command center. He knew once the operation was over Sleep and Brackish would have difficult decisions to make about where they ended up living now that they were married. Sleep would have a very difficult go of it as his wife had just started a new career in the area while Sleep's job was still in San Francisco. Eyes didn't need that kind of drama.

With Damien's address plugged into the GPS, Eyes shifted the car into gear and took the route indicated on the screen. The closer the highlighted line got to the end destination the nicer and more opulent the homes became. When he was directed to take the last left turn before reaching Damien's place it was obvious that anyone who lived in that neighborhood had a net worth that had at least seven zeros at the end of the number. The other thing that struck him was how sterile everything looked. Perfectly manicured lawns, shrubs, and trees. Not a thing out of place as if the entire scene was taken out of a magazine.

More than any of that, the most striking thing that stood out was the complete absence of children playing. Be it in yards, driveways, sidewalks, or even streets. Where were the kids with bikes, chalk, jump ropes, or a plethora of other items that would keep them happy and active? Had he been away from his country too long to notice a societal change? Had he been fighting for the freedoms of these kids only to have their parents not take advantage of being able to set them up in the neighborhoods where it was completely safe but instead choose to lock themselves and their kids inside, away from the beauty the outside world provided? Something struck at Eyes's soul and it hurt more than he wanted to admit to himself.

Pulling into the driveway of Damien's home shouldn't have shocked Eyes, but it did. The place looked as if it was a newer version of an 1800s southern plantation. There were columns holding a second story wrap-around porch that mirrored the lower level. Intricate lattice work wound around the entire upper porch while the lower one was open from the grass to the inlayed brick with a geometric design no one could deny mesmerized in its flow. Massive windows reached at least twelve feet high and were precisely spaced to give the entire face of the home perfect symmetry.

The massive front door opened in half, each side opening wide enough for three grown men to walk through. If both doors were opened, Eyes wondered if a semi would fit through it, both in height and width. He made an educated guess that it would. Damien walked out, his smile wide and seemingly genuine.

"Eyes," Damien called. He quickly descended the steps. Then he grabbed the six pack from Eyes's right hand so the two men could shake. "It's been a while, so I'm glad you could come on such short notice."

"Me too. We come back from foreign lands, get busy, and forget to check on each other. Seeing you again has reminded me how important that is. I've made a couple of dozen calls over the past month to men and women I should have gotten a hold of long ago," Eyes told him.

"I did the exact same thing," Damien said with a laugh and a clap on the back. "I guess great minds think alike." He paused for a moment to look at the front door he'd left ajar. "We'd better get inside before the dogs come barreling out." Damien pivoted toward the house.

The interior of the house made the exterior look ordinary. The chandelier that hovered over the foyer was majestic, rich light splitting and reflecting through the enormous room. It was directly over a mahogany floor with stairs curving up both sides of the room. It spoke of elegance and riches; the entry room had been created to stop people in their tracks.

"Nice place, D-Train," Eyes told him, meaning it.

"Thanks, brother, business has been good since I left you in Africa," Damien said with laughter.

"I'd say," Eyes quipped.

The men walked directly to the kitchen that was about the size of the bottom level of the home Eyes had grown up in. Like the missing kids, Eyes noticed there were no noticeable kitchen products or utensils. There was no refrigerator, no oven, no drawers. It looked as if a wall and an island were dropped into the kitchen and then left unfinished.

The question was answered as Damien pushed his hand into a false wall, pulled, and then the contents of a fully stocked fridge was revealed. Eyes, in awe of how seamlessly the device was built into the wall, didn't even realized he'd handed over the beer he was carrying as well as a container full of a shrimp salad.

"Let's get the obligatory tour of the house over with. My wife always tells me people love this type of home and want to see it but don't want to be rude and ask for themselves. I have to admit I've loved the place from the first moment we walked inside those huge doors. Sierra will be home any minute. She and our daughter, Samantha, went out for the day. But my wife's always happy to meet my old friends."

"Looking forward to meeting her. Before we go anywhere — what's up with this kitchen? Everything's hidden like some spaceship. Where's the stove, the dishwasher . . . hell, where's the sink?" Eyes asked.

"Crazy isn't it? "Damien said. "Watch this."

Hidden under the lip of the island Damien pushed a button and a portion of the Pyrolave countertop dropped down a couple of inches and then slid silently away. In the same motion a faucet rose, presenting the user on-demand hot water in addition to the regular hot and cold options.

"What in the hell?" Eyes exclaimed.

The two of them laughed at the absurdity of it and then went on the tour of the house that could've taken ten times longer if either of them cared about looking at the details of random stuff. The one thing that caught Eyes's attention was the numerous family photo's strewn across the entire mansion. More than a few of them had at least one of the Anderson family members in them.

Sierra and Samantha were in the kitchen when Damien and Eyes made their way back. Eyes was surprised to see the genuine love and affection in Damien's eyes as he spotted his wife. The man Eyes had known didn't show emotion, let alone love and excitement. He had a really difficult time knowing how to read Damien.

Damien left his side, walked swiftly to his wife, and lifted her in his arms before giving her a kiss that would make anyone watching blush. She was giggling when he let go of her. "I missed you," he said in a soft tone.

"I've been gone for four hours," she said with a giggle that took years from her face.

"That was four hours too long," he said. Then he frowned in a mock pout. "Are you telling me you didn't miss me?"

She laughed with pure joy. "You know I missed you," she said. "But aren't you embarrassed to be so mushy in front of one of your buddies?"

He kissed her again, this time short and sweet. "Nah, not at all," Damien assured her. "But I guess I should introduce the two of you," He turned, his arm wrapped around his wife. "Eyes, this is my wife, Sierra. Sierra, Eyes."

Sierra looked at Eyes with a brow raised. "Eyes?" she questioned.

Eyes stepped forward. "That's my nickname. Real name's Jon. Feel free to call me either," he told her. She took his hand with a surprisingly firm shake, his respect for her growing.

"I like Eyes," she said. "And this is my daughter, Samantha." The beautiful young lady stepped forward and shook hands, her touch light. She seemed pretty shy . . . *and* he recognized her.

"You look familiar," Samantha said, studying his face quizzically.

Eyes laughed, shocked she'd remember him. "I was at the paintball war with your family."

Her beautiful eyes widened. "Oh my gosh! That's it. You were like a ninja," she gasped. "Each time we went in I was shot within seconds. You probably got me at least a dozen times yourself." She laughed as she spoke, but she wasn't wrong. Even in a game Eyes and his team couldn't tamp down the soldier that was always in them.

"My buddies and I might be a tad competitive," Eyes said in explanation.

Damien laughed hard at those words. "A tad is the understatement of the year," he said.

"And you aren't?" Eyes pointed out.

"Didn't say I wasn't. I know how good I am. It's always fun when I have a nice challenge thrown against me. It doesn't happen too often." There was confidence and truth in his words and expression.

"You guys go ahead and talk war. I have a phone call to make," Samantha said before she left them.

Damien pulled out a couple of beers, Sierra opened a bottle of wine, and the three of them made their way to the back deck, which could have easily been a landing zone for a helicopter, maybe even two helicopters.

"So, Eyes, Damien told me the two of you go way back, that you two were in a Middle Eastern country together. He talked non-stop about you as a person but not what you two were doing over there together. Maybe you can fill in the blanks." There was a playful smile given to her husband as Sierra took a drink of her wine, the cool bottle already sweating from the heat of the day.

"Ah, darling, nobody wants to hear about that dry dessert and those miserable days," Damien said.

"Shut it," Sierra said with a laugh. She then turned her attention back to Eyes.

Eyes looked over to Damien to make sure this wasn't a moment where matrimonial bliss was going to take a hit if he told the truth. Receiving a small nod to go ahead, Eyes started his story.

"It was Africa, not the Middle East. I was on assignment in Mogadishu, part of a training operation with some of the local military, when this young punk, trying to act as if he were Tony Stark, began talking about military contracts he was working on."

"Who?" Sierra asked, looking back and forth between the two men.

"Iron Man. The First Avenger," Damien clarified, then mock-glared at Eyes.

"Oh. That sounds about right. He was a very cocky man when I met him," she said, poking her husband in the side of the arm playfully. Then her expression softened. There was more to that story, Eyes was sure, but it wasn't an area he was free to ask about unless they volunteered.

"He had a couple weapon upgrades he was selling to the US military, and the group we were working with was to test them out. Very similar to the Iron Man movie, when we were out on a run there was an attack on our team. Unlike Iron Man, Damien went straight into action. He wasn't supposed to be involved at all, but he was right in the middle of it with the few of us who were taking the fight to the enemy. It was by all regards a life and death situation that most people would've wilted under," Eyes said, saving many of the gory details that went with that day.

"Are you serious? Damien, is that true?" Sierra asked.

"One hundred percent true, ma'am. When we returned to base he could've easily asked to go home but he went right back to his business, acting as if what he'd just gone through was something that had happened multiple times in his life. The truth of it, I found out later, was he'd only shot a gun a couple times in his life before that moment. Men like Damien are more than few and far between, they're so rare they make diamonds look like grains of sand on an endless beach," Eyes said and meant it. For the story at least.

"Oh my gosh, Damien, why didn't you ever tell me this?" Sierra questioned.

"No big deal. I was doing work, a situation arose where I was needed, I helped where I could and that's that." Damien shrugged while taking a large refreshing drink of his beer. He finished it off, set it down, and was about to get up to gather another when his wife stopped him.

"Now that I know I have a badass in my house, I guess I can get him a beer," Sierra said over her shoulder while walking toward the house, laughing at her own words.

"She really didn't know?" Eyes asked, shocked.

Damien gave him a grim look. "I'm not proud of that time in my life. I was an asshole to the world, to my friends, and especially to women. So, I just act as if my past is over and done with. But no matter how I try to lock the past in a box, it does have a way of springing free with new surprises. But Sierra has helped me heal, to face the past and the future."

Eyes was really having a hard time seeing Damien as a bad guy. But then again, wasn't that what all the friends and family said of serial killers? The people closest to them never had a clue they spent their free time committing unspeakable acts of terror. Was Eyes only seeing the man he'd had such respect for years earlier while refusing to see the monster in front of him? He didn't think he was capable of being nonbiased.

"Glad to see you got a good one, D-Train," Eyes said.

"She's great. We had a pretty sordid start to our relationship that can be saved for another time, but I do have to say I'm definitely a blessed man."

"Speaking of being blessed, are you getting into the political field with that senator? It was Mills, right?" Eyes started in with the real questions he wanted answers to.

"Miller . . . I still don't know about that, but we've been able to help each other out some. We've opened up connections for each other. She has business connections that'll help me build my enterprise, and I have numerous people who've always wanted to be connected to a high-level politician, and they'll be more than happy to pay handsome amounts of money for that connection," Damien said flatly.

"Surely you're doing well without her connections," Eyes said as he looked at the lavish spread. Even the yard had been manicured and designed to perfection. "So, unless you want an even bigger mansion, I don't see the allure of politics."

"I'm never moving again. This is my forever home. More importantly it's Sierra's dream place," Damien said.

"Well, I truly am glad for you, old friend. This is the epitome of making it."

"I admit to being fortunate from the beginning and I don't mind getting more if I can. Probably would've lost it all if not for Sierra and the kids. She taught me to be less greedy. In fact, I'm at a point now where I give away as much as I make," Damien stated.

Eyes could see that Damien was getting lost in his thoughts and Eyes wondered where his mind was going. Was his old friend telling him lies or the truth? Eyes was unsure.

Damien broke the momentary silence. "You know, there are a multitude of ways to diversify your net worth. Sometimes people question the ethics behind some of the business dealings, but somewhere down the line, voluntarily or not, everyone's hand gets a little messy. I figure — why not pre-empt it, make as much money as possible and then do something good. That's what I do with the veterans center we met at. Almost all of it is funded by Joseph and Katherine Anderson, but I gift money for salaries, educational growth, and various programs the center offers."

Eyes brought the bottle of beer to his lips, downed a large mouthful of the pale ale, then dropped the bottle with a small amount of tension. He had to wonder if what he'd heard was really what he'd heard. There was little room in the world Eyes lived in to allow *any* ethics to be questioned.

"What are you saying, D-train?" Eyes demanded. Before he allowed an answer, he started again. "Are you telling me if you steal a box of diamonds, sell them, and then give the money away, you're okay with that?"

"Oh, no, come on Eyes, you know me better than that. I'm speaking purely business. Scenario — it isn't en-vogue to use Chinese labor in today's market, but outsourcing is the only way to make big money. Instead of China, I've found other labor markets, like India, Vietnam, or even Myanmar. It might cost more in those countries than in China, but not much more and who reaps the rewards? My company does, but then I turn around and give most of it away. This is what I mean by questionable ethics," Damien shared.

"Ah, I see. You know I'm not a business guy. Just a knuckle dragger who needs everything spelled out for me," Eyes said.

The two men looked at each other for a couple of seconds. A small tug of war in seeing who was going to speak next. Damien never had a chance to win, he knew it before even realizing the game was happening. That, and Damien was a natural conversationalist, while Eyes would pick and choose the time to talk.

"Hell, Eyes, why are we on this topic? This is a great day for me, getting to sit with you again. Let's get the food going and drink a couple more beers," Damien said while jumping to his feet and walking to his wife, who was bringing out a beer for each man.

Over the next couple hours Eyes, Damien, and Sierra told stories, laughed a lot, and had a great time catching up with each other. A couple times their daughter made her presence known, but she was more interested in talking to friends, as was the case with many teenagers.

As the evening wound down, Damien escorted Eyes to the front door, and as they departed Damien finished the night saying something that made Eyes's brain jump. "Business is what defines me. My wife and kids are my heartbeat, but the act of making and moving money is the drive. It's a strange idea for most and makes them cringe to hear it said out loud. Me, it drives me, and there are few things I won't do to grow my businesses and overall net worth. I can tell that bothers you. It doesn't make me a bad man."

Eyes knew this wasn't the time to delve into a deep conversation, or even argue with him about his philosophy. "I don't worry any about how a man does business or makes his money. You should know that."

"Though we haven't seen each other in almost fifteen years, what you think of me matters," Damien admitted.

"All good, D-Train. Give me a call this week so we can get together again. This was a great day. I'm glad we got to hang out," Eyes said with as much positivity as he could muster.

"Yes, soon, for sure," Damien said as Eyes made his way to his car.

As soon as Eyes was on the road he called Brackish, told him to do deeper dives into Damien. Then he called Chad and told him he wasn't going to bet on Damien being involved, but he also wouldn't bet against it. Damien surely was wading in waters that at least made him *look* dirty.

What did that mean? It meant they were still at square one. Dammit!

CHAPTER TEN

Green was bored out of his mind. What an interesting saying, one he'd heard many times before, but hadn't fully understood as he'd never really felt that way. How could people be bored when there was so much life to live? He'd literally sat on rooftops and in small rooms with his eye on a scope and his finger steady for hours upon hours at a time — and he'd never been bored.

But having lunch with Senator Miller was boring . . . and he had a feeling she felt it too. But unlike him, she wanted him for a purpose, and she was willing to be bored in order to further her agenda.

They were sitting in a swanky Seattle restaurant in open view where reporters could snap their picture, and she could get a big media buzz about her second time out with the mystery man nobody could find information on. The senator loved the attention and figured he was a pretty boy for her arm.

It was funny to Green that he'd found her attractive when he'd first met her. He now only saw her fakeness and plastic smile. He'd been slightly turned on by her at first, but now he couldn't find a single stirring of desire. And he knew that had far more to do with Mallory Black than either him or the senator.

It was fascinating how much Mallory was on his mind. Since their night together a few days earlier, she'd consumed his thoughts. And he'd rather be just about anywhere else in the world next to Mallory than spend a two-hour lunch with the senator, which was thankfully over half finished. Though that thought was a bit depressing. He wasn't sure he could keep up his act for another hour. And if she wanted to go somewhere again, he wasn't sure what he'd do — maybe set off a damn fire alarm.

"What got you so excited about the world of politics?" the senator asked as she speared some lettuce. Had she even put dressing on the salad? He didn't care.

"I've never been interested, but I was bored at work and decided to join a political action committee. I've been fascinated with the ins and outs of our political world ever since. So, I'm new to all of this," he told her. It was partially true. He'd always loved doing his job without having to know what went on back in Washington, D.C. But once he'd realized the power politicians actually wielded, he became more and more interested. There was so much damn corruption in the system. It really needed a reboot, and fast.

"Do you have any goals of running for office?" she asked. Her smile was pleasant, but he was under no illusions he was being interviewed.

He held up his hand and laughed just as his character would be expected to do. "No way, no how. I'm going to leave that to people a hell of a lot smarter than me," he told her.

She seemed satisfied by his answer. She couldn't date someone who might compete for the power she wanted. It took all he had not to roll his eyes.

"Hendrick, do you —?" Her words were cut off when an alarm sounded in the restaurant, making all conversation halt. Three men rushed toward them, encircling the senator.

"We have to go now," they said, not even glancing at Green. She nodded, not attempting to argue. Green sat there and watched as she stood, throwing her cloth napkin on the table, and then walked away without a goodbye or concern for him. After a stunned few seconds, he leaned back and laughed.

"What's going on?" he whispered. The conversation that had ceased a few seconds earlier had started again as people rushed about the restaurant.

"Sir, you have to get out. There's a fire in the kitchen," a harried waiter said as he ran past Green's table.

"Yep, fire in the kitchen," Brackish confirmed over his comms.

"Maybe wishing does become reality," Green said with a chuckle.

"With how boring that conversation was, I was wishing for a fire too," Brackish said. "You need to up your A game because right now I'd give you a C minus."

"I'm having a hell of a time acting interested," Green said, knowing he was safe to talk into the air as nobody in the place was paying the least bit of attention to him in their rush to get out the doors.

"That wouldn't have anything to do with a pretty young aide would it?" Smoke piped up.

"She's an FBI agent, Smoke, not an aide," Green said oddly defensive of Mallory.

"Hmm, I'm sure you're her hero with how you're defending her," Smoke said in a girlie voice.

"Blow me," Green said just as he stepped through the front door of the restaurant, finding a few dozen people milling about the huge parking lot as they looked at the building, presumably looking for smoke. Green heard sirens in the distance.

"Nah, I prefer women," Smoke told him. Before he could make a reply, another voice interrupted.

"Hendrick, over here," the voice called. He turned to find Mallory walking toward him from about twenty yards away. He pulled out his earpiece, done talking to his team as he moved to meet her halfway.

"Hello, Mallory," he said, feeling his spirits instantly lifting.

"Hi," she said, unbelievably acting a bit shy. He hadn't been expecting that. Mallory was confident in all she did and in how she portrayed herself. So, he didn't understand this new side of her.

"What are you doing here?" he asked casually, incredibly glad to see her. Damn, she was stunning even in her work suits. He seriously wanted to peel off her layers, exposing her beautiful body to him one button at a time.

"The senator sent me to apologize to you for the men rushing her out. Whenever there's any kind of situation like the one now, they have to get all high-level officials to safety," she said as if she'd had to say this to other people before.

"And the peons are left to burn?" he asked with a laugh.

"No, of course not," she said automatically, using her rehearsed lines before she seemed to remember she didn't have to be the aide when it was just the two of them. "Actually, they really don't give a damn about what happens to the peons. Just look at natural disasters. They'll move heaven and earth to get out important figures, and the rest of the population is left behind to pick up the pieces. Do you ever wonder how messed up it is that these elected officials are supposed to be servants of the people, but the only ones they serve are those who put money in their pockets?"

"I've always wondered how a politician who makes a decent salary that I don't fault, can then afford mansions, vacation homes, and travel all around the world," he told her.

"The people working their asses off pay for all of that, and they do it every single time they vote for yet another tax or another law the politicians push on them for their own gain."

"Didn't we once have a big old party to tell Britain we weren't going to be controlled?" he asked.

"Those days have been long forgotten," she said with a shake of her head.

"So, what now?" he asked as they walked toward the parking lot.

"What do you mean?" she asked.

"I was picked up and brought here, so I'm sort of stranded," he told her.

She laughed, her true smile showing. "I'm not worried about you being stranded anywhere,

Hendrick. I have a feeling you have a friend or two who can pick you up."

They reached her SUV and he leaned against the driver's door, unwilling to let her go.

"I could have a chopper pick me up if I wanted, but I *want* to spend the day with you," he told her, being more honest than he thought he'd be. Her smile fell as she tried to analyze him.

"Why?" she finally asked. Now he was the one who didn't know what to say.

"Because we have more to discuss," he told her. "And because I like being with you." Her cheeks flushed at his words. She stood there as if indecisive on what she should do.

"I don't have any more work today," she finally said, and he felt as if he'd just won the Super Bowl.

"Then I say we play." There was a definite double meaning in his words, but she seemed to like them. He was damned determined to get a kiss from her before the day was over. It would either be as spectacular as he assumed it would be, or it would be flameless, and they could move on with their lives and simply have a working relationship. He wasn't quite sure which he wanted more.

"What do you want to do?" she finally asked after settling her internal battle.

"I haven't had a lot of play time in the city so why don't you find something fun for us to do? It's a beautiful day and I'm game for anything."

"We can't get caught. There's no work reason I should be with you," she said as she hedged.

"Why don't you call the senator, tell her you're worried about me and going to try to get information from me. That will cover all of the bases if we get busted. In fact, why don't you lead her into telling you to take me out, make me comfortable, and get me to talk. You can act irritated about it," he suggested.

"Damn, you're good. Should I be worried at your manipulation skills?" she asked with a sparkle in her eyes.

"Very worried," he told her with a smug smile.

She picked up her phone and with quick wit and the right words, the senator fell right into the trap, eager to get Mallory to take him out. She hung up and looked at him with a wide grin and evil delight in her eyes that slightly worried him. Maybe giving her full-on power hadn't been the smartest decision he'd ever made.

"Hop in," she told him, hitting the key on her fob. He quickly walked around to the passenger door of her vehicle, worried she was bluffing him to get away from her driver's side door and would suddenly take off. Thankfully, she didn't lock him from the car by the time he reached the other side.

"Where are we off to?" he asked.

"I guess you'll soon find out," she told him . . .

***

Mallory wasn't quite sure what she was doing. But she'd been incredibly jealous when Hendrick had met with Senator Miller for lunch. She knew he was investigating the woman just as she was, but she also knew how charming the senator could be. It's why the woman had come so far in her career, why she'd gotten everything and everyone she'd wanted.

And Hendrick was a man. Would he fall for her charm?

When the senator had told Mallory to take care of the Hendrick situation, she'd been more than happy to do it, wanting to see how he was reacting to being left so completely behind once the first hint of danger had been discovered.

They went to the Seattle Aquarium, and she found herself sitting on the edge of a wall, playing with the various sea creatures the public was allowed to touch. There was something about this place that soothed her nerves. She loved water and most of the creatures that lived within the many depths of seas, rivers, and lakes.

What surprised Mallory was the burning attraction she felt toward Hendrick. It had been a long time since she'd felt that burn in her stomach, a need to be close to a man. She was so focused on her career and the steps she needed to take to not only be respected in her job but be the best. Some said it was more difficult for a woman to make that happen. Mallory's philosophy was it depended on the woman. She hadn't ever considered herself a victim. If she wanted something, nothing was going to stop her from getting it.

She was lost in her thoughts when something in the pool went by and splashed her, sending a spray of salt water up her nose, making her cough as she laughed. Hendrick's laughter joined hers in a perfect medley.

"You'd think I'd learn by the third time that happened," Mallory said as she scooted back. "But nope, I'm a glutton for punishment."

"I could stand here all day and watch you get drenched," he told her, still chuckling.

"Ah, my hero," she said before turning her gaze back toward the sea life playing before her. It was easier to focus on the creatures than the man. The more she looked at him, the more she talked to him, the more time she was with him, the more she fell for him. How in the world was that happening?

Mallory had never been a fan of falling at first sight. That meant a variety of things. She didn't believe in love, lust, or even like at first sight. She believed a person could enjoy another's company, but she didn't believe it was anything more than pleasantries. It took a while to get to know a person and know whether you were compatible or not. If both love and like were looked at more scientifically the world would have a lot fewer feuds on its hands.

"When I was a little girl I wanted to be a mermaid and live my life in the sea," she said, shocking herself by sharing such a silly childhood dream. He didn't say anything right away, so she risked a glance at him.

She was surprised to see his eyes burning as they trailed her body, which she told herself was perfectly covered. The look in his gaze was so intense she looked down again before their eyes connected. Would she jump into his arms if they were trapped in one another's gazes?

This so wasn't her.

It was at least a minute before he spoke again, and his voice was slightly husky. "I can see you swimming the seas as a mermaid," he told her. Then their eyes connected, and he seemed to settle a little as he winked at her. "You know, they don't wear tops."

She felt another flush as his eyes drifted to her ample chest that she covered with constricting tops and fitted suit jackets.

"The thought of that freedom appealed to me until I was about twelve. Then I realized all I'd be able to eat is seafood, which I can't stand, so I gave up on my dreams of swimming the seas around the world."

Hendrick laughed. "You didn't give it up when you realized mermaids weren't real?" he questioned.

She looked at him in mock horror. "What? Mermaids aren't real?" She gasped. "What are you talking about?"

They both laughed as a little girl gazed at the two of them in horror. "I was just kidding," Mallory quickly said. She leaned closer to the child. "But we do have to keep it a secret so the fishermen don't find them."

The girl's eyes flashed with appreciation as she nodded, her face serious. "Yes, we don't want that to happen," she said. The girl's mother sent a thankful look Mallory's way.

"That was a close one," Hendrick said when the child stepped away. "We can't be responsible for crushing the hopes and dreams of our youth."

"I guess we should be careful," Mallory said. "But I do still believe in mermaids, by the way."

She could tell by Hendrick's expression that he was confused. He wasn't quite sure if she was still joking or maybe a little crazy. She enjoyed keeping him guessing.

"Are you going to explain?" he asked as she finally stood, and they began moving through the aquarium looking at the many displays.

"I believe in magic," she said. "And sure, I haven't *personally* seen a mermaid, but I've seen a lot of things in life that take my breath away. So, I choose to believe there are many mythical creatures out there. After all, someone came up with the idea many, many moons ago. Was it because they'd caught a glimpse of a mermaid? Or was it all in their imagination?"

Hendrick seemed to really contemplate her statement, and she found she truly liked that. Finally, he smiled at her, his face breathtaking when his guard was down, and light danced in his eyes.

"I like that," he said. "I've always wanted to slay dragons."

She went serious for a moment, taking in the heat from his body as he walked next to her and a scent she couldn't quite describe. It reminded her of walking through the woods next to a stream at dusk. There were hints of pine, salt, and a freshness about it that made her want to swipe her tongue just once up his neck.

"That's a very noble profession," she told him, loving that he obviously embraced magic too, even if he didn't realize it.

They kept moving through the beautifully decorated aquarium when his stomach rumbled, and he laughed.

"I didn't get to eat my lunch," he told her a bit sheepishly. "By any chance are you hungry?"

"Starving," she said with a laugh. "I didn't realize it until you said that."

"Great, I saw a restaurant sign in the last hallway." They moved to that hallway then went down, finding a great place with a view of the sound. It was absolutely perfect . . . if not a little more romantic than she wanted. The place was dim in the middle of the afternoon since it was heavily overcast in Seattle, and little light shone inside.

"This is fancy," Hendrick said. "I like it. A perfect place for a beautiful woman."

Her body tingled at his words. He was either very smooth or spoke exactly what was on his mind. She hoped for the latter but had a feeling it was him being smooth.

"I've never eaten here. As I don't like seafood, this might not be the wisest choice," she said as they approached the hostess station.

"They always have non-seafood options," he assured her.

There was a window seat available as they were between lunch and dinner. They were seated and the hostess left, assuring them the waitress would be by soon.

"Since your dreams of becoming a mermaid failed, what was your second choice as a child?" Hendrick asked.

"I didn't have a plan B. I was very upset about giving up my mermaid dreams. In high school, I realized my favorite shows were all crime related. I thought of becoming an attorney but knew that sitting in an office all day would drive me absolutely mad, so I did a lot of searches on what my interests were and what jobs would work well for me. The FBI came up on every single one of them. So, I joined the military and then the agency. And here I am now."

Their waiter interrupted, giving them water and menus. He took their drink orders and disappeared again.

"What about you? What made you join the military, and then this group you're in now?" she asked.

He looked as if he was wrestling with the decision to tell her the truth or not. She'd learned in her many years of working with men it was best to be quiet and let them figure out things on their own. If they wanted to talk, they would. If they didn't want to talk and she pushed them, they'd put up a wall.

"I didn't have the best home life," Hendrick finally said after a longer pause, then became more comfortable. My parents divorced when I was three. I lived with my mother, but she checked out emotionally and never came back again. My dad was an absent drunk I rarely saw. He wasn't violent, but he was the definition of a deadbeat dad. I have one brother and one sister who still live in the small town I grew up in. Neither of them have any ambition whatsoever."

"I'm sorry, Hendrick," she said, truly meaning it. "Where did you grow up?"

"In Oxbow, Oregon. The town is so small they don't even have a school."

"I don't know if I've ever been to a town that small. I might've passed one while driving somewhere, but you drive through them so fast if you blink you'll miss it."

"If it wasn't for my teachers and my sports coaches, I don't know how my life would've turned out. But they saw something in me and pushed me to graduate, then helped me when I told them I wanted to join the Navy."

"It was your way out," she said, knowing that feeling. "It also sounds like you've always had what it takes to be successful."

"I don't necessarily know about that. I think I was far more motivated than others. I wanted out of that town and away from my family. So, I worked twice as hard as others because I wasn't letting anything hold me back from getting away."

"It also sounds like you were born with a healthy dose of competition," Mallory told him.

He laughed. She could sink into the sound of his laughter. That was a dangerous place for her to be. They were business partners and nothing else. She had to convince herself of that. It was more difficult the longer she spent time with him.

"Yes," he told her. "I'm certainly competitive, but it's hard not to be when I know the difference between men and boys is strength. I get what I want . . . when I want it. I have a feeling you're the exact same way," he said in that deep, low voice that made her stomach clench.

He leaned in, invading her space in a way she wished they were alone. But they weren't. She was very aware they were in public, and more than aware that if they did anything to blow either of their covers they both might be out of work.

"Hendrick . . ." she began but stopped at the fire burning in his gaze.

"You don't need to say it," he said when the silence dragged on for several moments. "I understand we're doing an important job. I wasn't expecting this curve ball thrown at me."

She was then puzzled.

"Curve ball?" she questioned.

He smiled as he leaned back.

"You," he said. "You're one hell of a curveball and I'm finding I want to take a swing."

Those tingles in her belly spread to between her thighs, and she wondered if she'd be strong enough to resist the attraction between the two of them. Her entire life she'd put her career first. This was the first time she resented that path. She'd always been able to put the female weakness, as she called passion, in her rearview mirror. But with Hendrick she wanted to throw all of her carefully laid plans aside.

"We can't have conversations like these, Hendrick," she finally said.

He didn't seem fazed.

"Why not?" he asked. "I've always believed in honesty."

"Because this job is a career changer for me, and I've worked hard and long on it. We need to stay professional." She put a stern expression on her face that had made many men back down. He didn't even blink. There was something wickedly sexy about a man who knew who he was and wouldn't allow anything to get in his way.

"Please," she said, hating to be pleading with him. Her attraction only grew when he backed down, changing their conversation to work and impersonal topics. He was giving her what she'd asked for, but their sexual tension didn't dim.

They left the restaurant, and the drive back to his place was silent. She put her vehicle in park and waited for him to climb out. He sat there, her throat tightened, and she couldn't utter a word for the life of her.

Finally, he spoke just when she thought the air around them was going to suffocate her.

"I'll respect you, Mallory, but this chemistry between us is unusual and incredibly special. I think we can both do our jobs and explore what this means. I don't want to give you false hopes of white picket fences, children, and animals running around, but I think we could make some magic happen between us as we do our jobs."

Her entire body throbbed with the need to say yes. A job was fulfilling, but it was one piece of a person's life. A human needed touch, needed their needs met. Could she have it all? She'd never tried before.

"I'll think on it," she told him. It was all she could give right then. She needed to clear her head and be out of his presence to think for a while. Maybe the day had been a fluke. Maybe when she woke up the next morning she'd realize how ridiculous she'd been.

"I'll accept that," Hendrick told her.

Then he leaned over and kissed her cheek. Before she could respond, he jumped from her vehicle and disappeared up his walk. The home didn't fit him, she realized as he slipped inside. She didn't know why that thought occurred, but it just didn't fit him.

She finally drove away . . . and his kiss burned long into the night. She couldn't imagine what she'd feel if his lips touched hers . . .

CHAPTER ELEVEN

"Hello, Brackish." Joseph Anderson answered his cell with a smile at the young man who'd already brought much levity to his life over the last few months. If the elder statesman enjoyed anything, it was a man who was supremely confident of his intellect and had a right to feel that way. Brackish fit that mold to perfection.

"Mr. Anderson. How are you today, sir?" Brackish asked with true respect and sincerity. Joseph could hear the smile in his voice as he asked the next question. "Feeling safe and sound in the mansion?"

"I'm well, thank you." Joseph paused for a moment as he chuckled. "You might be feeling sneaky and sly, but I'm much older and wiser than you, boy, and I have to say I feel the same way about it as I did when you initially talked of home safety. My security systems are more than adequate," Joseph boasted.

"I know you like to believe that. Is the wager still on?" Brackish asked.

"Yes, it is. You break into my house, I'll pay you to upgrade all of the systems," Joseph said, not at all worried about his top-of-the-line system failing.

"Any ground rules, sir?"

"Ground rules . . . Hmm. I'll send you a rough schematic of the ground floor. Don't disturb my bedroom or room three on the diagram. Katherine still goes through therapy and I don't need her interrupted or frightened. The object to retrieve is a globe, almost the size of a volleyball, carved out of lapis, it won't be hidden in a drawer or in a secret spot, but it'll be up to you to find it," Joseph said.

"Consider it done," Brackish said confidently. He then finalized the call. "We have a couple things going on this week so you can rest until nearer the end of next week. Be ready."

"Good luck, Brackish. Until then, be safe," Joseph said with a laugh before ending the call.

***

Brackish hung up his phone with a beaming smile. The first part of his operation was set to perfection. Joseph believed the team wouldn't strike for the next week and a half. Meanwhile, he was planning to strike in four days. This would test how good Joseph's systems truly were.

The conference room of the special ops compound housed the team and Chad. They'd all heard the call and were smiling once the connection ended. They were looking forward to having some fun with Joseph and whatever team he was putting together. It was always a positive to test yourself against others. It helped see where your strengths and weaknesses lay.

"Chad, can you get Jasmine on the phone? I have a plan to use her to do our recon. From what we saw of her during paintball, she might be more than happy to help get in on some undercover work," Brackish said. A sinister smile that held no weight, crept over his face.

"Oh, I like it. She's almost as lethal as me," Smoke said to the room.

"Well, I know she's cold-hearted," Sleep said as he rubbed his belly. "I think I have permanent damage from her shooting me in the gut. You know, I like the kid, reminds me of me. If she'd been a boy . . . umm . . ."

With that screwup of words the team realized the noose he'd just set around his own neck and the banter was on.

"If she were a boy, what?" Chad asked with a grin that told Sleep he was glad it wasn't him who'd said those words, and *really* glad no women were in the room with them.

"Yeah, Sleep?" Smoke asked with a smirk. "Is someone at this table being a chauvinistic pig?"

"I don't know," Brackish said as he flexed his arm. "There are just some things a woman can get away with that a man can't. That's not sexist, just reality because we're stronger."

The table erupted. "I've seen some damn strong women," Eyes said.

"Yeah, and they have skills that spin some men in circles," Chad reminded them.

"But not us because we're so smart, talented, and ripped," Smoke said.

"I don't know how smart Sleep is after his slip-up," Eyes said.

"Women might have skills, but this badass has more," Smoke said, standing and flexing his varying bulging muscles, making all of the men groan and make puking sounds.

"Do you ever get tired of being full of yourself?" Brackish asked as the laughter began to die.

"Nope, I'd date myself if it were possible. I don't think there's a woman alive who can handle all of this and keep me entertained," Smoke assured the team. Then he lost it with laughter as he dropped back down into his chair.

Smoke made the room fall apart when he lost his breath from laughing so hard. He had to slap the table, and hard, a couple of times to get his brain to kick back into the natural rhythm of breathing. Green nearly fell out of his chair laughing at how ridiculous Smoke was and that made Chad let out a deep throaty laugh that sounded like a hippo calling its mate. They had to look like a pack of wild hyenas.

After a few more rounds of insults, Brackish got the room to quiet down. Grown men, who'd seen the worst of the worst of what the world had to offer, were wiping tears of laughter from their eyes, but they easily composed themselves in a nanosecond to do their jobs.

"Okay, let me start over," Brackish said while giving a final wave of his sleeve over his eyes. "Chad, the idea is to ask Jasmine to take a few of her cousins and her little brother over to visit their grandparents tomorrow. I think she'll be fully onboard with helping. She's a thrill seeker. We'll tell her to go under the guise of seeing her grandparents, and while they're visiting, she'll start a game of hide and seek throughout the entire house. She'll be the first to hide, but what she'll really be doing is looking for our globe while mapping out the guards' locations."

"Brilliant plan," Eyes said.

"Love it!" Green exclaimed.

"Perfect setup — way to use locals," Sleep offered.

"Nice. She'll definitely be onboard," Smoke shared.

Chad looked around the room at the men he'd been leading and wondered how he'd gotten so lucky to find such a perfect mix. It was a great feeling to lead men who could weave between serious and hilarious with ease. While this was a big deal for Brackish, the only reason the other men remotely cared was because Brackish did, and that was enough for them. If one was in, they all were.

"It'll work flawlessly. Let's send her a text to see if she's available. I know that kid never answers calls," Chad said.

Hey Jazzy, it's Chad, have a secret mission for you if you're interested. Call me ASAP.

Within five seconds of pushing the send button, his phone was ringing, Jasmine's name flashing on the home screen. Chad turned it so the entire table could see then flipped the screen back, hit the accept button, and put the call on speaker so everyone could hear.

"Hey, Chad, what's going on?" Jasmine asked almost out of breath. "I'm in." They all chuckled at her enthusiasm. She didn't even care what it was, and she was in.

"Are you okay, Jazz?" Chad asked.

A couple of audibly deep breaths were heard before Jasmine started again, "Ha. Yes. I'm doing fifty-yard wind sprints. Pushing myself to see if I can be as fast, if not faster, on my twentieth as I was on my first."

"What number are you on?" Chad asked.

"Thirty-three," Jasmine said nonchalantly.

Each man sitting there gave knowing nods. They all knew the internal fire she was displaying, and they fully respected it. Jasmine was going to do some great things with her life. She showed the same grit each of them had shown from a young age.

"Keep pushing yourself. If you have a minute before getting back to it, I have the men from the paintball games with me right now and they're going to ask you to help with something. I'll let Steve discuss the details with you. No pressure at all, but I think you might be interested," Chad said before sliding his phone to Brackish.

"Hi Jasmine, it's Steve. How are you?" Brackish asked.

"Good. What's going on, Steve? How can I help?" Jasmine replied with clear enthusiasm in her tone.

"We're going to break into your grandfather's mansion . . . with his approval, to prove we can. He thinks his security is up to the task. We think otherwise." He paused for a long moment. "And we don't ever lose."

She giggled, excitement clear in her voice. "Oh, Grandpa's good," she said. "I'm wondering if I should be on *his* team or *yours*."

That made all of the men laugh again. She was fire and wit, and she'd grow into a fine young woman. She was nearly there.

"He might be good, but we're better," Brackish said. With Jasmine on Joseph's team, though, it would make their job a little harder, but they were up for any challenge. They hadn't told her the day yet.

"Hmm, I am my grandfather's favorite . . ." She paused long enough to make them all sweat. Then she laughed again. "But I'm also highly competitive and I'm his favorite because I always do the unexpected."

"So . . ." Brackish said, waiting for her answer.

"So, I'm in on team ninjas."

"Team ninjas?" Brackish asked, trying to keep his tone serious, and having a difficult time of it.

"Every team has to have a name," she said, and they could practically see her rolling her eyes. One second after bringing a woman on their team and they were already being bossed around. It caused more chuckles.

"Okay, we'll meet at this location," he said, and rattled off an address. Then he gave her the basics of their plans. She hung up the phone after a gleeful goodbye.

"That girl will go far in life," Smoke said.

"Have you decided to mentor her?" Chad asked.

"I don't know. She's the little sister I never knew I wanted. If all little sisters were that spunky then brothers would complain a lot less."

"True. She'd really thrive if you took her under your wing."

"I was thinking the same thing," Chad agreed.

It had been assumed Jasmine would go into the family business, but the team saw something different in her. They saw a warrior. With the proper training she could be one of them. She and Smoke had bonded at the paintball match, and Chad almost felt sorry for any man Jasmine dated because she not only had a father and uncles who'd kill for her, but now she had a former Army Delta Force man who'd interview potential dates. It might just be wiser for Jasmine to be a nun. It certainly would be safer for all of the young men out there.

"Smoke you're going to make a great father one day," Eyes taunted him. Smoke didn't take the bait. He just leaned back.

"I don't need my own kids. I have plenty of you suckers to lend me some."

But it was true. Whether Smoke knew it or not, he was already showing his extraordinary paternal tendencies. He'd make a damn fine father, uncle, and godparent. He was meant to teach the next generation.

Chad interrupted them with a laugh. "Ha! Look at this text from Jasmine. I'm loving her transformation from beautiful teen into womanhood."

"I just ran two fifties in a row, the fastest I've had all day. Let's get this going and kick some major ass!

"Ah, that's my girl. I'm gonna mold her into the baddest of the bad," Smoke said.

There was no doubt he'd do just that. Jasmine had just inherited a new uncle and the world had better watch out.

****

Four Days Later

"Mr. Anderson, Mr. Chad Reddington and some of his friends are here to see you," the butler announced.

Joseph folded the top part of the newspaper he was reading to look at his butler, not sure he'd heard the man correctly. He wasn't expecting company.

"Say again?" Joseph asked.

"Mr. Reddington and five men are here to see you, sir," was announced again.

"Please send them in," Joseph said while standing.

He made his way from the desk that had been with him for decades to the sitting area of his office. Standing near a recliner, he looked around. They wouldn't announce themselves before trying to break into the house, so he was confused. Coming through the frame of the door in single file the sight was one to behold, one that could most certainly defeat small countries.

"Good day, gentlemen. What brings you to these parts?" Joseph asked.

In between handshakes and seating, Brackish said, "I've come to receive my reward."

Joseph's head quickly snapped to the far wall of his office. The recognition of the globe sitting on the table created a sense of relief. Then confusion took over.

"What reward? The globe's still sitting here," Joseph said, looking over at the object he'd been checking on multiple times a day.

"Is that *your* globe?" Brackish asked. His eyes opened a little more than normal, indicating that maybe Joseph shouldn't be so sure about his assessment.

"Maybe you should look," Sleep prompted.

The men sat, smiles on their faces, looking way too relaxed for Joseph's liking. Under normal circumstances Joseph would never allow anyone to play him for a fool and it *never* happened in his own office. So, for him to start to lose confidence in his thinking was unnerving, especially in this environment.

"Joseph, you *really* should look," Chad said, giving a head nod toward the globe.

"You're all insane, I can see it sitting right there," Joseph huffed but reluctantly rose from his recliner, making his way to the object.

Joseph had put the globe as far from the door as possible, past his desk, in the corner of the room. There were no windows near it, and the only way for someone to retrieve it was to walk completely through the room. He'd even had a CCTV camera put directly on the globe, dedicated to its safety.

The closer Joseph walked to the item the less secure he was in its originality. His pride took a hit well before he reached the table it was sitting on. This wasn't *his* globe. Joseph forced himself to walk all the way to it and was surprised at the elementary nature of the poorly painted orb. The only writing on the surface was a little star in the vicinity of Seattle reading *you are here* next to a gold star.

Joseph muttered under his breath. "Son of a bitch, you guys are unbelievable." He turned to stare at them in disbelief. "When? How?" Returning to his seat, Joseph placed the replacement globe on the coffee table in the center of them and gave it a little spin.

"This morning at three, I walked in here, switched the globe and walked out. In fact, here's your globe," Brackish said as he reached under the couch and pulled out Joseph's stone globe. Everyone smiled.

"Three in the morning?" Joseph gasped. How could someone walk into his home without knowing about it? He knew right then he was going to give Brackish the keys to the kingdom for the security of his home and recommend to his sons they let him look at the security to their businesses and homes as well — if Brackish wanted the work he'd be busy for years.

"Yes, three in the morning. I was able to break the electronic security protocols fairly easily. Don't take offense, almost all of the security systems are built the same and when you know how to break one you can break almost all of them. Whoever built yours did a better job than most, but it was still fairly elementary. From there, knowing you had CCTV set up in various locations around the estate I simply went to the server room, re-routed the feed to play on a loop. At that time of night no one would expect there to be anything but darkness and no movement. To your guards, everything would appear normal," Brackish shared.

"How did you know exactly where it was?" Joseph asked. There was no possible way even Brackish could get through his entire house in an hour.

Brackish smiled. "I had a bit of help."

"What help?" Joseph asked.

"We recruited Jasmine and she did a stake out."

Joseph gasped. "Jasmine? *My* Jasmine," he thundered.

"Yep, your Jasmine. We think she's going to be a damn fine spy someday."

"No, she wouldn't help," Joseph insisted.

"Yep, Grandpa, I helped, and I kicked butt. You had no idea. When I was over the other day I did recon and found where you were hiding the globe," Jasmine said as she entered the room.

Joseph looked stunned, and also impressed. Brackish noted that Jasmine had been right. She certainly was her grandfather's favorite. He didn't think that little girl could do anything wrong in her grandpa's eyes.

"The catch is I think your granddaughter is a former KGB member. No way that girl is eighteen and only getting ready to go to college," Sleep said with levity.

"What?" Joseph asked, more confused than ever.

"You see, we only asked Jasmine to locate the globe and report back to us. Making us a fake globe to trick you was all on her. She brought in the art supplies in a suitcase and handed it over to me when she reported the location," Brackish said.

"Are you serious?" Joseph asked, a mixture of pride and frustration at losing on his face.

"Yes, yes he is," Jasmine said, very proud of herself, as she should be.

"I never thought of you as a spy," Joseph told her.

"Grandpa, ever since Grandma got hurt I've known something big has been going on. I see all of these news reports of drug busts, and big-time dealers getting caught, and the news saying the details to how they were apprehended aren't available to the public. Anyone can surmise that must mean they don't know who's getting the credit because if they knew they'd say. Each of the agencies responsible for things like this love to pat themselves on the back in the news, and since none of them have done that, it makes me think someone out there is doing this without wanting credit. Now, who do I know with enough money and influence to want to help rid the city of drugs all while some super-trooper Greek-god military guys show up together, out of the blue, and are now hanging around you and Chad?" Jasmine asked as calm as could be.

"We..." Joseph started but Jasmine put her hand up, requesting him to pause.

"I said at the hospital the night Grandma was hurt that I'm not a little girl anymore, Grandpa. I know I don't have years of life experience behind me, but I'm not a fool. I want to help wherever possible. My proposition is that you give Steve whatever he was going to get for obtaining the globe, he does whatever it is that you want him to do, and you both share with me what's going on," Jasmine finished.

If the jaws of the men could have hung any lower, they would be tasting the carpet. Each of them was speechless. Impressed but speechless.

Joseph couldn't help but smile at his granddaughter.

"My love, before another word is said I need you to walk back out that door and close it behind you," Joseph asked sweetly, and Jasmine did as requested.

Joseph made a quick phone call to his son, Jasmine's dad, told him the entire situation, to which he laughed hysterically, and then gave his blessing in sharing whatever information Joseph wanted to give, noting that his daughter was a woman now and while he'd do all he could to protect her, it was time to let her take on responsibilities that were much bigger than they'd let her take in the past.

The phone call was disconnected, and Joseph looked at the team before him, asked for their input, and it was Brackish who replied, summing up what they all were thinking. "She's young, but youth shouldn't be an instant detraction from allowing information to be shared. Many young men and women have risen to the occasion when faced with large responsibilities. Aside from that, we all know whatever's shared here, none of us are thinking she'll be walking into any place that could have any degree of physical danger. Besides, I'm scared of what will happen to us if we say no — she's scary smart and will probably trail us. It's smarter to let her know what we're doing, where we can keep an eye on her."

"Jasmine," Joseph called.

Jasmine found her seat next to Smoke again and was told what the men were doing with fighting crime in the city. She wasn't given deep details, but she was given more than enough to ask question after question after question. Some of them she didn't receive answers to, others led to more questions.

After a while Joseph turned back to Brackish, still completely in shock they'd managed to get into his home so easily even with the help of his eldest granddaughter.

"How did you get past the guards?" Joseph asked, though he knew the answer to the question before he formulated it.

"If you expect two men to watch over the entirety of your grounds then we should have another conversation. Right, or wrong, the appropriate number of guards you have can only be answered correctly by you. What you're comfortable with is the only answer there is. None of us sitting here will tell you what to do, we have our own ideas, but the idea of your home coming under physical attack from an outside entity isn't all that high in my opinion," Brackish replied.

Joseph sat back, deep into his chair, and went into a part of his mind he hadn't needed to for quite some time. He questioned the safety of his home and what that meant for Katherine more than anything else. There weren't many men as good as Brackish, but he made his way into the house with no difficulty at all. He was impressed with the special ops team, but he was also going to fall into a dark mood if he didn't address this issue immediately.

"I don't live in a world of fear and don't think I need to live in a prison in my own home with armed guards stationed every few feet around my property, but I admit when someone is right, and you were right, Steve. You said my security isn't up to what it should be, that you could easily break in, and you did," Joscph admitted.

"It isn't something that brings me joy," Brackish admitted.

Joseph gave out an exhausted exhale. The year overall had been taxing on him and this was one more burden to think about. Even in his moment of self-pity he laughed at how ridiculous he was being for having the thoughts and emotions while sitting in front of these men who'd been through hell on earth and were still going strong.

Joseph stood, went to his desk, slid a drawer open, pulled out a small pad, walked back to the recliner, started writing on the pad, then tore off the paper and handed it over to Brackish.

"I don't want you taking any of your time away from the operations currently going on but if you want to start upgrading my security, this is my offer. It's thirty percent higher than what I currently pay my security team, plus a one hundred percent bonus for bringing this to my attention," Joseph said.

Without showing any indication if the amount written on the check was more or less than what he thought it should be, Brackish stood, took a step toward Joseph, extended his hand and said, "It's a deal. When I'm done no one will ever be able to hack into any of your systems ever. If they do, I'll give you every dime back, plus interest."

"If any of you'd like to take on the oversight of my physical security, I'm willing to discuss that now as well," Joseph said, looking over the other men.

"While I shouldn't speak for the men, I'm going to. I won't be able to help, I have a career I enjoy very much and I'm building it into something amazing. Green has just started his newest company and he won't be able to focus on this. Smoke has his own company going as well. I know Brackish will defer to us, not that he couldn't do it, but his love is in the cyber world and I'm confident that's where he'll want to stay. That leaves Sleep, who recently married a hottie, who is also *way* smarter than he is, and isn't going to be moving anywhere again any time soon. So, when we complete our task he's going to be out of a job because as of right now I'm firing him from the one down in SF," Eyes said with his world-renowned goofball smile.

"That's true, but I'm still better looking and smarter than you. I get to go to sleep every night knowing that truth," Sleep retorted.

The men laughed, ribbed each other, and enjoyed the fellowship of the moment. There'd be more conversations about the physical security of the Anderson mansion, as well as their other properties, but the rest of their time together that day was one of telling stories and making fun of each other — only in the way that men who trusted each other completely could.

And Jasmine was right there with them. None of them knew what exactly that meant, but they all saw the light in her eyes they'd had at the beginning of their careers. She just might be working with them someday soon.

CHAPTER TWELVE

Mallory felt tension throb through her as she downed her third vodka and cranberry of the evening. She was at a baseball game in an owner's booth watching as Senator Miller laughed, flirted, and played the dutiful politician, while practically hanging from Hendrick's arm like an extension of his body.

Dammit!

She never should've gone out with him a few days earlier, never should've shared with him, laughed with him, and opened herself up to him. She looked at Hendrick Meeks in a whole new light and didn't like it one little bit. They had a job to do, and she couldn't do that job if she fell for her partner.

That word stopped her. He wasn't in the FBI, and he wasn't her partner. They were only working together. She'd come prepared to the game, knowing he was going to be there, and that the senator had gotten all green lights to pursue the man. She'd been with the senator the day before when she'd been ranting that Hendrick hadn't called or texted. She was used to men panting at her feet, and Hendrick playing it cool was driving the senator crazy.

It wasn't as if the senator was in love or even in like with Hendrick, though. She'd had another man brought into her place the night before to "scratch her itch" as she liked to say. That made Mallory realize her own itch hadn't been scratched in over three years. She might wither up and die if she didn't have an amazing orgasm with a man worshiping her body real soon. And though she was trying not to look at Hendrick as the man who could get the job done, she just couldn't help herself.

She was far from sexy at the baseball game, choosing comfort and business casual at the same time, wearing a fitted, somewhat short, black skirt and baseball jersey the senator had insisted all of her team wear.

Mallory's hair was up in a ponytail, which she despised, and she wore flats, knowing she'd be doing a lot of pacing. She found a secret thrill in the power of heels, even on the job, but they were very impractical. She couldn't very well chase a bad guy in three-inch stilettos.

The room erupted in applause as their team took the lead for the first time in three innings. Hugs, fist bumps, and high-fives were exchanged as liquor flowed. The crowd parted as the senator's phone rang and she stepped outside the suite. Mallory's eyes collided with Hendrick's, and the heat in them nearly melted her to the spot.

They held gazes for several moments when the door opened, and the senator stepped back inside. "I have to take care of something. I should be back in about twenty minutes," she said, her eyes only on Hendrick.

Mallory looked away with disgust. This was what they wanted. They needed the senator to trust Hendrick, to pull him in closer. But the thought of him going home with her was enough to make her stomach heave.

Hendrick said something and the senator left the room, escorted by her twenty-four-hour guards, and Mallory needed a break. She'd been fantasizing about Hendrick for three days in a row and she felt as if she couldn't breathe.

She looked up again to find his eyes on her, something flashing between them hot enough to blow up the entire stadium. She quickly turned and fled the room just as another eruption sounded in the stadium when "Home Run" was yelled over the speaker system. The few people who'd been in the hallway rushed back into their suites and Mallory sprinted away, finding a quiet corner away from everyone.

She let out a sigh of relief as strong hands snaked around her waist and spun her, making the remaining air rush from her deprived lungs. She gazed up in shock at Hendrick's intense eyes and hard lips. He was so damn tall, towering above her, his strong arms flexing against her sides, and his chest crushing hers.

"Wh . . . what are you doing?" she gasped, her voice hungry and urgent. She wanted to kick herself, but she couldn't even breathe, let alone think rationally. She was a trained agent, and this wasn't acceptable.

"You've been driving me mad all night with your hungry looks while I have to pretend to be interested in anything that vulgar woman says," Hendrick growled.

She was shaking in his arms which she'd never done before. "Stop, Hendrick. If someone sees us . . ." she began, stopping at the look in his eyes.

She was straining to retain her composure when he reached up and grabbed her chin firmly with his strong fingers. He didn't hesitate before bending down and *finally* claiming her lips in a kiss that both invaded and possessed at the same time.

His tongue was sharp as it navigated her mouth in probing swipes that had her knees trembling and her arms clenching around his neck. Within seconds her body was more awake than it had ever been, and she clung to him like a vise. Shock at him capturing her lips evaporated as his free hand ran down her back and squeezed her ass, pulling her against his body, making her very aware of how turned on he was.

He wasn't only hard, but the bulge pressing against her was big and tempting. There was nothing sweet and exploring in this touch. It was wanton and needy, calling to her in a way nothing had before.

Mallory was a strong woman who ruled her life and didn't take prisoners. She'd always been in control . . . until now. She squirmed against him as he backed them up against a wall and moved his hands, grabbing her hips and pulling her up, making her skirt crawl up to her panties as she lifted a leg, wanting his arousal pressing against the part of her that felt as if it were on fire.

She wanted to be taken . . . wanted to be kissed . . . wanted to lose all control. She wanted to be his.

His hand slid under the hem of her skirt and ran over the bare skin of her ass that was barely covered by her red silk panties. She'd never been more grateful for her secret love of lace, silk, and satin. She was ready for him to take her right there against the wall and be damned with the consequence. He was ravishing her in a way she hadn't known she needed until that very moment.

His finger began to slip beneath the elastic of her panties when a yell in the hallway was swifter than a bucket of ice-water over their heads.

"Dammit, why don't they just hand the game over!" a drunken voice shouted as heavy steps moved toward them.

Hendrick wrenched his mouth from hers as he leaned back, setting her leg on the ground and tugging on her skirt at the same time he covered her body from view of anyone walking past them.

She couldn't see the man as he moved down the hallway, but she was shaking in Hendrick's arms, partially from the reality of what she'd been willing to do in a public place, and mostly from the effect she was still having with him so close to her.

"I'm sorry," he finally said. "That got out of hand really quick. You've been killing me all night as I've stared at your legs, at the sexy pout of your lips, and the way that jersey clings to your breasts. I lost it. I won't let that happen again."

If it wasn't for the huskiness of his voice and the thickness of his erection still pressing into her, she might think he was fully composed. He was recovering a hell of a lot faster than she was.

"I don't know how that just happened," she said, her voice breathy and needy.

"We finally kissed," he told her before he smiled, taking the breath she'd been gaining right back from her. "And we'll definitely do it again."

"That was quite pleasant, but I don't think it's a good idea," she told him. The longer they stood there, the more composure she gained. That was better. She wasn't some dreamy-eyed teenager, making out with the injured baseball player while the game went on in the background. She was a confident woman on the job.

He laughed at her words and she glared at him.

"It was more than pleasant, and you know it," he told her. He pulled back and she chilled at the loss of his body heat. He gave her a look from head to toe before nodding. Then he reached up and brushed below her lip, probably wiping away lipstick. She was sure she looked as if she'd just been ravished. "And it will *certainly* happen again. For now, we should get back. There's a bathroom just around the corner. You might want to fix your hair or everyone in that suite will know what just went on."

Her cheeks flushed with color as she reached up and yanked her rubber band from her hair. She was sure it was a mess. He'd had her against the wall, and she'd been a wriggling mess in his arms. How in the world was she going to get through the rest of the game? They had at least an hour left. And how was she going to react when the senator came back and put her hands all over Hendrick? A shudder passed through her at the thought of that.

She left him standing there without another word and was horrified at her reflection. At least she was alone in the large bathroom. She fixed her hair and makeup as best she could, but there was nothing she could do about the heightened color in her cheeks. She definitely needed another drink — that was for damn sure.

The two of them entered the suite again just as a foul ball sailed overhead and landed in the glove of a very happy child. The big screen flashed his grin, clearly showing his missing two front teeth. The boy's father lifted him in the air as the fans cheered.

Mallory found a smile as she grabbed another vodka and cranberry and moved over to stand with a group of men just as the senator glided back into the room, immediately spotting Hendrick and walking to him. She said something, pulling him from the person he'd been speaking with and he leaned back and laughed, his merriment echoing through the room.

Spite filled Mallory. She knew they'd just been kissing to within an inch of their lives, but jealousy still flowed through her. The poor man next to her didn't stand a chance.

"What did I miss while I was gone?" she asked in a flirty voice Mallory despised. The look in the man's eyes was satisfaction enough for her to bear it though.

She flirted as he laid out in detail the last inning, and she sipped her drink, forcing herself not to guzzle it. Mallory loved sports, but not when her hormones raged and she desperately tried not to watch as the senator and Hendrick touched, laughed, and made a show for the group better than the game they were watching.

It was the eighth inning when a voice whispered in her ear. "Are you driving me crazy on purpose?"

A chill slithered down her spine as Hendrick's hot breath flowed over and in her ear. She turned, her face composed even with the buzz she was feeling.

"Whatever do you mean?" she asked with enough sugar to fuel an ant for life.

"You've had your hands all over this idiot for the past hour. He's barely standing and just stumbled from the room. Remember my hands were the ones bringing you pleasure not very long ago," he told her.

A merging mixture of desire and anger filled her as her core tightened and her blood ran hot.

"Your hands have been busy with the senator. Go away," she whispered.

"It's a damn good thing I'm wearing this jersey or everyone in this room would know the condition you've left my body in. You can flirt all you want, Mallory, but I'm the only man in here who can bring you the satisfaction you're craving right now," he warned.

The senator sidled up to them before she could respond. Mallory was thankful for the jersey as well, because her nipples were so hard they'd put on a show the entire suite of people would be able to read loud and clear.

"Mallory, I haven't had a chance to chat with you tonight. Are you enjoying the game?" the senator asked.

Mallory had to force herself to remain calm at the drunken look the senator was wearing. Mallory knew it was all a show. The senator didn't drink anything other than wine when she was in privacy. She always maintained a strict demeanor when in public. And though people might think she was drinking, her aides knew to give her nonalcoholic drinks only she knew she was holding. That allowed her to act as she wanted. She was putting on a show for Hendrick, probably hoping he was going to take advantage of her, and she could blame the alcohol for her actions. It was disgusting.

"Very much, but I think I'm going to call an end to the night. We have a lot of meetings tomorrow," Mallory said. She finished the last of her drink and set the glass down.

"You don't want to leave before the end of the game. This is a close one," the senator said, but she could see the woman didn't mean it. There was nothing the woman would like more than for the game to end so she could take Hendrick home.

The thought of that literally made Mallory sick. She was a fool. They were doing their jobs. And Mallory didn't think it would be a hardship for Hendrick to seduce the senator. They'd both get what they wanted. Mallory wasn't sure why the thought of him touching Anna was killing her a bit. It had to be the alcohol.

She didn't say anything more, just turned around and left as she ordered an Uber. There was a small part of her that hoped Hendrick would find an excuse and chase her down. But as she reached the parking area, she realized that was idiotic too. She'd worked too long on this case to throw it all away. She was a professional. It was time she remembered that.

Maybe she shouldn't see Hendrick anymore.

She was almost home when the message appeared on her phone, making her heart skip a beat. *I'm picking you up Saturday morning. Don't worry. We won't be spotted by anyone where we're going. We're going to play soccer.*

She hesitated. Hadn't she just been telling herself she wasn't going to see the man away from the senator anymore? She firmed her shoulders and began typing a reply. She hit send before throwing her head back and sighing.

What time?

She was a fool. And she might end up jobless when this was done. But for some reason, she couldn't find it anywhere inside of her to care.

CHAPTER THIRTEEN

Mallory looked out her window each time a car passed by her house. Hendrick was due to arrive any minute and her lack of patience was being felt by the carpet under her pacing feet. She couldn't believe she was so enamored with the man she was acting like a schoolgirl getting ready to go on her first date.

She couldn't stop thinking about their kiss at the ballgame. It had been hot and sexy and everything she'd ever dreamed a kiss would be. So instead of acting like the mature adult she was, she'd spent the morning changing her outfit and shoes, and then fixing and re-fixing her hair and makeup.

Of course, she didn't care too much for a bunch of cake on her face, so the waterproof mascara and liner and a hint of lipstick was what she'd settled on.

She assumed she'd be sweaty and possibly muddy within the hour, so she didn't understand why grooming seemed so necessary.

Hendrick Meeks. That's why. Dammit.

But after a game of soccer, he'd told her they would be off to another adventure, so she'd gone through her clothes again, choosing two outfits she had stashed in her backpack so she could change. He'd refused to tell her what they were doing after soccer, but had said to bring nice clothes, preferably a dress, but saying a pair of dress jeans and heels were just fine. She wanted to pack yoga pants and a hoodie to be defiant. She might be able to act as if she didn't care in front of him, but she knew the truth.

She was waiting with the cliché bated breath.

As she was glancing in the hallway mirror for the eightieth time, her ears caught the sound of a car stopping and a door shutting. He'd arrived. Was she going to have him come inside? Could she trust herself enough to show him around, give him a tour of her small but modern home? Nope. That wasn't a good idea as her clothes, including her panties and bra, were currently thrown on the bathroom floor.

She'd gotten home late the night before, had been more than a little buzzed, and beyond sexually frustrated, and cleaning had been the last thing on her mind. Then she'd woken late after tossing and turning for hours and had been in a rush to get ready before Hendrick arrived. Hendrick was most definitely not coming inside . . . at least not yet.

He knocked on her door, and she found herself flinging it open within a second. She should've stood in front of it and taken some deep breaths first. The sight of him made her knees a little wobbly.

"Good morning," Hendrick said in that voice that did beautiful things to her body.

"Good morning; you're right on time. I just finished getting ready," Mallory said. She was having to constantly remind herself she wasn't a teenager on a first date. They were partners working on an important case.

She stepped outside, firmly shutting the door behind her, bringing the two of them beautifully close. She glanced up and instantly found herself lost in the man's sexy gaze. She'd been in such a hurry to block him from her home she hadn't thought that she'd basically be flinging herself into his arms.

"In a hurry to see me?" he asked as he reached out and touched her waist, making her skin tingle.

"In a hurry to burn off some steam," she said, her husky voice betraying her.

He smiled, his fingers caressing her through her clothes for a few moments, before he took a step back, making her able to take in a soothing rush of air.

"Okay, let's go burn off some energy," he told her.

They walked to the car with Hendrick's hand behind her back. She didn't try to brush it aside, finding she liked the feel of his large fingers touching her. She knew how beautifully they could grasp her thighs and hips.

She shook her head to clear it. If she spent the day with thoughts like that, she was officially screwed. As they got to the car Hendrick stepped in front of her, opened the passenger side door, and held the handle until she was inside. She was grateful when he took the long way around the vehicle, giving her time to calm her nerves and try to get her hormones under control.

Silence hung heavy between the two of them as he slid into the driver's side of his roomy vehicle.

She wasn't sure she could handle a completely silent ride. In all of their interactions so far, the two of them had been able to delve into numerous topics, keeping the conversation flowing during their time together and not feeling awkward. But always, there was an air of sexual tension between them. And it was hanging so thick that it seemed neither of them could formulate two words, let alone entire sentences.

"It'll only take us about thirty minutes to get there," Hendrick said after he pulled out onto the quiet street. She smiled as she looked at the map on his navigational screen. He didn't need to say a word as it was telling them their arrival time. Maybe he was trying to break the silence between them.

"Good. I need to move. Sitting too long in a vehicle today will drive me crazy," she said. He nodded. And then they went back to silence. After about ten minutes, Mallory had to repress a smile as she thought about the awkwardness of the moment. It felt almost as if they were at a middle school dance. Boys on one side, girls on the other, both hoping the other would break the stalemate and cross the room to ask for a dance.

Finally, after thirty minutes felt that like ten hours, they pulled into a nice park outside of the city.

"This is beautiful," Mallory told him. "I haven't been here before."

There were large groups on multiple soccer fields. "I hadn't planned on joining an actual game, just kicking it around between the two of us. I haven't been here before either," Hendrick said as he turned to her, his eyes lit up. "But if you're game we'll ask to join."

"I haven't played in years. I'd love to play a game," she said, finally feeling the tension between them float away. There was nothing like a good active game to get your mind off sex — or more accurately, a lack of sex.

They stepped from the car, went to the back of the vehicle, changed their shoes, then approached a group of people who were still setting up for a game. Mallory noticed there were no females. She hoped they wouldn't mind her joining. It had been a while, but within minutes she'd show them she was good if they gave her a chance.

Hendrick approached the group with confidence. "Mind if we join?" he asked.

"Both of you? Sure, just so long as you know this is a little higher skill level than other pickup games. Don't know if either of you have played in the past but if not, I'd recommend waiting for another half hour-ish when the other players who go to field B start showing up." The man wasn't arrogant, just letting them know the skillset needed to have an enjoyable game.

"I don't know about this two-footed oaf, but I've played a game or two," Mallory said while digging her elbow into his ribs.

The young man laughed, then turned to lead Hendrick and Mallory to the field. "Also, not that it matters to anyone here, but we don't do a lot of talking. We play hard," he said with a laugh. "About seventy-five percent of the players don't speak much English. We have guys from Mexico to Russia and everywhere in between. There's a guy from Japan who knows how to say Starbucks, Seattle, and Futbol. That's it."

"Sounds good," Hendrick said with a laugh.

"I don't like chattiness when I play," Mallory said. "I get a little competitive."

"Then you're on my team," the kid said. "I'm Seth, by the way."

"Great to meet you, Seth," Hendrick said as he shook hands. "I'm Hendrick and this is Mallory."

"Perfect, let's do this," Seth said.

Within five minutes teams were formed and gathered to their respective sides. Eight men on one side, seven men and one woman on the other. In their own way of communicating, mostly by a couple of guys physically placing others in a spot, it was settled on who'd play where. It wasn't a shock to Mallory she was put on defense, as far away from the attacking position as possible.

She also wasn't surprised to find Hendrick put in the middle. Hendrick was most certainly a man who stood out among other men. At six two, Mallory was sure he was normally the tallest in most situations. In terms of soccer players, he was a giant. Most of the players were closer to Mallory's height than Hendrick's.

Forty minutes into the game Mallory had touched the ball a total of two times. She was getting ticked. She despised being coddled, and she really hated when men treated her like a delicate flower. She could hold her own, and she'd had more than one bloody nose in her life from playing fast and hard. What was the fun in playing a game she didn't get to participate in?

Halftime was called and the players walked to their respective spots to pick up their drinks as different languages flowed around them.

"I'm losing patience," Mallory told Hendrick who looked perfectly happy. Of course *he* was, he'd been handling the ball the entire first half.

"What?" Hendrick asked, obviously clueless. Typical male.

"If my own team doesn't give me a chance to work some magic on the ball soon, I'm going to start kicking them," she whispered.

He laughed. "We might not be invited back if that happens," he told her.

"I don't care. What's the fun in playing if I can't play?"

He shrugged. "Be more aggressive." His words should've ticked her off, but he was right. If she wanted to prove herself, as she had to do a lot in a male dominated workspace, she had to go the extra mile.

She let out another sigh. "Dang it."

"What now?" he asked, laughing again as he guzzled his drink.

"I forgot my water and Gatorade on my kitchen table."

"Lucky for you, I brought extra," Hendrick said before he took a drink then handed it over to her. She didn't hesitate to grasp the bottle. She was thirsty and not even thinking about germs. Heck, with how their tongues had been tangling the night before, there were no germs left that hadn't been swapped.

Just as their break ended, the few clouds that had been lazily hanging in the sky disappeared, and the summer heat became noticeable. The sun was no longer hidden, and it warmed up real fast as players made their way back onto the field.

Hendrick took his shirt off and threw it to the ground next to his drink. He walked ahead of Mallory and she found herself tongue-tied as she gazed at his muscled back, the skin toned and tight and narrowing perfectly into his shorts that hung over his beautiful ass.

Several of the other men threw off their shirts as well, but Mallory didn't care. There was only one man she was devouring with her eyes, and now she might be screwed on showing her prowess on the field. She couldn't see the ball if she couldn't take her eyes off of Hendrick. She finally reached him on the field.

"Come with me," he told her, taking her by the elbow and leading her to the attacking position. There were only a couple of complaints from the man Hendrick moved out of his position. But with one look from Hendrick, the guy stopped arguing. Damn, Mallory didn't want to be turned on by that — but she was.

"She's a striker this half," Hendrick called to his teammates.

If there were any arguments from the other men, they didn't verbalize them.

Hendrick started to turn away, but Mallory reached out and barely got hold of his bicep in the tips of her fingers. He turned his head to look at her and she whispered her thanks. He nodded and she turned away from him, wanting to concentrate on the game. So that meant no looking at his naked flesh.

It only took ten minutes before just about every man playing had their shirts off. The heat was becoming a deciding factor in who was in shape and who thought they were. In the new position Mallory was running a lot more. Her body was overheating quickly, but she refused to give in to exhaustion.

A ball was passed to her, she dribbled around one defender, then another, passed it to a player streaking to her left, then cut toward the middle and found herself wide open. Calling for the ball multiple times the other player ignored her and tried getting past three defenders only to have the ball stolen from him. The same scenario played out again, and again the ball was stolen from him. This time she confronted him.

"Dude, pass the damn ball. The last two times I've been wide open," Mallory chided.

A man on the other team came up with irritation and condescension in his eyes. "Woman, you do not talk to him that way. He's my cousin." She opened her mouth to snap at the man when he repeated himself. "*You* do not talk to him. You shouldn't even be here. This is a man's game, not a place for females. Learn your place."

Mallory stood there in shock before she glanced around to see if the others were watching this scene play out. But no one had noticed anything wrong. She wanted to yell, hell, she wanted to throw the man to the ground and show him just how tough she was. But Mallory knew the strongest thing a person could do most of the time was walk away. She turned and started back to her position, but instead ran over to the sideline, grabbed the Gatorade, and chugged the rest of the contents.

As she looked back at the field of shirtless men, she decided she was going to cool off herself. The man's pompous attitude had given her an attitude of her own. She was just as fit as any of the men out there, and she was good at what she did. So, she pulled off her shirt, leaving her in a perfectly modest sports bra. It was black, nothing was showing, and women worked out in them all of the time at gyms and while running. There should be no issues.

As she came back onto the field the play was coming back toward her, and she sprinted hard at an angle for the player to get her the ball while at full speed. Just as the ball was passed to her, and she was on her way to the goal, a dark streak came up next to her, slamming a shoulder and elbow into her side.

The purposeful and violent impact lifted her into the air. With the speed she was sprinting and the impact of the hit, her balance was completely thrown off. She was only able to get her forearm in front of her face a fraction of a second before landing and tumbling over herself.

The world rotated a couple of times before coming to a complete stop. While lying on her back, she took a moment to check for injuries and gain her bearings. Then she jumped to her feet, ready to fight the idiot who could've caused serious damage. It wasn't the first time this had happened in a game, but it was the first from a man. She wouldn't take it from a woman, and she sure as hell wouldn't take it from a man.

The man who bulldozed her was the same man who just talked down to her, and before she could get to him and defend herself, he was circled and yelled at by some of the other players. The only thing she could see that stood out was Hendrick face to face with that man.

With one hand Hendrick was picking the guy up by his hair, the other hand squeezing hard around the man's neck. There were too many voices to decipher what was being yelled. One thing for certain was Hendrick didn't hesitate to defend her. She could defend herself, but she had to admit she liked that he was sticking up for her. What the man had done was completely reckless and uncalled for.

The scuffle on the field dissipated quickly, though some harsh words in different languages were still calling out to each other. Mallory was in a bit of shock at all of it. Hendrick turned, then made his way over to Mallory.

"Are you okay?" he asked, his body visibly shaking, the adrenaline from the moment obviously still raging through him.

"I'm good," Mallory said, looking into Hendrick's eyes that were as deep blue as the sky at first morning light.

"I don't know what that asshole was thinking, but it took all of my restraint not to pummel him to within an inch of his life," Hendrick said.

She smiled. "You do remember I'm FBI, right? I can pummel too. I was the bigger person earlier and walked away. After pushing me, I was going to show him some of my special training." Hendrick smiled, but she saw that he was still too worried to really find humor. She wasn't sure why that pleased her so much.

Hendrick slowly brought his hands to her jaw, gently cupped her chin, and maneuvered her head, brushing her hair away to look closely at her skin for injuries. She could smell his sweet, musky scent, and it was driving her insane, washing away any and all injuries she might've barely felt. She sucked in air and her lungs burned. The more she was near this man, the more she needed him. Was she a fool not to take what they both wanted?

Their eyes locked and she couldn't seem to stop herself from taking a half step closer to him. He was blotting out the sun with his body, but the heat coming from him was too much to bear. She reached up and gently grabbed his elbows, locking the two of them together.

"I'm fine," Mallory said again in a husky whisper. She wasn't physically hurt, but she was aching in a way that only Hendrick could help.

He looked at her, really looked at her, and she knew he was reading all of the signals she was throwing out. His gaze roved over her face, down her neck where sweat was trickling in little drops straight into the V of her chest. That made her nipples tighten, and his eyes locked onto the swollen nubs trying to break free from their confinement. She wanted him to see all of her, to touch all of her, to take away this ache she'd been feeling from the first moment they'd met.

"Yes . . . yes you are fine," Hendrick said softly, finally looking back up to her eyes.

He leaned against her, the sweat from their bodies sliding between them as they reached for each other and sent the heat factor off the scale. He leaned down, about to close the final inches between them when a voice called out, making Mallory want to growl with frustration.

"Hey, is Mallory okay?" The words dashed a splash of cold water on them which they definitely needed in a very crowded park.

"Are you okay, or do you want to get out of here?" Hendrick asked.

Mallory reached out and took Hendrick's hand, intertwining their fingers, then leaned up and kissed his ear. "I think it's time for us to leave."

"Amen," he said. He turned to the other players.

"Mallory is fine, but we're finished. Enjoy the rest of the game."

With that, Hendrick took Mallory with him to gather their gear, then quickly moved back to his car. She burned with anticipation. Hendrick opened the door for her, then rushed to the driver's side of the vehicle. He started the car then pushed the windows down and cranked up the air conditioning to help cool them off.

It didn't take long for Mallory to react to the cool air washing over her chest. Green noticed her nipples grow hard and push against the fabric she desperately wanted off of her. When she saw the look in his eyes, she felt her hunger grow even more.

"Where are we going?" Mallory asked, seduction dripping in her tone.

He turned and smiled, and she was glad he wasn't driving yet. They might just crash with how jumpy both of them were.

"Somewhere that's going to keep you very, very wet," he said.

She felt her body slip over the edge, and she wondered if the man could talk her body into coming. He might, because with every stroke of his voice it was like a slide of his tongue over her clit. She clenched her thighs together as she reached out and rubbed her fingers along his thigh.

"You'd better drive fast then," she told him, before looking down at the arousal his shorts refused to hide. It pulsed beneath the thin nylon. She ran one finger over the hard flesh and they both shuddered.

"If you want to get home alive, you can't do that," he said, his voice strained.

She reluctantly pulled away as she looked around the park. She wasn't sure either of them would make it home. But this place was far too crowded for an afternoon tryst. She'd have to control herself . . . if she could.

CHAPTER FOURTEEN

Mallory was shaking as Hendrick pulled up to her house. Neither of them said a word as they moved to her door. Her fingers trembled, taking three tries before she was able to get the key into the lock and open her door.

As they stepped inside, she was unsure what to say or do. She didn't normally bring men to her home. If she liked someone and they were dating, it might progress, but nothing like this had happened to her before. He took the uncertainty away from her when he grabbed her, pulling her against his body. The heat that had escaped from them in the frozen car quickly returning.

"I haven't had a single moment I haven't craved you since you were wrapped in my arms last night, panting against my lips, your body hot and inviting."

Her eyes locked with his and a bead of sweat dripped down his brow, her hunger growing by leaps and bounds. She'd never been so turned on in her life. The explosion she was anticipating would surely rock her world and leave a crater in its path.

Speechless, she willingly fell into his arms. Her fingers bit into his thick biceps as their mouths collided. She pulled his lip between her teeth and nibbled, making a moan escape him that did beautiful things to her insides. His hands clenched her butt as he tugged her close, pressing his arousal into her. She ran her hands up his arms and tugged on his hair, ready for him to take her right there against her door. But then he pulled back, causing her to whimper.

She opened her eyes and stared into his smoky blue ones. They were normally so clear, but right now it looked as if storm clouds were rolling across them. "I need you in the bedroom right now," he growled, the sound a call to her core.

On shaky knees, she ran to her bedroom with him right on her heels, his enticing fingers never falling away from her back. They practically fell into her room, and Hendrick pulled her close, his lips descended as his hands slid down her back.

She needed a shower, but she couldn't delay what was coming. Maybe they could ease the ache and then shower, and then have a second round. She wanted this man unlike any other, and she didn't care how she looked or how messy she was.

His lips trailed over her jaw and he began licking and nibbling her neck, making her cling to him as he devoured her with his tongue, lips, and teeth. She spread her legs to keep from falling as she ran a hand up his side, his muscles rippling beneath her touch.

"More, I want more," Mallory said as she pushed him. His eyes widened in a bit of shock before he allowed himself to topple onto her bed. She climbed over him, feeling bold, sexy, and in control. She knew he was allowing it, but that didn't lessen the impact it had.

He pulled her down to him as she writhed, their bodies locked together, few clothes between them. He grabbed her head and kissed her again, making her lose her breath as his tongue circled her mouth and his hands gripped her hips, tugging her into his hard body as he thrust and gave her a preview of what would soon be inside her.

He tore his mouth from hers and she leaned forward, unwilling to let go of the connection, but then his hands slid up her back and beneath her sports bra. She lifted her arms and he easily pulled it over her head, her breasts spilling out against his chest. The touch of his fine hair against her nipples sent a surge of wet heat to her core and she groaned.

Before their mouths could connect again, he lifted her up and pulled her closer, his mouth closing over her hard nipple as he sucked it deep into his mouth and flicked his tongue over the tip again and again until she cried out. It was so good, so unbelievably good.

He scraped his teeth over her tender flesh, licked it, and sucked again while his hand ran up her thigh and beneath her shorts, straight to the edge of her panties. He moved his head to lavish attention on her other straining nipple as he slipped inside her panties and slid his finger along the wet heat, her moan filling the room.

"I need you now," she gasped as she pushed against his finger that slipped inside her heat. "I'm ready . . . right now." She didn't need more foreplay. She needed him.

"Not yet," he said. "I finally get to touch this body and it's not ending fast."

She groaned in frustration, then gave him a wicked smile. If he wanted to play, she was more than willing to play. But she wasn't going to be the only one tortured, and his sweaty, musky body was doing things to her that should send her to the ER.

She pushed away from him, and he tried to stop her, but she grinned and trailed her finger over his lips and down his chin as she leaned down and nipped the corner of his jaw, making him groan as he reached his fingers in her hair and pulled.

She kissed her way down his neck, the taste of salt and musk the most beautiful aphrodisiac she's ever experienced. His stomach quivered as she licked the muscled flesh, turning her body to mush. She loved that she was the one making this large, beautiful man tremble beneath her touch.

She reached into his shorts and he lifted his hips. She pulled the shorts and underwear down with shaking fingers, then gasped as he sprung free, his glorious erection silky smooth, large, and throbbing, the tip shiny with his arousal.

He kicked his shorts away as she gazed at him in hunger.

"Mallory," he gasped as her fingers circled his base and moved up and down his skin, fascinated with the ripples in his flesh and the beads of moisture escaping his round tip.

"Yes?" she purred as her face drew nearer, the erection calling to her like a beacon at sea.

"Come here," he demanded.

Everything within her felt a need to obey his command, but she was too mesmerized. She closed the distance to the body part calling to her and encircled his tip with her mouth moving down his shaft as she sucked and licked him. His entire body jolted as her tongue traced his head and slid against the ridged crest at the top.

The animal cry escaping him urged her on as her fingers tightened on his base and she sucked him hard while moving her hand in a rhythmic motion. She got lost in him, in his taste, in the feel of him, in the sounds escaping his throat. She could suck him all night, it felt so damn good.

"Enough!" he thundered as he sat up, his hand gripping her hair and pulling her from his pulsing staff.

With a quick motion he flipped her over to her back, and she looked into his eyes, making her body respond in kind to the demand and pure lust of his expression.

"I need you now," he told her. He yanked her shorts off her, tossing them over his shoulder before he stood, making her shake as she lay on the bed, watching him. He reached into his discarded shorts and pulled out a condom, and she smiled, almost laughed. If she hadn't been so achy she would have.

"You had a condom in your shorts?" she gasped.

He slid the condom on in record time as his gaze burned into hers. "A man can dream," he replied, his words teasing, but his voice too needy for a joke. He stood there for a second allowing her to take him all in from her submissive position.

Never would she have thought she'd be so happy to be where she was, below a man while his gaze raked over her. She was always in control. But she had a feeling she'd be willing to give Hendrick anything he wanted — anything at all. When the look between them became too much for her to take, she closed her eyes and waited for him to climb over her, to take her the rest of the way to heaven.

Her eyes snapped back open when she felt his wet tongue run up her inner thigh as he murmured his approval at her taste and scent. Her body arched as his lips whispered over her pulsing clit before his tongue swept out and circled the throbbing flesh.

"Sex. I want sex right now," she called, her body on the verge of exploding. She wanted him inside her, and she'd never been a woman who could come multiple times. She didn't want this to end with a flick of his tongue, she wanted to have him buried deep as he claimed her. "Please . . ." She was about to cry she needed him so badly.

He swept his tongue along her one more time before crawling up her body. His weight pressed against her as his knee parted her thighs wide. She spread them more as she lifted her feet and wrapped them behind his back, completely opening herself to him.

"Open your eyes," he whispered, his hot breath rushing over her ear before he leaned back. It took a lot of effort, but she cracked them open, his eyes nearly on fire in their erotic blaze.

She felt his tip at her entrance and tried lifting her hips upward, but he was in complete control. She begged him again to make them one. Her eyes threw open as he suddenly thrust forward, pushing his entire length deep, deep inside of her. She gasped as she rocked the edge of an orgasm. He pulled back a little and thrust again, and she was shocked at the pressure that was ready to blow.

"Yes, more," she begged.

And he gave her more. He pulled out farther, then slammed inside of her. She clenched him tight as she pulsed around him, her body soaring as she came, her voice crying out in pure delight. He rocked gently in and out of her as she shook and pulsed. And then she fell back against the bed and smiled, true joy filling her.

"Oh . . . my . . . gosh," she said, practically purring. "That was way too fast, but the best orgasm I've ever had." She might regret that honesty later.

"It's not over," he said, a mixture of pain and pride in his voice. She opened her eyes to look up at him where it seemed he was barely holding on to control.

"Of course not. You need to come," she said. She should push him over and ride him, but she didn't think her jellied muscles would comply.

He smiled through the possessive look he wore. "It's not over for you either," he said, his tone filled with smugness.

"I'm not one of the lucky ones to come multiple times," she said. "But that doesn't mean I don't love to see your pleasure even after mine is finished."

His look only intensified. "Then be prepared to feel a new experience," he promised.

Unbelievably, she felt a new clenching between her thighs at his bold words. She'd only had a few sexual experiences in her life, but she'd spent some time on her own with various toys. She'd know by now if she could orgasm more than once.

But Hendrick began moving again, slow and steady strokes, deep then shallow, hard, then soft. He moved in and out of her as he leaned down and took a nipple into his mouth and sucked while one hand gripped her ass and slid between her cheeks to run up and down the slit. Her thighs shook as she felt that build up again, her eyes glued to his when he moved back up and looked at her with satisfaction.

"More," she gasped, awe in her voice as her body sang in sweet desire. Her core was igniting again, and it was even more sensitive than it had been the first time. She was going to get greedy. She'd never want to let this man leave her bed.

His face went feral as he grabbed her hip hard, slanting her to where he wanted and then began to thrust harder in and out of her, groans escaping him as he began to lose control.

"Yes, more!" she demanded, loving that she was the one making this beautiful man lose all semblance of control.

He gripped her as he buried his head against her neck and bit down on her shoulder. And then it happened. She exploded, lights flashing behind her eyes, stars shining, an eclipse overtaking her. It was unlike anything she'd ever experienced. She felt as if she was hovering over the earth, living somewhere between reality and the heavens. She'd heard stories of sex taking a person to another world, but now she knew it was true.

He gave out a guttural cry and she felt him pulsing hard and deep within her as his own orgasm ripped through him, his muscles clenching, his body shaking. They trembled together as they both soared to the stars, then floated back down to reality.

They were both panting as if they'd just run a marathon and when he shifted, she whimpered, not wanting him pulled from her, not wanting their connection to end. He licked her neck, his face still buried against her.

"I weigh twice as much as you, so I'm just shifting, not pulling away," he assured her. He shifted his weight, his beautiful erection separating from her, making another whimper escape, but he kept her pressed tightly against him. She wiggled, needing to be flesh to flesh with him, needing this feeling to last as long as humanly possible.

"Holy hell," she breathed, unable to open her heavy eyes. She still tingled from head to toe.

"Yeah, I don't think there are words," he told her with a satisfied sigh.

"Stay for a while," she said, hating the weakness she felt right then, hating how much she wanted to be held by him, but not hating that feeling enough to let him go.

"There's nowhere else I want to be," he assured her.

He pulled the sheet over them as he tucked her tightly against him, and then she fell asleep. It didn't matter if it was the middle of the day, she'd just had a workout that was worthy of an Olympic athlete training marathon.

She also just might've fallen in love. Could you be sexed to stupidity? Could sex make you love someone? Hell, she didn't know. She just knew she wasn't willing to push him away anymore — not as long as he'd have her.

CHAPTER FIFTEEN

Green was still walking on water after his night with Mallory. He'd been smiling at people as he passed them in the street, making people stop in their tracks, and he felt as if he could conquer the steepest mountain climb. He hadn't been able to see her for a full week, but he had no doubt the next time they came together, they'd make magic again.

But he couldn't think about Mallory right now because he was in the conference room with the rest of his team, and they were preparing to clean up the streets that night. He had tonight to beat the bad guys and tomorrow to get the girl.

"Listen men, the mission is a go at Rainier Beach tonight. The major drug deal going down is between two rival gangs. Outside of major drugs being passed, the two groups are splitting the territory. The main bosses are meeting in the auto body shop at the intersection of MLK and Merton," Eyes said as he pointed at the intersection on the big screen in the conference room.

The special operations men had scouted and poured over the terrain of the area for the last week. This was the final run through. Every detail was laid out, every movement for each man was walked through with minute scrutiny under every foreseeable outcome. The schematics of every building in the area were found, and then for each open location the men had gone into the shops and garages acting as customers to confirm which exits were open or closed. They walked the aisles to see what routes would be best to use in case they had to run through them.

"We'll be full tactical and, as always, expect a firefight. There's no love lost between these people, and with one wrong move they'll end up in a bloody civil war that would leave us nothing to clean up. While we can't stop it if it starts, we don't want a war happening because of us," Eyes continued.

The four men that would be in the field had been through all of this more times than they dared to count. Brackish, the fifth man, would be their eyes from above. There was a plan to deploy ten small drones flying in a pre-coordinated pattern. The LED lights would be removed from them so no trace could be seen by anyone. There were small cameras placed inside the garage, and a van, seemingly beat up and in need of repair, was placed in the parking lot, close to the road, that held a massive device that could see through walls, especially walls that were cheap sheet metal — as were the ones at the car garage.

"Sleep and I will be homeless men, pushing shopping carts full of trash. I'm sure they'll try to move us along, but we'll delay and loiter as long as possible. They can't kick us off the train track seats, so we may spend time there. We'll act the part better than Hollywood. Green, you'll be across the street at the construction company parking garage in the back. There are plenty of areas up there that have a clean line of sight to the entire area. Smoke, just south of him is the building you'll be stationed at. Behind it you'll find abandoned dump trucks and tractors. Take up your spot there," Eyes said, finalizing the plan.

"I'm going to be in the building next door in the armored truck ready to pick up Eyes and Sleep once everything goes down," Chad added.

Earlier that week Chad talked to the owner of the business and paid him a handsome amount of money to lease the space to *work* on his own vehicle. The pitch was that he didn't have room at home to do the maintenance but didn't want anyone to touch his vehicle. For a cool $2500 the owner had been more than happy to let him have the bay for five days.

"Once the two leaders are confirmed inside the garage, we'll release the gas, knocking out everyone inside before they can alert others. The cameras and van will give us the confirmation we need before starting with the lookouts and foot soldiers. As that information's relayed to us, Green and Smoke will disable the vehicles with their electrical charged rounds. Those shots need to be completed within ten seconds. From first to last shot we cannot let any of them get away. As chaos starts to unfold, the ants will either run or start shooting each other. Sleep and I will need to put as many down as possible. We've tested the chemical agent inside the miniature darts, and it'll knock out a grown man within fifteen seconds, most of them dropping within seven," Eyes continued.

"I bet three thousand dollars I put more down than Eyes," Sleep interrupted.

"I'll take that bet," Brackish said, pulling out his ante.

"How will you know how many you get?" Smoke asked.

"Easy enough for me to review the information coming back from the drones," Brackish replied.

"Then I'm in for Eyes," Smoke said as he pulled out a wad of cash and threw it into the center of the table.

Green leaned back in his seat, put his hands behind his back, staring up at the ceiling. After a few moments of serious contemplation, he came back to the table, pulled out his money, carefully stacked it into a neat pile, and said, "I have three thousand on Sleep to put the most down, but I have another two thousand on Eyes having the coolest shot and/or drop."

This created another round of bets and bantering between everyone at the table. They had to do this type of stuff which would seem odd to the outsider but quite normal to those who deal with the highest level of stress. By the time all bets, side bets, one offs, and posturing was done, there was more than forty thousand dollars bet between them.

"Green, Smoke, once we have confirmation everyone's incapacitated, haul ass over here and help us bundle them up and put a tie on them. Brackish will make the call to Sheriff McCormack as to the location of the event and how many total individuals are detained. We'll also be compiling every piece of data on both of these gangs and handing it over to the authorities so the arrests will stick. If there are any questions, comments, additional input, or anything else, say it now. If not, let's gear up," Eyes finished.

People were all different in their own way of preparing for things. From getting up in the morning and starting their day to going to bed at the end of the night, everyone has their own customs, quirks, and intricate things about them. The same is said for those preparing for battle.

Eyes was always stoic, silent, and internalizing his steps with painful detail. Not moving, not looking at anyone, he was the epitome of a leader thinking of a great chess match with all of the possible outcomes, and how to keep each piece of his team in the right square so they'd make it home safely.

Sleep talked, and talked, and talked. Not to say he wasn't thinking as well, but his internal stress release was verbalization. Stories, jokes, nonsense, whatever he was thinking was being said. Those who went through their first preparation with him didn't know what to think, but once they saw the warrior he was, they felt the great void when his voice was no longer there.

Green was the quickest to get ready, not a thing out of place, meticulous attention to how his gear was set, but he did it quickly and then would watch his teammates prepare. If something was placed incorrectly on someone, or they were missing a piece of anything, he was the first to recognize it and help them get set.

Smoke moved around the area, not heavy or large movements but calculating ones, almost as one would think a ballerina would move, light and purposeful, energy always sitting just beneath the surface, everyone anticipating the explosion to come. His eyes were at ease; he knew what he was capable of and that confidence led to smooth easy movements.

Brackish geared up in his own way, knowing the information he was receiving came with a responsibility everyone relied on. He created backups and tested platforms and responsiveness, power input and availability, camera positioning, and computer dialogue. Those tests were performed multiple times before he'd bring them online for the team.

Chad always got ready by himself. This mission was no different. It was his first action in more years than he cared to admit to himself, let alone to anyone else. Due to that, adrenaline coursed through him as he prepared to do what needed to be done. By the time he was finished, his mind was focused and set on the task at hand. He double checked himself, head to toe, speaking out loud each piece of gear he touched, ensuring there was nothing missing.

The men met in the main lobby of the command center, did a gear check on each other, said a quick prayer, and then made their way to the vehicles they'd be using. The expected meet up of drug dealing gang members was five hours away, but they needed to be prepared far ahead of time.

"Radio check — team member one," Brackish called out in his microphone.

"Check," Chad replied.

Brackish did the same check for each member as the screen showed they'd made it to their location, and each replied in the affirmative for comms being good.

"Operation Rust Bucket is underway," Eyes called out over the radio as he and Sleep got out of their vehicle, fake beards and wigs on, shopping carts loaded with crap over the top of a box that had gear and toys hidden inside. Since it was still warm, even at 10:00 PM, they wore light long sleeve shirts. If they wore short sleeve their muscular toned arms wouldn't match the homeless drunken look they were pulling off very well in their own humble opinions. They had to walk a mile before reaching their destination.

Chad made it to his vehicle, thanks to a little magic from Brackish to turn off all security alarms the manager had set. He hated sitting and doing nothing, but he knew it was needed and he was more efficient where he was than in the middle of the action.

Smoke and Green had to be a bit more creative in the way they got into position, but they did it without being seen. Even after numerous dry runs the two of them still went through the steps of verifying length, angle, and wind speed from their respective spots to the parking lot they'd be sending shots to. Smoke was shooting his little EMP rounds from four hundred sixty-three feet. Green's shots were almost two hundred yards longer than that. The two of them tested those rounds at a range over the last week, Green had fine-tuned the ballistics and taught Smoke what the drop rate was. The team knew if Green was comfortable with the shots then there were no issues with the high-tech bullets.

At 12:30 AM the first car arrived. Over the next fifteen minutes all of the players were in the parking lot. The two leaders and three additional men from each gang, who all were carrying oversized bags, went into the garage and left the other members in the parking lot to stare each other down. None of them would dare draw on the other gang, but the words, looks, and signs thrown at each other were contentious.

Brackish watched the gang members on the hidden cameras and waited until drugs were presented, passed between each other, and money exchanged before he pushed the four buttons that released the completely odorless gas. Before the eight men could make a signal that they were in any kind of trouble, all of them were unconscious. Of course, the entire mission was being recorded, including voices via microphones placed in little places all over the garage.

"Phase one, complete," Brackish said to the team.

Eyes and Sleep timed their cart pushing perfectly. One of the unbalanced wheels on the shopping cart squeaked with each step Sleep took. The sound broke through the gang members berating of each other and they didn't like the interruption, even from a couple of trash-picking homeless people.

"Spare some change or maybe a drink?" Eyes called out to the group of men.

Multiple phrases that meant the same thing as *get the fuck out of here* echoed back to him. He smiled under his beard and couldn't wait to put these men down. He was about to disappear from their view as he approached the van holding the massive X-ray vision, when a police car pulled up to the intersection.

At the exact same time a brilliant flash coursed across the sky. They knew a chance of some heavy rain was possible, but the lightning wasn't expected.

The police officer looked over at the overflow of vehicles in the parking lot of the garage, and all of the bodies attached to it, and knew something was wrong. Everyone could see him reach for his radio and talk into it. That's when every plan that had been previously made was flushed down the drain.

A rumble from the sky barreled around them. The clouds released heavy drops of rain, slow and methodical at first, but the cadence quickened, and within seconds there were sheets of water falling on them.

The officer turned his spotlight toward the men in the parking lot and that was all it took for the first shot to fly. The round made impact with the windshield of the police cruiser, which then set off a volley from everyone with bullets flying in all directions. Three men ran directly toward the police car and they were going to take down the cop, but Sleep was on them, and put two rounds of chemicals into each one.

Seeing their members go down and suspecting the police of shooting the men lying in the street, more gang members joined in. The flashing lights on the police car and the heavy rain made it next to impossible to see far.

Another massive arc of light cut through the sky, lighting up the entire parking lot. It allowed Green time to ascertain his target. One round sent, one car incapacitated. He put another round into the chamber of his gun, but it was impossible to see any other cars with the water cascading down on top of him.

The police officer tried reversing the vehicle, but it wouldn't move. More and more rounds impacted the car. Eyes and Sleep knew he was in a bad situation, so they took the fight to the men. They dropped man after man. Each time it happened the other side thought it was their rival gang. For a moment they'd forget about the cop and again turn on each other, not once looking at the homeless guys.

"Guys, abort. There's a line of cars coming up MLK from the south, and a line of police cruisers coming from the east. It's going to turn into a mad house real quick," Brackish calmly said into the comms while watching live feeds from his monitors. Two of their drones had gone down due to the rain, and three of them went black with their video feeds, but they were already on their way back to base.

"We aren't leaving that cop," Eyes commanded.

Another massive rumble pounded around them, hard enough to vibrate in their chests. More shots rang out, more yelling.

"Chug, get the hell out here, get to the police officer on your side, and have him jump in. Sleep and I will take leave when we see you safely gone," Eyes yelled into the microphone.

Doing just that, Chad floored the gas pedal, ran through the garage door, crashing onto the street. He slid to a stop on the driver's side door of the cop car within seconds. The officer had been hit and looked to be in shock. Chad jumped out, pulled the officer from his car, and helped him into the back seat of the armored vehicle. A machine gun started putting rounds into the passenger's side window, all of the energy of each bullet being sucked up by the thick bullet proof glass.

Chad jumped back into the SUV, put the vehicle in gear, ran over a curb, and made a smooth exit. More rounds sank into his vehicle, but they didn't come close to penetrating it. He let the cop know he was one of the good guys and was getting him out of the war zone he'd been in the middle of. The cop was still in shock, but he radioed his fellow officers, telling them he was being taken to safety.

An entire armada of lights could be seen racing toward them. Eyes knew he and Sleep had to put down as many of the men as possible before that line of cars arrived. Just then his worries about the cars stopped in a flash.

Smoke had seen the vehicles coming as well, and since they had their lights on, they made for easy targets. He wasn't as adept at figuring out all the measurements when shooting at a distance like Green was, but he knew if he got the first car down it would stall the entire train. The distance, the monsoon, and the speed of the vehicle all created challenges. His first two shots missed by far, his third shot was close, but his fourth shot was a direct hit to the engine of the lead vehicle compartment, stalling it in its tracks. The sudden stop caused the next three vehicles to crash into each other. From there Smoke hit each of those stopped cars.

"Great shooting, Smoke!" Green said.

Sleep and Eyes continued putting down gang members, and they got almost all of them by the time the police arrived. The first officers on scene only had to deal with two gang members. Those two had decided they'd rather live than deal with the entire squad of vehicles full of police that could be heard coming real fast.

"Pull out. Sleep and Eyes, play your part, give your report to the officers, and then get out of there. The rest of the team leave now," Brackish said.

Each member of the team acknowledged the order, and they quickly packed up and were gone. Another mission, another success, even with the twists and turns. They were doing good work, *and* making the city a safer place.

***
One Week Later

The special ops team were all smiles as they sat around their table in the command center. Even Chad was grinning as he held reports.

"Don't make us wait, Chug," Smoke said impatiently.

"Don't tell him that, Smoke, or he's going to draw this out forever. And we have a party in Vegas to get to," Green said.

Chad rose his brows. "Party?" he asked.

"Don't play dumb. You know you're coming," Sleep said. "It's bachelor party time."

Chad laughed. "I'm bowing out of this one, boys. I like my marriage, and my wife doesn't approve of a bachelor party unless she gets to have a bachelorette party, and I'd rather have her alone than ogling naked men in Vegas."

The table of men laughed. "Yep, I'm not super thrilled about our weekend either. I'm going to worry so much about Avery, I'm not going to have any fun," Sleep grumbled.

"Worried a Vegas stripper will take her away?" Eyes taunted.

"Not in the least. As I said before I'm worried some idiotic drunk will dare lay hands on her and then I'm going to beat him to a bloody pulp."

"If he's foolish enough to touch your wife he deserves it," Brackish said as if smashing a man's face in was no big deal. Of course, none of them thought it was a big deal. There should be honor among men, and if a woman was wearing a ring, that meant hands off.

"Okay, tell us," Eyes insisted.

Chad began. "After the police sealed off the area and talked to Sleep and Eyes, buying their story that they were homeless, they were left scratching their heads. They couldn't figure out why all but two of the gang members were lying on the ground, moaning and throwing up, and talking about magical bullets falling from the sky."

Smoke laughed. "Anything I touch has magic in it," he told the group.

"Hey, the criminals in the lots were all Eyes and me," Sleep piped in. "You got the vehicle parade that was coming in as backup."

"That was magical," Smoke insisted.

Chad interrupted, knowing the back and forth could go for hours. "The police were also confused when they found the gang leaders passed out in the garage with no visible evidence of what had happened to them."

"That's because nothing I create is traceable," Brackish said with a satisfied smile.

"It wasn't until the next day when the rain stopped and the sun shone that they found the casings from where Sleep and Eyes had been stationed, right where the officers had spoken to their homeless eyewitnesses."

"I bet that blew their minds," Eyes said with a smirk. They knew they'd left nothing behind that could possibly be traced back to them, and their disguises had been top-of-the line. The best face recognition software in the world wouldn't be able to figure out their true identities.

Their forensic team concluded the homeless men had been the ones to put down thirty-nine of forty-one gang members without lethal force. The men were paralyzed for twelve hours."

"That's it? What a bummer," Green said.

"That's a long time to be paralyzed, especially with the cops taking you into custody," Brackish said with a smirk. He was working on something stronger though, something that could incapacitate someone for twenty-four hours.

"That afternoon they received all of the video transmission from the night before, and after reviewing it, they saw the video evidence corroborated the forensic evidence. They've concluded a special ops team was on a mission. They've also concluded the team was certainly ghosts and it was a waste of their time and budget to pursue them."

"I thought they'd at least try," Brackish said with a pout. "It's always fun to be hunted."

"That's like a grizzly bear being hunted with a BB gun," Eyes said. "How can that be even a little challenge for you?"

"I didn't say it was a challenge. I just like it when people try," Brackish said. "Maybe we should piss off the CIA. I love going head-to-head with them." A gleam entered his eyes.

"With the way the world's going right now, that might actually happen," Chad said, no humor in his eyes. Brackish came to attention. All he needed was the official go and it was on. He'd love to dive into the CIA databases.

"Let's stick locally for now," Chad said with a laugh. "The bottom line is there are about five hundred years of jail sentences added up so far, taking these men off the streets permanently. That means business can come back to the area, and people living nearby can feel safe again. This is all because of you guys. You're truly cleaning up this city. I know you don't get a pat on the back, but you get the reward of walking down the street, knowing people are alive because of you."

For once the men were quiet as they looked at Chad, his words sinking in. They were so focused on their mission they didn't often stop to think about the long-term impact they made on people's lives. It was a pretty humbling experience.

"Great job, men. Now take the entire week off. You've earned it. Just make sure I can get hold of you if anything arises. We're getting closer and closer to the end of this mission, and you should be damn proud of yourselves," Chad finished.

Fists lifted in the air as the men called out shouts of victory. Their path wasn't finished yet, but the end was in sight. Taking down those two gangs was like conquering one wave in a massive ocean, but it was still a win, and a good win at that. What would come next?

"Aren't you boys forgetting something?" Chad asked as the men stood to leave the conference room.

All of them stopped in their tracks, each searching their brain for what was missing, what they had forgotten.

Chad pulled out stacks of cash and said, "The bets you all had on the bust."

The men slapped each other's backs, jokes instantly being made about who was about to get paid.

"I reviewed the tapes multiple times specifically for this purpose. First bet was on total number. Eyes won by two. Second bet was on best put down. This was difficult and I'll show you why when you return from Vegas but I had to give it to Eyes. Third and fourth bets were the weird ones and split between Smoke and Green," Chad informed them.

As he pushed the pile of cash across the table he started to smile at himself, not able to contain the thought in his head.

"Sleep, it's almost as if you weren't even there. I feel bad you lost so bad to these guys," Chad said.

The laughter exploded through the room before Chad stood, raised a hand, and finished the conversation, "Sleep, Brackish, because this is a dual bachelor party, and I know you guys are barely able to make ends meet with not making any money, I want you to have this, from me and the guys."

He pulled the stack of money back, reached down and put another pile on the table, equal in the amount and handed one pile to Sleep and one pile to Brackish. The last words he said before all the men started razzing each other was, "Don't spend it all in one place."

CHAPTER SIXTEEN

Green went from one of the best moods he'd been in in a long time, to one of the worst.

Women!

Yep, that one word described it all. Women could bring intense joy and pleasure, and they could also drop a man to his knees begging for mercy. Right now Green had women problems — yep, women were making his life hell at the moment. He had his mission woman, and she was an absolute pain in his ass, and then he had the woman he couldn't stop thinking about who was ticked at him.

He was sitting on a luxury jet about to land in Las Vegas with four men he respected, truly liked, and enjoyed being with. He was about to have three days of freedom — no work, no stress, no worries. But instead of being excited about the trip, all he could think about was Mallory.

"Green, if you don't get that sour expression off your face, I'm going to have to punch you," Smoke said as he leaned back in his seat and glowered at Green.

"I hate that I couldn't get Mallory to call me back after that damn photo op the senator staged. And I'm on shaky ground with the senator anyway. When I told her I was going on this trip, she got all pissed off, saying she didn't think a man who was supposed to be devoted to her should be partying in Las Vegas."

"So . . ." Eyes said, looking confused. "Which woman are you with?"

"I *want* to be with Mallory, but I've charmed the damn senator so much she believes we're a couple now. I was supposed to get her to like me but not want this exclusive thing. I can't sleep with the woman. There's no way I'm going to blow Mallory's cover, and I'm starting to show my disdain for the senator. If she kisses me one more time I might puke on her two-thousand-dollar heels."

"Wait? When did you and Mallory become a thing? And what photo op are you talking about?" Sleep asked. "I don't remember seeing anything."

"The photo came out this morning. Mallory and I got in a fight over it. I told her I can't blow my cover, but I'm not going anywhere alone with the senator. I told her the senator is just a mission to me, that I'm not sleeping with Anna. She says she believes me but the damn photo this morning puts me on shaky ground. To make matters worse, she knows I'm working on a special ops team, but I can't give her any information on the team, which to an FBI agent doesn't look good. And, of course, she can't find any information on us, even working in the FBI, so she's losing trust in me. I'm all sorts of screwed right now."

"Back to the photo!" Smoke said, jumping back in. "What in the hell has Mallory so riled?"

Brackish laughed as he pulled out his iPad that connected to the internet even while flying at thirty-two thousand feet above land.

There was a photo of Green and the senator locked in what appeared to be a pretty hot kiss next to a pool at a hotel. The caption read; *Pool side kiss. The future president and mystery man swimming in the deep end at the crack of dawn!*

"Yep, if I was Mallory, I wouldn't be happy with that image either," Eyes said with a whistle.

"What are you doing with the senator at five thirty in the morning?" Sleep asked.

"I didn't stay the night with her. I got a call at 0500 telling me there was an emergency and I needed to get there fast. So, I slipped on my jeans and a sweatshirt, didn't bother to brush my hair, looking as if I just got out of bed, which I had, and rushed to the hotel. She told me to meet her by the back door. She walked with me to the pool wearing only her nightgown and robe and grabbed me and kissed me. She had the entire thing planned. She wanted it to look as if I'd stayed the night and was just leaving after a wild night. I don't know what her game is with this one though."

"She wants the press to think she's found a worthy man to be on her arm. The iron-clad story Brackish has made up for you is foolproof, and you're perfect for the senator. You aren't showing enough interest, so she threw down a couple aces on the table," Sleep said.

"Mallory knows the game though. I shouldn't have come on this trip. I should've stayed and insisted on seeing her alone."

"She can't risk it right now," Eyes said. "The press is going to be watching you more than ever now," he pointed out.

"So maybe I should just say screw it and go into the middle of a strip club and get photos with a dozen dancers all over me," Green said with defiance. "Then the senator would dump my ass."

"Yes, that would end the interest of the senator for sure. She can't deal with that kind of bad publicity, but it would most likely end it with Mallory too," Smoke said. "But I'm game if you are. I don't mind a dozen lap dancers doing my bidding. Hell, since I'm not dating a senator I might just do that anyway."

Green glared at the man who oozed sexuality. "You know what, Smoke? I think you're far more talk than action. I think you make all of these comments because you're actually a big teddy bear. We all saw how you've taken Jasmine beneath your wing. A true bad boy doesn't love kids and little lost kittens."

"It was one kitten," Smoke said with a glower. "What was I supposed to do, leave the poor thing crying in the rain. She was right there at the door, freezing, wet, full of fleas, and starving. I can still be a bad ass *and* have a cat."

The tantrum made Green and the others crack up.

"However, will Stormy survive with you gone this week?" Eyes asked. The kitten Smoke had saved two months earlier was now a member of their team, living in the operations center, sleeping with Smoke, and ruling the entire compound. She had the best toys, food, and medicine available, and all of them had heard Smoke talking sweet to her when he thought no one could hear.

"Mock all you want, but she's better than a guard dog. You mark my word," Smoke said.

Green had to admit he liked the little orange feline. She was full of spit and vinegar, and she could be a terror or super sweet curled up in any of their laps. And she had attacked Eyes a couple weeks ago.

"I hate that beast," Eyes said, rubbing his hand over the thigh of his jeans in remembrance. His words made everyone laugh again.

"Maybe if you weren't a sleeping whore you wouldn't have been attacked," Smoke said defensively. It had only been Eyes and Smoke in the operations center that night but Eyes's scream had gotten Smoke on his feet prepared for battle in seconds.

"No, your demon spawn was probably taught to terrorize," Eyes said.

"We have fifteen minutes until we land. Tell the story again," Sleep begged.

"I hate all of you," Eyes said, looking out the window as Vegas came into view.

"Eyes woke up in the middle of the night and stumbled to the bathroom. Apparently Stormy likes to drink from the freshly flushed toilet, so he did his business, then flushed when Stormy jumped up on the seat and scared the shit out of Eyes. He let out a scream like a little girl, stumbled backward, and slipped. The cat screeched at him, and he tried to correct himself by pushing forward. The momentum sent him flying forward, his hand landing in the toilet." Smoke was laughing so hard as he told the story he had to stop and regain his breath.

"I ran around the corner just in time to see Eyes jerk his hand from the toilet as Stormy swatted him right in the face. He yelled again as he fell backward this time and slid in the water splattered on the floor. The cat was smart enough at this point to sense danger, and she ran from the room. I swear there was a smile on her lips as she passed by me."

Everyone laughed again as they heard the story. It didn't matter how many times they heard it, it still filled them with joy.

"You go ahead and laugh, but I swear that damn cat tried to kill me. She might actually be a secret spy sent to us like a Trojan horse," Eyes said. He looked around as if afraid the kitten was going to come out of the vents and attack at any moment.

"Stormy's safe and sound being babysat by Uncle Chad this weekend. Apparently, he's taking her to Joseph's house to get playtime with the kids. I told him I'd personally tear off his limbs one by one if anything happened to her while I was gone," Smoke said.

He said the words like it was no big deal, but the team realized the man would be devastated if something happened to the cat. Who would've thought he'd be a cat lover?

"Buckle up. We'll be touching down in about five minutes," the captain called.

"Okay enough of our life in Seattle. Now, my boys, it's Vegas time, and we all know that what happens in Vegas, stays in Vegas," Eyes said, a gleam in his eyes.

"Oorah," Sleep said, making them all laugh again.

"You can't say that. Only Marines do," Green pointed out.

"I have some bad ass brothers in the Marines, and they gave me full permission," Sleep countered.

It didn't matter. They landed. And the fun was about to begin.

They stepped from the jet and found a large Hummer SUV waiting at the private terminal to whisk them away to the MGM Grand. It was midmorning in Vegas, and they had three full days to get into as much trouble as humanly possible. They had another two full days to recover from getting into all of that trouble before they reported back to work. So, they were going to live life to the fullest.

The limo was large, but with the five of them inside it, the space shrank considerably. There were several bottles of whiskey lined up and Sleep was the first to reach for them.

"What time are the women arriving?" Sleep asked as he looked at his watch.

"They won't tell us anything," Brackish said with a growl. "They've left their phones off and refuse to speak to us the entire time they're here. They said they've got bodyguards, won't be going anywhere unsafe, and that this is time for them and time for us. Of course, I already know where they're going and can follow them throughout the entire city with the cameras but I'm desperately trying to respect my wife and let her enjoy her bachelorette party."

Brackish's fingers twitched on top of his modified iPad even as he said the words to his team. He was a newlywed after all, and he loved being with his wife.

"It's going to be hell for me too," Sleep said. "I married Avery because I actually do enjoy being with her."

"That doesn't mean you can't have some fun with the men too," Eyes pointed out. He laughed but there was something in his eyes that made Sleep slap his back.

"We're brothers to the end. No more talk of women . . . until we check in to make sure they're safe at night," he said, making all of them laugh.

"I can agree to that . . . I think," Brackish said with a sheepish smile.

The limo took them to the MGM Grand, and they were whisked through check-in then rode high in the elevator up to the bi-luxury suite that towered over the strip. They had a personal butler who was willing to cater to all of their needs 24/7 for the duration of their stay. It wasn't a bad way to start the trip.

"We have a pool table and fully stocked private bar. I'm digging this so far," Eyes said as he wandered the huge suite.

"I like the room, but I don't plan on spending much time in here," Green said. "If I'm going to be in Vegas, I want to do it all."

"I agree. We have fine food, fine women, fine rides, and even finer money to be taken from the casino. Before we grab some grub and get this party started, let's toast our recently married brethren," Eyes said.

"Amen," the rest of the team added as they took out cold beers and held them in the air, made toasts, and drank to each of them. They took about an hour to unpack, shower, change and then they hit the elevators. This time the elevator took them down, and the excitement level rose.

Their first meal in Vegas was at Wolfgang Puck Bar and Grill. They ordered one of each appetizer on the menu and a couple pizzas that were delicious but barely scratched the itch of their hunger. These men knew how to eat, and they weren't ashamed of it. But they had their first activity, and they didn't want to get sick. They were about to get fast and furious.

"Hurry up, Smoke," Eyes yelled as Smoke stuffed the last bit of pizza in his gullet. "Our appointment is at four and we're barely going to make it in time."

"I thought bachelor parties were all about drinking and strippers," Smoke yelled. "Why the hell do we need to traipse all over the city?"

"Says the man who doesn't have a wife at home," Sleep said with a laugh. "If I spend a three-day weekend drunk with naked women around me, I won't be married anymore."

"Good excuse," Smoke said, then finally stood. "I guess that's why I'm never getting married. I don't want to have to choose the right thing."

They all laughed as they stepped outside where their limo was waiting. The driver already had their itinerary, so they climbed in and were off. Their next stop was a brand new, state-of-the-art Formula One race world. The owners built a small city people could race through, then they were able to move to new locations that allowed different racetracks to be routed.

There were at least twenty different iterations, meaning a person would have a new experience every time they came to the track. Between the different tracks and the multitude of different cars to choose from, no one would ever get bored.

"Whoa, you didn't say we were coming here," Smoke said, his eyes open in awe. They'd finally managed to impress the man. "We all chose an activity. This is mine," Eyes told the group. "It's been far too long since I've opened something up fast and hard."

"That sounds like a personal problem," Green said as he patted him on the back. "I don't have a problem with fast, hard . . . or slick."

"I don't know why I bother to say anything," Eyes said as he moved forward.

"I've reserved the cars," Eyes said. "I'm taking out the McLaren Speedtail; Smoke, you have the Bugatti Chiron; Sleep, you have the Aston Martin DBS Superleggera; Brackish, you have the Ferrari 812; and Green, you have the Lamborghini Aventador." The men all looked at the cars as they tried not to drool.

"Who wants to race?" Brackish asked, the most excited the group had ever seen him.

All four of the men held up their hands. They got the rules rundown, then climbed inside their high-powered machines. As soon as the wind whipped through their windows the rules no longer applied.

They got the cars back to the office an hour late and didn't feel a bit remorseful for it. Their bank accounts and the huge deposits they'd put down helped the manager not freak out on them. They were walking away when Eyes smiled with joy. "Beat that," he told the group.

"It's going to be hard to beat," Smoke said. "But I'm always up for a challenge."

They made it back to their hotel, changed again, then did some gambling and decided to hit the nightclub scene. Eyes and Smoke were the only two excited for the club. The other three of their group had to take a lot of ragging about being whipped.

Green didn't know what he was. He didn't actually have a woman, but instead two women who wanted something from him, and that left him standing there not knowing what in the hell he was supposed to do about it.

"Come on, guys, this is the Cirque du Soleil's Light Nightclub," Smoke said. "Do you know how hard it is to get in here? We not only have true VIP entry but can do anything we damn well please. When Joseph says he has connections, the man isn't kidding."

"Is this your activity for us?" Sleep asked with a laugh as they approached the loud club that had a line around the block to get in.

"Hell yah, it is," Smoke said. "I was too afraid you guys wouldn't come to the club if you knew about it beforehand. This, this right here is where we separate the men from the boys when it comes to alcohol consumption."

"You're probably right," Brackish said as he looked up at all of the security cameras. "I can't wait to get back and break into these bad boys. I bet it's better than watching real television. Can you imagine the crap that goes on in places like this?"

"I've seen *The Hangover*, and I have no plans of bringing a tiger back to our room, at least like the one in the movie," Sleep said mischievously.

They moved inside the club and Brackish's attitude changed as he was in pure heaven. The high-tech lights, cameras, and speakers were drawing him in. He wanted to see how much money and time they'd put into the technology for the club. Of course, that's what he was interested in.

"How long do you think it'll be before he gets escorted out?" Sleep asked as Brackish circled around looking up.

"I'd give it thirty minutes tops if he doesn't quit acting like he's trying to case the place," Eyes said.

"How long do we let him sit in security guard jail?" Sleep asked with a laugh.

"Hell, a night in their crappy holding cells would be a dream come true for Brackish. He'd have them all interrogated by morning," Green said.

"True," Eyes said as all of the men nodded in agreement.

They should've been having the best time of their lives, and it wasn't a complete disaster, but they weren't as young as they'd once been, and while the DJ was incredible, and the aerial acrobatics show was amazing, it was also loud, making it hard to speak, and the girls were just too young. Smoke went out there and danced, and even he didn't look as enthused as he'd been going on about being. But the drinks were smooth and went down easy.

They stayed for three hours before reaching their limit. The five of them drank more in that timeframe than the party of ten in the booth next to them who'd been there for five hours. They went back to the casino and stayed up until dawn at a great blackjack table, tipping the dealer more than most people made in a good month, and continued downing enough alcohol to fuel a jet.

They all crashed in the early morning hours and had a rude awakening when Brackish set off an obnoxious alarm, making each of them jump up in bed.

Eyes blearily looked at the clock, finding it was only ten in the morning. "Brackish, we've been asleep for four hours. What the hell?" he yelled.

"The day is young and it's my day today," Brackish said.

"This ought to be good. Are we going to some tech fair?" Green snapped as he got up. His head was pounding. He moved to the sink and downed a glass of water and some Advil.

"I think you'll love today," Brackish assured him.

The men got up, showered, dressed and headed out. They hadn't eaten much the day before, so their first stop was the buffet at the Pink Flamingo Casino.

It was fun to get away from the main strip, and it had a hell of a buffet. The guys were sure the casino reconsidered all you can eat by the time they were finished.

"Hell, I could live on buffets," Smoke said as they walked from the place.

"I've never had all you can eat crab legs. I might've cleared them out," Sleep said as he rubbed his flat belly.

"I definitely cleared out the shrimp. Damn, that was good," Sleep said.

When the limo took them to their next stop, all of the men smiled. "Now, this is more like it," Green said. "This is my idea of heaven."

They were at The Gun Store that featured both an indoor and outdoor range. Brackish had chosen the package that allowed them to shoot WWII classics, including the Thompson. They had machine guns, AKs, and tommy guns. It was paradise to each and every one of them. They had two full hours of shooting as much ammo as they wanted, yelling out quotes from their favorite movies.

"I'm gonna make him an offer he can't refuse . . ."

"You wanna play rough? Okay. Say hello to my little friend . . ."

"Now if I ever, I mean if I ever, see you here again, you die, just like that . . ."

Smoke made them all laugh when he said his quote. "You don't understand. I coulda had class. I coulda been a contender. I could've been somebody, instead of a bum, which is what I am."

They all walked from the place with smiles and high fives. Of course, Green beat them in most of the competitions, but Sleep came in for a final win with a short-range shootout. And they were all winners because they were having fun.

Their second day in Vegas went by in a blur with more drinking and more gambling. Brackish hit huge at the roulette table after placing five thousand dollars on a single number – black twenty — which hit. The payout was thirty-five to one. His takeaway was one hundred seventy-five thousand dollars. His kid was getting fifty thousand in his savings account, his wife fifty thousand to spend on what she wanted, and he was blowing seventy-five thousand on the remainder of their trip. Day two ended on a high note . . .

It was their third day when everything went wrong . . . very, very wrong, for Green at least. For the rest of the crew, it was a show that rivaled anything they could've imagined on the strip.

CHAPTER SEVENTEEN

Mallory was beyond humiliated to be dragged to Las Vegas by the senator, who'd been pissed for two days that Hendrick had decided to go on a bachelor party adventure with his friends. The senator showed her possessive side, and Mallory felt absolutely miserable with not understanding her feeling about Hendrick and this mission.

Her job had always come first. There'd never been a division of loyalty. This time, though, it was different. This time she didn't want to be undercover. She wanted to come out in the open and tell the world she had feelings for this man who'd managed to dive deeply beneath her cool surface without her knowing it was happening.

She knew Hendrick had to maintain cover, but did that mean he had to sleep with the senator when Mallory's own bed was still warm from their bodies lighting it on fire? She'd seen that picture of him outside of the senator's hotel, not only had she seen it, but that photo had been cemented in her brain, and she'd felt a pang in her heart.

No, she wasn't in love with Hendrick. How could she be? She barely knew the man. But she didn't sleep with just any man, and what the two of them had shared together had been unlike anything she'd ever experienced. She felt betrayed at what he'd done. And with how possessive the senator was being, it was clear who was telling the truth about what happened between the two of them. She'd never thought she'd be a jealous woman. She absolutely hated feeling that way now.

"Good. We're touching down soon," Senator Miller said as she adjusted her makeup and fixed her flawless hair. "Hendrick says they're having a low-key day at the pool today. I'll see just how honest the man is."

She licked her lips like a predator set on her prey.

"I'm sure he's just hanging with the boys," Mallory said with no emotion.

"Why would he want another woman when he has me?" the senator asked with a cackle that had never really annoyed Mallory until lately. Now, the sound was worse than nails on a chalkboard.

She so wanted confirmation that the senator had slept with Hendrick. Then she'd know for sure they had no chance. There were a lot of things Mallory was willing to do for her job but sleeping with the enemy wasn't one of them. She'd known Hendrick would have to flirt and taunt the senator, but she hadn't thought the two of them would be at a hotel together in the morning.

She was so damn confused. Not just confused, she was hurt in her heart, something she'd never anticipated happening. She needed to talk to him — but she was afraid to do that. It didn't help to have the senator right there in her face telling her how amazing Hendrick was.

They landed in Vegas and the waiting limo took them straight to the MGM Grand. The senator stepped from the car and walked straight in the lavish lobby with a snobby look on her face.

"I normally stay in The Nobu Villa at the Nobu Hotel," the senator said.

Mallory was in shock as she gazed at the endless marble floors of the hotel with high painted ceilings and a centerpiece with a golden lion. This was luxury, and she normally would've been excited to come to the city of sin where she could drink and laugh and let herself go, but this was the opposite of excitement.

One of the senator's aides checked them in while she stood back and listened to Anna Miller continue as if she was royalty and this peasant hotel wasn't good enough for her.

"I heard that room goes for thirty-five thousand dollars a night," Mallory finally said, remembering when she'd read an article of the most luxurious rooms in the world to stay in.

The senator waived her hand in the air as if that much money meant nothing. To her it was chump change. Mallory couldn't imagine being so cavalier over throwing more money into a single night than many people in the world made in a full year.

"Yes, but money comes easy to someone like me," the senator said with a fake laugh that made

Mallory's jaw clench. "I only stay where I'm treated how a queen should be treated." She laughed again. "Of course, being president as I will be, is even better than having royal status. Hell, that's the epitome of royalty."

"I once dreamed of being a princess mermaid," Mallory said. She'd never know what it was like to be treated like royalty, but she wouldn't mind a taste of that. She'd once believed being with the right man could make a woman feel like a queen every single day. She'd started to think that way with Hendrick. Was that dream over?

"Only those who take the reins can be royalty," Anna said. "Don't you read history? Vying for the crown has always been bloody. I'm not afraid to run my sword through whoever I need to in order to get what I want."

A shiver ran through Mallory because she had no doubt the senator was telling her the truth. She'd lie, steal, and cheat to get exactly what she wanted when she wanted it. Mallory decided discussing burning lots of money was a better conversation than killing people. She didn't want the senator to talk too much and then feel the need to eliminate her.

"You know . . . a lot of famous people have stayed at the Nobu, such as Jennifer Lopez and Justin Bieber. They might be artists with their faces all over television screens, but they don't hold true power. Hollywood simply does the bidding of the right politicians. They're our puppets and they happily dance on their strings when we pull them. If you want real power in life you run for office. It's quite refreshing how naïve so many are. I quite enjoy it." The senator was talking more to herself than giving any type of career advice to her underling.

Mallory felt sick to her stomach. She knew Washington, D.C. had a lot of power over the people, but she still believed in freedom, still believed people made their own choices in life. The people elected the officials, didn't they? That meant the people had the true power. But with the way the senator was talking, she was starting to change her mind on that.

"If you don't please the people though, they won't reelect you," Mallory pointed out.

Anna laughed, this time true joy in her voice. "That's where Hollywood comes in again, my sweet little assistant. You have a lot to learn in the world of politics. If the people start to grow restless, we just feed them what they need to hear, and voila, we're gods again."

That sick feeling in Mallory's gut grew worse. She thought back to all of those times she'd followed the advice of those she'd respected. In her youth, she'd been very susceptible to actors, musicians, and sports gods. Once she'd gone to college and joined the FBI she'd wised up to who to listen to, but had she been foolish not to pay more attention? Probably. She was getting real life lessons right now; she'd been getting them since she'd joined the FBI.

"Does it make you feel bad to deceive people?" Mallory asked.

The aide came back and handed over the key, and Anna began walking with Mallory at her side.

"I don't deceive anyone," Anna said as if she meant it. "I give the people what they truly need, even if they don't know it's what they need at that moment. And in order to do this I need to be pampered. If I'm happy, those I *serve* are as well." She put extra emphasis on the word *serve* as if that was an utter joke. It truly was. This woman wouldn't serve a single person in her life.

Mallory began to question her own sanity and lack of insight. Had the senator always been this way and she hadn't picked up on it? Or was the senator's hard exterior faltering a bit with her jealous rage over Hendrick?

They made it up to a beautiful penthouse suite that featured over a thousand square feet of space, an exquisite bathroom with the deepest tub Mallory had ever seen, and views of the strip that took her breath away. Her room was close by, and she was sure even with it being smaller, it would still be spectacular.

"Ugh. I hate that this is where I'll be spending the night. I need to get Hendrick back to my room though, so I can stomach this place for one night," Anna said. She gingerly placed her purse on the table as if she was afraid it would get germs. The surfaces of the room gleamed with cleanliness and expense.

"I've never been in a nicer room," Mallory said, too in awe to maintain a dismissive air.

Senator Miller laughed. "My room at The Nobu is over ten-thousand square feet with three bedrooms, and a private deck with a Japanese maple tree. There's also a sauna, massage room that I've had a lot of fun in, a massive terrace with its own bar, a Zen garden, and a multitude of dining areas including a sushi bar of course."

"That sounds like a mansion on top of a hotel," Mallory said. She'd love to walk inside and see it. Did people actually live in places like that year-round? It was unimaginable to her.

"It's nice, but I only reside in beautiful places. My home in Washington State is lovely, but my DC home is where I belong," Anna told her.

"How do politicians, who make decent money, all end up multi-millionaires?" Mallory asked. She knew the answer, but she wanted to see how far the senator was willing to take her confessions. Mallory was about to find out.

The senator gave her an assessing look as if she was judging whether she could talk or not. She then moved to the window and looked down below her just as she did from every pulpit she spoke on.

"We get bought," Anna said with a chuckle. "Or at least the different lobbyist *think* they're buying us. They deposit nice large sums of money in our accounts and then we make laws based on what they want. The bigger the deposits, the more willing I am to do what they so nicely ask."

"I thought that was illegal," Mallory told her, making sure to keep her voice calm, as if she was simply curious, not ready to arrest the woman on the spot.

"When you run the country, you make your own laws. What the public doesn't know, can't hurt them, right?"

"But won't they see how you live?" Mallory asked.

"They don't open their eyes up to know the truth. We tell them our version of the truth, have our media allies hammer it home, and then our message is sealed. Did you know if you repeat a lie enough it will become the truth in the eyes of anyone, even the truth can't undo the lie? You just make sure your message comes across loud and clear *first*, and then no one can taint the waters with the boring truth. It's too late by then." A smug laugh accompanied the senator's words.

Mallory was horrified at what the senator said. How could she discuss the lives of those she was supposed to care about as if they were nothing but ants she was willing to burn in order to build a bigger mansion? She could because she had everything she wanted even if it was at the expense of those paying for her supposed service.

"I need to change. Meet me back here in thirty minutes. We're heading to the pool," Anna said, clearly done with her gloating. Mallory nodded and turned away without another word. She was glad the senator was done. She wasn't sure how much longer she'd be able to keep the absolute disgust from her face.

She went to her room that was half the size of the senator's, and still more luxurious than her bedroom back home, and she changed into her modest swimsuit before sliding on a robe. She never had been one to show off everything she had in public. Some of the bikinis people wore horrified her. But at the same time, she felt anyone had a right to express themselves however they wanted. If others didn't like it, they didn't need to look.

Mallory was back in the senator's room in thirty minutes, then had to wait another twenty. When Anna stepped from her room, Mallory couldn't stop her gasp. What was the woman thinking to be wearing what she was wearing in public? She was running for office. Of course, with that outfit, she'd probably have no problem at all drawing in the male vote.

Her bright red bikini showed far more than it hid, with her ample breasts staying perfectly in place beneath the small triangles that covered her nipples and not much more. The bottom of the matching material rose high on her curvy hips and showed everyone she passed there wasn't a single hair left on her body. When she turned, the small material only went out about two inches from the crack of her behind, showing the senator wasn't afraid of doing squats.

She slipped on a thin robe that barely hid anything but gave a smoky appearance that would only make people look harder to see the goodies she possessed.

"I know I look good and I'm not ashamed of showing that at a pool where it's perfectly acceptable, even for a senator," Anna said with a laugh.

"I'm sorry," Mallory automatically said as she jerked her gaze away.

"That's okay, I know I'm hot. Look all you want." The way she said that sent more disgust through Mallory. Was the woman hitting on her? No way!

The senator ran one of her bright red fingernails down Mallory's arm before turning. "Let's go."

Mallory had known the senator had some odd sexual exploits her team had to ensure were covered up, but she hadn't known quite how twisted the woman was. How did she hide her dark side when she lived in the public eye? It was crazy.

Mallory and the senator, along with a couple of bodyguards who were always silent, stepped out the doors onto the six acres of area dedicated to an outdoor oasis. The pool area featured four pools, three whirlpools, and cascading waterfalls. Along with all of that there was a lazy river, cabanas, chairs, and trees everywhere, giving the illusion of privacy and being on an island.

They moved past laughing guests, and a few people getting poolside massages.

"Oh, I need a massage. It's been an entire week," Anna said with a sigh. "I think I'll order one for this afternoon . . . or just have Hendrick give me one. He has incredible hands."

Mallory had the strong urge to stick out her arm and shove the senator into the pool they passed. She knew she'd be fired, and probably arrested immediately. But it was almost worth it to ruin her perfect makeup, and to simply shut up the incredibly clueless, snobby woman.

"I think it's been over five years since I've had one," Mallory said, clenching her fingers together to keep herself from enacting her petty moment.

"That must be why you're so high strung. I'll remedy that quickly," Anna said as she called her aide close. Mallory was also her aide, but apparently not on this trip. Apparently on this trip, she was the senator's wingman and talking companion. She was where she'd been wanting to be — and she hated it.

Massages were scheduled within minutes of Anna's aide calling. When a person carried as much power as the senator did, they could have anything they wanted on demand. It was truly crazy.

They moved around the pool a bit, unable to find Hendrick and his friends. The senator quickly grew impatient and told her bodyguard to find him. When he came back, he gave her the news with no expression on his face. Mallory wondered if he was a spiritless oaf only doing his job or if he had to grit his teeth as much as she did. She'd probably never know.

The men were at a cabana — and they weren't alone.

Senator Miller changed direction, never hurrying her step. A woman like her wasn't in a hurry. The rest of the world was supposed to wait for her, not the other way around.

When they turned a corner and found Hendrick's Park Bungalow Cabana hidden back from the rest of the people, they both froze. Hendrick and another man, a very pleasant looking, very muscular, dark skinned man, were inside . . . with women sitting on both of their laps. The gentleman with Hendrick was laughing at something the woman on his lap said, and she brushed her chest against his massive chest, causing his arm to snake around her and pull her a little closer.

The woman on Hendrick's lap took that moment to trail her pink nail down his chest, reaching the waistband of his shorts before he reached out and clasped her fingers. Mallory didn't move. The senator wasn't frozen like she was.

"Hendrick," the senator said with ice in her voice. "Are you enjoying your . . . *boys'* . . . day?" she asked, hesitating on the word boys as there were clearly hot women with him.

Hendrick jumped, the woman nearly falling from his lap. He steadied her as she rose and glared at Anna, and past to where Mallory was slowly stepping forward, not knowing what else to do. Hendrick looked from Anna to Mallory and back again. Then he smiled sheepishly.

"Yes, we've been having a great time," he said with a shrug. "What are you ladies doing here?"

"I wanted to spend the day at the pool with you," Anna said, quickly dismissing the woman who'd been with him as if she was a peon who didn't deserve a moment of her time. "I wasn't expecting any other females to be present. I knew you'd like the surprise visit."

She spoke so haughtily the woman who'd been glaring seemed to register danger. She didn't say another word before she hastily retreated. Probably a wise idea.

"I know this looks bad," Hendrick said, still not seeming worried. "But my boy, Jon, went on a mission to see how many women he could fit in the cabana. Carl and Steve all but ran for the hills when the ladies started showing up. Tyrell and I were getting them all back out, so Jon went to find more. You literally just stepped up as I was trying to remove Candy from my lap." It was a very simple explanation, but Mallory wasn't buying it. From the stiff set of Anna's shoulders, she wasn't either.

"*Candy* . . ." Anna said so ruthlessly it made a shiver travel down Mallory's back. ". . . just happened to fall on your lap?"

"Well, no, she climbed on, but I didn't want to be a complete asshole," Hendrick said. His eyes flashed to Mallory for only a second before going back to the senator. This gave her time to really study him. Mallory was confused. He looked as if he was trying to appease the senator, but he didn't seem enamored with her.

Was that his act? Was he trying to make her more interested in him by playing it cool? Or was he really doing a job and only keeping the hook in her while he still tried to bust her? She was so damn confused.

"All of this is true, except for me trying to get the women out of here. The more the merrier, I say. Come in both of you, and we can all have some fun," Tyrell said, a smile that burned genuine resting on his lips.

The senator ignored him completely. "We need to talk, Hendrick," Anna said. She moved forward and brushed her finger down his chest. Mallory wanted to puke. This was twice in five minutes she'd had to watch women trail their fingers down his impressive body. It should be her fingers, and *only* her fingers, doing just that. She had the urge to grab Anna by her hair, drag her to the pool, then hold her under the water.

Anna leaned in and tucked her head into Hendrick's chest at the same time she dropped her robe. "But we'll do it later. I like this cabana and I want to go swimming," she purred. She was claiming her man.

Hendrick looked over Anna's head and his heated gaze met Mallory's, a look in his eyes she couldn't read. It seemed he was pleading with her for understanding, but she didn't know what to believe anymore.

Horrifyingly, she felt tears prick her eyes. She refused to show him how this affected her. She nodded at him as if she was doing her job, and he was doing his, and then she turned and walked away. She didn't hurry her pace until she was out of sight with the cabana and then she rushed to the other side of the pool, flung her robe off, and dived into the refreshing water.

She swam for several minutes as she let a few tears fall, the water washing them away as she continued dunking her head. When she got herself under control, she emerged from the water, grabbed her robe, wrapped it around her, and left the pool area.

She wanted to go home, but she knew she couldn't, so instead she went to her room. She'd wait for the senator's next call, wait to find out if it was later that day . . . or not until morning.

CHAPTER EIGHTEEN

Sunday.
Monday.
Tuesday.
Wednesday.
Green had had enough!

He was about ready to abort his mission. Just as soon as he had that thought, he pushed it away. He knew that wasn't going to happen. Not in this lifetime or the next. Once he began something he didn't give up on it.

But he was pissed off.

The bachelor party in Vegas had started out fantastically. It had been everything a bachelor party should be and so much more. They'd raced fast cars, shot incredibly cool guns, ate so much food they should all be walking around looking like Oompa Loompas, and drank the equivalent of a large bar inventory. And then Mallory had appeared out of the blue.

He'd called . . . and called . . . and called.

And she hadn't answered. And now he was pissed — beyond pissed.

After the senator showed up and made it clear they were going up to her room to solidify their relationship, he'd been left with no choice but to end the farce. He wasn't willing to sleep with her and he couldn't put her off any longer. As soon as they'd been alone in the cabana she'd run her hand over his cock and he'd grabbed it, pulling it away, much to her disapproval.

He'd been hard as she'd touched him, which had made her lick her painted red lips that matched her bikini, one he normally would've admired. But his hardness hadn't been about the senator at all. It had been about the beautiful curves of Mallory's ass swaying as she walked away from him in her modest swimsuit that made him want to slowly peel it off of her as he kissed and licked every new inch of skin he unwrapped.

When the senator had tried to kiss him with Mallory still in sight of his lusting eyes, he'd pulled back. Her look of outraged shock had probably been the first real emotion he'd seen on the woman's plastic face. She wasn't used to rejection.

He'd told her clearly and concisely he didn't feel anything for her. It wasn't going to happen. To give the woman credit, she hadn't thrown a fit or screamed at him. She'd simply lifted her brow in a haughty manner, then laughed. She'd then told him she'd only wanted him for the photo ops, he was too beneath her to keep her interested in more than a mild fling. She'd then turned, not bothering with her flimsy robe, and walked away.

He'd immediately tried getting hold of Mallory, but his calls had gone straight through to voicemail. He knew he could bring Brackish in to work his magic and override any block Mallory might've put on him, but he didn't want the men involved. He wanted to solve this one on his own.

But now it was four days later, and he was done playing games. She hadn't been home, wouldn't answer her phone, and he wasn't above spying now.

He marched into Brackish's Dr. Evil room, as he liked to call it, with even more monitors added since the last time he'd been in the place. He wasn't sure how Brackish kept up with all of the technology, but the man seemed mighty pleased by it all.

"I need to know where Mallory is," Green said.

"I'm fine, how are you?" Brackish replied as he kept typing on his keyboard.

"Dammit, Brackish, I'm going out of my mind. Will you please help me?" Green snapped. "I've already blown my portion of the mission with my inability to tolerate the senator's hands on me, and I've fallen for the damn woman's supposed assistant. So, can you please tell me where Mallory is?"

Brackish chuckled. "I love a man willing to beg," Brackish said, making Green want to punch Brackish through the wall and into the next room.

Instead of having a comeback, he waited impatiently as he tapped his foot on the ground while Brackish spun around in his chair to another computer and began furiously typing. He turned back to Green in less than a minute with a smile on his face.

"I have the information. What are you willing to do for it?"

Green glared at the man. "I'm willing to keep your pretty face intact if you speak fast," Green threatened, making Brackish laugh heartily.

"I want to keep torturing you, but I can see you're about to have a total meltdown and unfortunately for me, or maybe fortunately for you, I know exactly how you're feeling," Brackish said. "She's heading to the airport. She and the senator are scheduled to fly out on a private jet in one hour."

"Where in the hell are they going?" Green asked.

"Washington, D.C. Apparently there's a huge gala tonight," Brackish said.

"Can you call Joseph and get me an invite to the gala and the use of the jet. I'm going there now," Green said.

"Is this for the mission?" Brackish asked with a smirk.

"Is there any doubt?" Green asked with a straight face. "I'm on the political action committee, aren't I? I'll need to know the hotel where Mallory's staying as well and have a room booked, preferably right next to hers. If you can switch the system to giving her a different floor than the senator, and rooms that have a connecting door between them, even better."

"Of course," Brackish said with a chuckle. "Consider it done. Look for the invite and reservation in your email. Better pack a tux, it's a black-tie event."

"Done." Green rushed from the room to hurriedly pack a bag and get to the airport where he knew the jet would be waiting. Maybe he could get Mallory to ride back home with him instead of the senator. He could have Brackish come up with a foolproof cover story that wouldn't make the senator suspicious.

It took Green about an hour to get packed, make a few calls, and arrive at the airport. Even though this was utterly last minute, there was one of Joseph's private jets sitting there, crew ready to take him to DC. Green had made a crapton of money in the past several years, but the power and money Joseph Anderson had was unbelievable. It was crazy what that man could do.

Did he want that kind of power? Not really. Then he'd never have a life. He liked things just the way they were. He could have just about anything he wanted when he wanted it — that was if he could get the damn girl.

He was boarding the jet when he finally caved and asked Brackish to do what he hadn't wanted to ask him to do. He knew he'd never hear the end of this. But at this point he was left with no choice whatsoever. He sent a quick text, then cringed as he imagined Brackish doubled over in laughter.

Please unblock my number from Mallory's phone.

He waited, and a message came back in under a minute.

Done. The one word was followed by about a dozen different emojis that were all laughing at him.

Green should've enjoyed the luxurious ride to Washington, but all he wanted was to see Mallory, so each minute felt like an hour. Finally, he landed in DC and grabbed the rental car he had waiting, doubled the speed limit to reach the hotel, and checked in. He wondered if he'd beat her to it. There was only one way to find out. He sent the text.

We need to talk now. No more excuses, no more ignoring me.

He sat there like a teen as he waited to see the bubbles appear on his phone showing she was opening the message . . . and hopefully responding.

After about a minute he heard noise in the room next to him, and he smiled. She was there. If she didn't answer the message quickly, he was pounding on the connecting doors.

I'm out of town. This will have to wait.

He opened his door, and there was only one small piece of wood between them. Well, the door wood was small at least.

Open your connecting door.

The bubbles spun on her phone as he heard her steps near their connecting door.

What are you talking about?
Open the door and you'll find out.

He held his breath, and then he heard the magical sound of a door unlocking. And then the door was opened, and there she was, looking at him with a stunned expression.

"How in the world did you make this happen?" she finally asked, her voice breathy. She held a myriad of expressions from hope to disbelief in her expressive eyes.

"I've got connections," he told her. And then he grabbed hold of her, pulled her into his arms, and kissed her as he'd wanted to do back at that pool in Vegas, which seemed to be a lifetime ago, though in reality had only been four days.

She was only stiff for a moment before she melted against him, her arms wrapping around his neck as she kissed him back, clinging to him as if she'd missed him as much as he had her. There was nothing more he wanted to do than drag her over to his bed and possesses her again, show her they were meant to be together.

Green wasn't sure when it had happened, but he'd fallen for this woman, and he'd fallen hard. He was mortified to think he'd wanted to be a bachelor forever, not wanting to deal with the drama of a relationship and not wanting to give up his freedom.

Now, he was completely on the dark side, needing this woman more than he needed food, air, water, or money. He wanted her, and as long as he had her, he knew he'd be just fine in all aspects of his life.

After long drugging kisses, Green pulled back and lifted his hand, cupping her cheek. "I didn't sleep with the senator. She called me over to her hotel in the morning, that photo op all planned out. It's always been a mission for me. The first night I met her, I did toy with the idea of sleeping with her. But after that drive home with you, I couldn't do it. From the moment I met you, I haven't seen another woman. I want you — and nobody else."

Her eyes widened as she witnessed the truth in his eyes. "I have no idea how you did this to me. I've been a confirmed bachelor for a very long time, but with you it's different. I could give it all up to be with you."

She gasped as she leaned a little closer to him. "I'm sorry. I shouldn't have overreacted," she whispered. She buried her head against his chest as she kept talking as if she wasn't able to look him in the eyes and show vulnerability.

"I've fought so hard for so long to prove myself in my work life that I've pushed away from any type of relationship. I didn't want one to hold me back. I didn't want to take a backseat to some male." She took in a shuddering breath and kept on talking. "And then you appear out of nowhere and I can't stop thinking about you, wanting you . . . and feeling jealous. I've never been jealous in my life. As a matter of fact, I've always been under the strict belief that if you have a reason to feel jealous, you need to leave the relationship. If a person wants to go, they will go, and if they're a cheater, they'll cheat. So, there's never been a reason for me to be jealous, I always walked away."

He cupped her chin, needing her to see him.

"Any man who let you walk away was a fool. You're worth fighting for," he told her. "I wasn't going to give up, not ever. And I told the senator I'm not interested. She wasn't going to stop until she got what she wanted, and I didn't want her, and I couldn't play the role of the doting boyfriend anymore."

"You blew your mission . . . because of me?" she gasped.

"Yes, but just that part of it. We're still going to get her. But I couldn't tolerate her hands on me anymore. I care about you, Mallory, and I want to see where this can go. You're worth more than this mission, more than anything I have."

He was shocked when tears sprang to her eyes. She wasn't the type of woman to cry easily. He pulled her close and hugged her, needing her to know what she meant to him.

"I'm sorry I responded emotionally. I never do that. I hope you'll forgive me," she told him.

"There's nothing to forgive. It's hard to be honest from the start and be vulnerable. I never realized that until you. But I've never had someone I wasn't willing to let go of before you either," he assured her.

She smiled up at him and he finally took a step back. "We have an event to go to and if you keep looking at me like that we'll be very late," he warned.

Her smile fell away. "You're coming to the dinner?" she asked.

"I told you I have connections," he said with a laugh, feeling more joy than he had in quite a while. "Can I escort you to the ball?" he finished with a bow that made her giggle.

236

"That won't look so good to the senator," she warned.

"I don't care. We'll figure that out when we arrive."

The trusting look in her eyes was bigger than anything he'd ever received before. "Okay, I'd love to go with you," she said.

He stepped forward, gave her one more kiss, then backed away quickly. "Go get ready and I'll hope to wow you with my impressive tuxedo," he said with a waggle of his brows.

"Mmm, you might make my panties wet . . ." She paused for a long moment as she stepped through their connecting doors. "If I wear any, that is."

Screw it. He was going to have her right then. He took a purposeful step toward her right as she shut the door in his face and clicked the lock into place. He heard her laughter through the barrier she'd wedged between them. Great, now he had to try to get into his form-fitted tux with a massive hard-on. *Down boy.*

Mallory controlled that night from the second she stepped back through the doors connecting their rooms. She wore a classic black dress that was both sexy and sophisticated at the same time with a modest neckline that dipped enough to showcase her pearl necklace and matching earrings. The dress hugged her breasts, stomach, and hips, before it flared out and rested just above her knees.

The lacy, three-inch, black heels that molded to her feet and made her legs seem endless gave the dress a bit of naughty that assured him she'd keep those on later when he took her to his bed. Her lips were shining with red gloss that made him want to feast on them all night.

It was a good thing his jacket was long enough to hide the evidence of what she did to him by simply walking into a room — especially when it had been a week since he'd last tasted her. He assured himself he'd get his fill that night, and the night after, and every night for as long as he could have her.

"We'd better go. I took too long," she said. "The senator left a while ago, and I don't expect her to look for me. I'm there to fetch if she needs it, but at events like this she'd much rather have very wealthy men attending to her every need."

"Good, we can make an appearance separately then sneak away together. I want you back here in my room where I can make you scream over and over again," he said, his voice husky and low.

"Hmm, maybe it's my turn to make you scream," she said, before she whirled around and walked to the door, making him drool as he followed her. The woman had a natural sexuality that was more appealing with her being so unaware of it. Whoever had invented heels needed a thank you note from every male in the world, because they brought so much pleasure. He chose to walk behind her down the hallway just so he could enjoy the view.

"I love your car," she told him as he helped her inside before climbing in and pulling out onto the road that was drenched as a hard summer rainstorm pounded the car and shortened the visibility to a couple hundred feet.

"If we're going to drive through a monsoon, at least we're doing it in luxury. I don't like being on the freeways in storms. There are too many idiots out there," he said as he pulled off the main road and made several turns until they were on a road with no lights and no houses in sight.

"I've only been to DC a few times, but this seems like an oasis in the middle of city life," she said. The storm's fury increased its tempo as they slowed more, the windshield wipers unable to keep up with the driving rain.

"Once you're out of the city in most of these large metropolises you can find a lot of beauty to find," he said.

Before she could reply, there was a loud noise, and the car swerved hard for a moment, causing Mallory to let out a small gasp as she grabbed for the dashboard. He reached for her as he pulled the vehicle onto a gravel road and moved a dozen or so yards to make sure no passing vehicle would run into them.

"What was that?" she asked. Her heart had to be thundering. His own had picked up a few beats.

"We blew a tire, the front left one," he said with a sigh. The windshield was coated in rain as he turned off the wipers.

"Oh, that really sucks," she said.

"Do you know how to change a tire?" he asked with mischief.

She folder her arms. "Actually, I do," she said with smile.

"Want to prove it?" he asked.

She laughed hard. "I'm sorry to be the one to inform you that there's no amount of taunting that's going to challenge me to change a tire in this rain. If I were alone, I'd do it, but in this weather, not a chance when you're sitting there perfectly capable."

He laughed with her, falling more in love with this woman by the second. That thought sent a jolt of fear through him that made facing the warm summer rain much more appealing. He wasn't falling in love with the woman. It was simply lust and like. That was all.

"I'd better get this done," he said as he began undoing his shirt.

"What are you doing?" she asked, her eyes going wide as he exposed his chest before pulling the shirt off. His jacket was already in the back. He didn't like wearing it while he was driving.

"I can't ruin my clothes, so they have to come off," he said. He was undoing his belt, and damn, he loved the look of lust in her eyes.

"You're going to change the tired naked?" she gasped.

"There's no one around and it will be like a warm shower . . . with tools. You've seen my body before."

He pulled up on the seat and pulled his pants and underwear down, his erection springing free and standing up. Her eyes focused on one part of him, and with the way she was licking her lips, she wasn't offended by the view.

He hadn't had car sex since he was a teen, and he knew it was a bad idea to start it right then. But he knew if he didn't get out of the car fast, they'd never make it to the dinner. He didn't want to risk blowing Mallory's cover. So, he did the only thing he could right then . . . he ran.

Green jumped from the car, the rain warm enough for him not to shiver, but cool enough to calm his libido . . . a tiny bit. He pulled out the jack, lifted the car, and got the ruined tire off. He still sported a bit of an arousal, but he ignored it as rain slid down his body and he got the new tire on. He was trying to hurry as he tightened and checked the spare tire for air before putting all of the parts back into the trunk. He took a deep breath before shutting the trunk lid and moving to the driver's door.

And then Green knew they were going to be late . . . they were going to be really late.

Mallory was leaning against the driver's door, her hair hanging over her chest, soaking wet, and not a piece of fabric covering her body. A streak of lightning ripped through the sky, and he got a full view of her luscious breasts, her nipples peaked, ready for his touch. Her legs were spread, and water ran down her body in waves, making little rivers pool over her bare mound before falling to the ground.

He didn't say a word, just stepped up to her and pulled her against him as he smashed his mouth against hers, drinking her in as he cupped her ass and pulled her close. He moved forward, setting her on the still-warm hood of the car, his arousal pushing against her. He nipped on her lower lip before sucking it in his mouth as his hands roved up and down her back, then moved to her sides and slipped to the front where he could hold the weight of her breasts.

He flicked her nipples before he kissed his way down her neck, licking her taste and the rain off her body before he moved over the curve of her breasts while he squeezed it. Finally, he dipped lower, and took her beaded nipple in his mouth, sucking and nipping the sensitive skin as she squirmed in his arms and screamed her pleasure.

He pushed her back, loving the gasp escaping her lips as he held tightly to her hips and ran his mouth down her belly. The rain splashing over their bodies, only adding to their pleasure. She lay there before him on her elbows, her head tilted down to keep the rain from pooling on her face. She watched him as he opened her farther, then buried his mouth at her core and licked and sucked her until she screamed again.

She shook beneath him as he brought her to orgasm, then kept on going. She released again when his fingers dove in and he sucked her pulsing clit. He eased off her and stood up, looking at the sight she made splayed out on the hood of the car, her body red, her nipples hard, her legs quivering.

He needed more.

"Tell me you're protected," he begged. Foolishly, he didn't have a condom.

"I'm protected," she assured him, lust burning in her gaze.

He'd never trusted a woman with that before. But he did trust Mallory. With a need that consumed him, he flipped her around, letting her feet barely touch the ground as he grabbed her hips, his thumbs digging into the tender flesh of her ass.

He kicked her feet apart and pressed closer, thrusting forward, sinking fully within her tight heat. That first plunge was heaven and hell. He had to calm himself before he lost all control. He stopped and waited, and she wiggled against him.

"More," she demanded as she turned her head and looked at him with such need, his heart raced, and he lost his breath.

"Patience," he said as he slapped her ass, making her gasp. She looked at him in shock before a devilish smile flashed across her lips.

"I said more, now," she taunted. He was shocked. It seemed his professional FBI agent liked a little naughty during sex.

He slapped her other butt cheek and felt a flash of heat surge around his arousal as she tightened, nearly making him come. She wiggled back against him, and she won.

He held tight to her hips as he pulled out and pushed in. He was done playing. The feel of the rain pounding down on them, the look of absolute lust in her eyes, and the way she clenched him were all his undoing.

He pumped in and out of her at a fast past, hitting against her body harder and harder with each thrust. Her scream of pleasure echoed around them as her body clenched him hard, heating him as she let go, her orgasm taking control and holding her in its power. He surged again and released deep inside her, his own control long gone, his orgasm ripping a call from him that mingled through the storm with hers.

The pleasure went on and on as he remained buried deep inside of her, their panting breaths barely audible in the downpour. When he could finally move again, he pulled from her body, causing a murmur of disapproval as she slid from the car and stood, her legs a little wobbly.

"That's the best flat tire I've ever had," she said after a moment. Then she winked at him. "And excellent triple A service."

Green laughed hard as he pulled her against him and lifted her in the air, spinning around. There they were in the middle of nowhere — naked, soaked, and sated — and she was able to make him laugh. He was never letting this woman go.

"We aim to please, ma'am, please leave a good review," he told her, as he put an arm below her legs and lifted her up, moving to the back of the car.

"I'll be sure to do that," she said.

He opened the back door and folded them both inside, where they soaked the leather seats. He pulled out his bag and grabbed a blanket, placing it below them and wrapping them in it.

"I always carry an emergency bag for a moment like this," he said.

"Mmm, I do love a man who comes prepared." He kissed her again but pulled back as he started to grow hard once more.

"We have a dinner to get to, so we'd better dry off."

She seemed disappointed, but she used the blanket to dry herself, then they did the tedious task of dressing in the car. Mallory climbed to the front without having to get in the rain again, and soon they were back on the road.

She fixed her makeup with the items she'd packed in her purse and they arrived at the dinner forty-five minutes later.

They entered the place, getting some strange looks from other patrons, as their hair was soaked, but there wasn't a drop of rain on their clothes. They smiled at each other for the entire time they were there, staying far apart in case the senator was watching. That just added to Green's anticipation for the rest of the night to come.

Round two wasn't very far away.

CHAPTER NINETEEN

Chad wasn't shocked by much anymore, not after everything he'd seen in the military and as a civilian. People just didn't surprise him. But today, he was standing in the command center as activity swirled around him.

Brackish was good — he was damn good, and just in case any of them ever forgot it, he was reminding Chad why he was the best of the best.

Brackish had broken the code, solved the riddle, and put the final piece in the puzzle that had been evading the team for far too long. Damien was being framed — there was no longer any doubt.

Someone had put millions into an account under his name, an account he hadn't known existed. It had been hidden under multiple umbrella companies that were hidden under shell companies that were hidden behind so many different layers, only Brackish could've gotten to the bottom of it. The entire criminal system was brilliant, and the amount of time taken to do this was remarkable, but once Brackish began pulling a thread, he always saw it through to the complete undoing.

"What's next?" Brackish asked as he turned and stared at Chad.

"Get Damien on the phone, now!" Chad demanded.

"Already on it," Eyes said as he hammered the phone and dialed Damien.

Those three rings were the only sound that could be heard in the suddenly still room. Panic wasn't something any of the team often felt as they were calm when the rest of the world was blowing up. But things were moving fast now, and they had seconds to save one of the Anderson family members.

"Hello." Damien's voice rang through the speaker system of the office.

"Damien — it's Eyes. Get your wife and daughter and get in the car, now! Don't pack anything, don't call anyone, and absolutely don't delay for even a second. Leave now. I'll give you an address while you're driving," Eyes demanded. The tone of his voice was unmistakable and no one who knew him would ever question what he was saying. Damien had seen Eyes when a battle was raging. He immediately came to attention.

"My family isn't here, but I'll send them the address once you send it to me," Damien said, giving the team a sigh of relief.

"Go find them, now, Damien. It's life and death. This isn't a drill. Get out of your house and get them to safety," Eyes commanded.

The team could hear Damien moving as he spoke into the phone. Keys were rattling and his breathing had sped up. He was listening.

"What in the hell is going on, Eyes?" Damien asked.

"You're being framed, Damien. It looks like you're being set up to take the fall as the money man behind a major drug ring," Eyes said. "And your death is the final nail in the coffin. They've hid it well, but my team is better."

There was no voice on the other end of the line as rustling could be heard. And then dead silence, but the call was still going.

"Damien?"

No reply.

"Damien, are they there?" Eyes felt terror fill him. We're they too late?

"Damien grunt if you can," Eyes said as he motioned with his team to load up. They moved fast.

There was a click of the phone.

"Shit!"

He dialed Damien's phone again, but it went straight to voicemail.

Eyes whipped his head around to their tech genius. "Brackish, can you track his phone? It just went cold," Eyes said.

The men were ready to go. They were prepared for whatever was coming next.

Brackish started hitting keys on the computer then replied, "Looks like the phone is dead, which tells me that either he, or someone else, has cut his service, or someone broke the phone, took out the sim card, and it's gone."

"What about his wife and daughter, can you get a signal from them?" Eyes asked.

"Already on it," Brackish said, not even looking up from the screen on his computer.

Eyes knew getting to Damien would take too long from the command center, so he tried calling Green, who was out in the field. Hopefully, he could get to Damien's house in time.

"Let's move," he said to Chad, Sleep, and Smoke. "Keep us on comms, Brackish."

"Will do. Go." Brackish never looked up as he worked his magic on the computer.

"Chad, you go with Sleep in one vehicle. Smoke and I will be in the other. Brackish, turn everything on. I want each man traced. If you find his wife and daughter, we'll split apart."

They were in their vehicle when Green answered his phone. He spoke before Eyes could say a word.

"Eyes, there's something crazy going on. Not sure of details yet, but I need you guys to start tracking my location. I'll call back when possible."

This night was quickly getting out of control. He looked at Smoke, who was ready to go, sitting next to him.

"Damien might not be trained to our level, but he's no slouch. He didn't give up his phone without a fight. He's resourceful, though. He knows we're coming, and he should be able to find a way to keep them talking until we get there."

The men were racing hard toward Damien's home. They pushed the vehicles to their limits. Eyes driving, Smoke next to him in the lead vehicle. Sleep driving, Chad the passenger, followed behind. They got through the light traffic and near the neighborhood where the Whitfield's lived.

They shut their vehicle's lights off about two blocks from the residence, and they slowed to nearly a crawl. As they looked down the intersection running to the house, they were met with a surprise. Three identical cars were in front of Damien's home. No lights on, no one inside the cars, just shut down and unattended.

"That his house with the cars? Something's definitely wrong," Smoke whispered.

"Yes, it is," Eyes said, bringing the vehicle to a stop, using the emergency brake so not to use their brake lights and alert anyone watching from the windows.

"Brackish, who are the nearest police to Damien's place?" Eyes asked into his mic.

"There are no on-duty police indicating any activity within eight miles of that place," came the quick reply.

"Call McCormack, give him the details, and tell him not to call this out over the radio. We're going to need help here, but I don't know who's listening. Tell him to come quietly and without a parade," Eyes said.

"On it."

The four men exited their vehicles, came together, and created a plan, keeping as out of sight as possible. They needed to keep civilians safe.

"I'm going to the front door. Once I know you're in location, I'll knock and ask to see Damien," Eyes said.

"Copy," the three men said before they moved to get into position.

Eyes walked directly to the front door and knocked. He'd removed most of the pieces of gear he'd had on minutes before, knowing anyone who opened the door wasn't going to be friendly. He couldn't look like a threat.

The massive door of the house opened, and standing before him was a large man, easily towering over Eyes, wearing a simple pair of jeans and a light jacket. A quick assessment revealed that his right-hand knuckles had been recently used, and he was carrying a handgun, no larger than a 9mm, in a shoulder strap that wasn't concealed much.

"Hi, um . . . I live next door, a friend of Damien's, coming over to see if he's okay," Eyes said, moving his arms around too much, giving him a look of someone who might be genuinely anxious after hearing strange noises.

"Everything's fine, go home," the beast said.

"Yeah, okay. But is he here? I'd like to see him if you don't mind." Eyes paused as if he was scared, but not willing to leave his friend. "Who are you? I haven't seen you before, and there were some loud noises a few minutes ago."

"Listen, neighbor, you need to go back home now. This is a family issue, and we're here helping," was returned.

"Oh. Okay." Eyes said slowly as if he wasn't sure if he believed the man or not. The large man's eyes narrowed. Eyes looked beyond the man into the dark house for any information he could see. He saw another man look over at the door. The guy had the same build as the man standing in front of Eyes. They were obviously hired men with all brawn and no brains.

"I didn't catch your name, friend," Eyes said again, taking a step forward, now at the threshold of the door.

"No, you didn't, and you aren't going to. It's time for you to leave," the big man said before starting to close the door on Eyes. It didn't work as Eyes put his foot in the jamb.

In a flash the big man grabbed the front of Eyes's shirt and tried pushing him away from the door, so he'd be able to close it. He hadn't been expecting Eyes to have fighting skills, so the man's face changed to shock when Eyes moved like a snake striking.

In a flash, Eyes pulled the guy from the threshold, down the steps, and had him bound like a pretzel within a few seconds.

"What in the hell is going on in there?" Eyes asked coolly, his stuttering act gone.

"Go to hell," said the man, struggling in an attempt to get to his weapon. It wasn't going to happen.

Eyes leaned in, putting pressure on the man's elbow, stretching it out in an unnatural angle, causing the man to cry out in agony "I asked you what in the hell is going on in there," Eyes repeated, authority ringing in his tone.

"Piss off, I ain't talkin'," the man said through gritted teeth and strained muscles.

A quick pull and twist broke the man's elbow. Before the scream of pain could be heard, Eyes moved to wrap his arms around the neck of the man. He wasn't going to kill him, but he applied enough pressure to knock him out. Then he secured the man in zip ties, put his handkerchief in his mouth, and zip-tied that around his head to secure it.

Eyes jumped up and got inside the house rapidly with barely a sound. Before he could get the door latched a hand slid inside it, startling Eyes. He grabbed the wrist and pulled on it hard.

"It's me," the barely audible whisper said.

Eyes immediately calmed. Green was there.

Green shifted inside, and they closed the door, then made their way to the bottom of the staircase. The other men in the house hadn't seen anything go down and weren't aware of their presence, but it wouldn't take them long to begin to search for their missing teammate.

In the distance they could hear the harsh sound of a conversation echoing through the house.

In a specific sign language that SEALs knew well, Eyes told Green to go up the stairs and search the rooms. Green did as requested while Eyes crept toward the kitchen. Eyes was glad he'd previously been in the house. He knew the layout and knew where someone could jump out at him.

Eyes paused as a voice spoke. "We aren't going anywhere until your wife and daughter get here and then we're all going for a little drive. I promise they won't feel a thing. You, on the other hand, you're going to watch them die, then your death will be very, very slow and painful." The glee in the person mocking Damien was as evil as it got. These types of men feasted on pain and misery.

Staying in the shadow, Eyes knelt down, keeping as much of his body in the dark as possible.

"Why are you doing this?" Damien asked. From the sound of the words, it was clear to Eyes Damien's jaw was either broken or badly damaged.

Eyes made it to the junction between the hall and kitchen to find five people standing around a chair where Damien was sitting, his arms and legs bound.

"I'm going to go see what the hell Jerry's doing. It looked like he was going to pop that little man's head off," one of the voices said.

The man, who Eyes had seen a few minutes before, was walking from the kitchen. Eyes made a pivot, eased himself into a closet, left it open just enough to get out, and waited for the man to pass. When the man did, Eyes slid out of his hiding spot, snuck up behind him, and struck like a viper, the power knocking the man off his feet. He fell face first to the floor. Eyes was able to catch the fall enough to not make a loud sound that would carry back to the kitchen.

Eyes secured the man, then drug him to the closet he'd just been inside. They needed as many of these men secured and unable to fight as they could get. There was no telling what was going to happen once everyone came face to face. It was an incalculable variable.

Returning to the spot at the entrance to the kitchen, Eyes arrived in time to see someone wind their arm back, make a massive arcing swing, and connect with Damien's face.

Eyes got down on his hands and knees and crawled between the island and the wall where the fridge was. He continued down the line, stood, and in a flash took two huge steps, grabbing the back of the chair Damien was tied to, spinning it around him, and then standing in front of the group of people who held his friend captive.

Eyes's blood went cold as he saw who was standing among the three remaining goons.

Few times in Eyes's life did he have a hitch in his thought process, but at the moment he was so stunned he was stumped. This day had been too full of surprises. What in the hell was going on?

Senator Anna Miller gave him a cold stare, not seeming in the least afraid of this new change in circumstances.

He paused for too long, the goons with the senator leapt forward, ready to take him down. It wasn't the first time Eyes had been in a three-to-one fight. It hadn't been fun in the past, and it wasn't going to be fun right now. They all fell to the floor as they each attempted dominance.

Eyes slid his arm under an attacker's chin, then cinched his arm, locking the man in. Fists were raining down on him from the other men, but luckily their hits weren't connecting in the right places. He couldn't stay in this position long, it was just a matter of time before things went bad for him if he didn't gain control over the situation, and fast.

Eyes kicked at one of the men's legs, but the move didn't have the intended effect, instead bringing the man down on top of him. Eyes smashed his forehead into the nose of the man, instantly breaking it and causing him to scream and spray of blood all over Eyes's face.

Just as he brought his arm over the man spewing blood, the last man walked up to the pile of fighting bodies. The sole of a boot blocked out the lights in the room, and Eyes knew he was about to get his face bashed in. Just as the boot started coming down, a crunching sound blitzed into his attacker.

No more than three seconds went by before the massive sliding glass door in the kitchen exploded, glass falling down in tiny shards. Three men came through the door like a Michael Bay movie. Sleep, Smoke, and Chad, holding long guns, stepped into the room in unison, stopping all the fighting.

Green had made short order of the man he'd tackled seconds before. And then in another few seconds all of the men who were so-called *security* for the senator, were on their knees, hands behind their backs, zip ties locking their hands in place.

"Four men outside have been secured," Smoke said.

"No one was upstairs, we're clear there," Green added.

"Nice try, you son of a bitch," Eyes said into the ear of the guy who'd almost stomped his face. He put an extra pinch on the zip tie holding the security man's hands.

The senator, who'd been looking so cocky just moments before, now seemed a bit rattled. It was almost fascinating watching all of the emotion flitter across her face. She was rapidly recovering her composure though, faster than most people would.

"Hendrick?" the senator's voice questioned as Green moved forward with confidence.

"Don't say a word," Eyes shot out to Green. He knew this would now turn into a legal battle that couldn't be avoided, and he needed to make sure his men didn't incriminate themselves in any way.

He turned to all of them. "None of you say a word. Take the guys to the front door and connect them with the others. You, check the senator for weapons. You and you, take a route and make sure everyone's completely secure, then get back here asap." He didn't use their names. He wanted the senator to have zero information.

Sleep and Smoke nodded their heads, confirming they'd return fast. Chad checked the senator for weapons, not caring about her personal space by patting down every inch she could possibly hide something. He found nothing. Eyes didn't want Green in the room at all and knew that Chad would be able to work with Sheriff McCormack once he arrived. Green was the only face the senator recognized other than Damien's.

"Are you okay?" Eyes asked Damien, looking over his bloodied face.

"Just a scratch here and there," Damien said.

"I thought the same thing but wasn't sure how soft you'd gotten over the years," Eyes said.

Damien's smile fell and was replaced by rage. A fire overtook him, and he was about to become unleashed, but Eyes stopped him, putting his hand on his shoulder, keeping Damien in his seat.

"No, D-Train, not here, not now," Eyes whispered in his ear.

Eyes brought his attention to the senator, his focus burning into her. His own rage was trying to escape. Whatever was happening, this woman was at the head of using his friend as a pawn in something bad. He wasn't sure what it was yet, but he'd do his best to help Damien figure out what in the hell was going on. Eyes also worried about Green, who was now wrapped up in the mess. He knew Green was clean, and they could prove it, but this entire thing was going to be a massive cluster.

"What's this all about?" Eyes questioned the senator.

She smiled, the way a snake would look at an injured rabbit. "Whoever you are, you're so far removed from any importance in my world, I can't think of a response that would be worth using on you."

Brackish's voice jumped into Eyes's ear, "Tell her you know about her company — Redsnow Consulting."

"You might not have any response for me, but I know about Redsnow Consulting, and more than you can imagine," Eyes said with a smirk he knew would get under her skin.

The senator went from cocky to aghast in a single heartbeat. She'd believed that company was so far removed from any person she was attached with that hearing someone utter the name in front of her had to be a kick in her gut. She took a step toward the island, reaching for it, using the surface to help maintain her balance.

"Yeah lady, you're going down," Eyes said with a smile. It wasn't his goofy smile his team knew so well, it was a return of a smile that was snake-like, that knew it had injected venom into its prey and the end was near.

"What's this about?" Damien asked.

"We'll talk to you about it when she's in jail," Smoke said over his shoulder.

Sheriff McCormack called into the house, "Clear?"

Eyes responded in the positive, telling the police officer to come in and arrest the woman for false imprisonment, which was enough to take her for a ride to the jail. By the time she was there a host of new charges would be sent over.

That didn't mean she'd stay in jail, but at least it was a start.

The senator was shell-shocked, but wise enough to not say a word as she was read her Miranda rights while the sheriff slapped handcuffs on her and walked her to the police car. The senator's security team was loaded up and taken away as well.

All the members of their team exited before the rest of the police showed up, and Damien and Eyes gave statements just as the media vans arrived. Eyes flipped his hood over his head and looked down at the ground before grabbing Damien and loading him into his car.

"Don't want to be recorded," Damien said as he looked at Eyes in a knowing way.

"Nope," Eyes said simply.

"Are you going to tell me who those men working with you are, and why you're acting like a SEAL?"

"Nope," Eyes said.

"Good enough for me. You guys saved my life and the life of my wife and daughter," Damien said as he reached out and patted Eyes's shoulder. There was a suspiciously choked sound to Damien's voice. Eyes gave him a few seconds to recover himself. "Thank you. Those words aren't nearly enough, but they're all I have. Thank you."

"You'd do it for me," Eyes told him.

"Without hesitation," Damien said.

Eyes drove Damien to the hospital and his wife and daughter were waiting as they arrived, their tears flowing as they wrapped Damien in their embrace and took him inside. Eyes slipped away. He didn't have to ask Brackish to handle the clean-up as he'd already made the calls to get the house cleaned and the door repaired.

Eyes had never been more thankful for the team he was on and who he worked with. They not only had each other's backs every single day, but they could communicate without words. Eyes knew this was far from over, but he felt closer and closer to solving the entire puzzle.

He didn't care what it took, they'd find all they needed to take the senator completely down. She was a menace to society and any longer in office and she'd be unstoppable. The only reason they could get to her now was she was so new in the political world and didn't have all of the protection in place so many long-time government servants had.

They were going to get her — and they'd find out why Damien was such a target. They'd find it all out . . .

CHAPTER TWENTY

Joseph Anderson looked around and since no one was watching, he pulled out a cigar, prepared it, sucked a nice plume of smoke in his mouth, then let it back out and smiled. He was good — he was damn good.

"Someone's looking mighty proud of himself." Joseph choked on the last of his cigar smoke as he spun around to see Sherman Armstrong walking up to him with Avery's mother, Bobbie, on his arm.

"You nearly gave me a heart attack, Sherman. What are you doing sneaking up on an old man like that?"

"I'm out having a stroll in this tropical paradise," Sherman said. The smile he sent to Bobbie made Joseph's heart proud.

"It looks like the two of you are enjoying this paradise together," Joseph said with a chuckle. Bobbie blushed as she looked down.

"We're . . . um . . . we're just friends," Bobbie finally said.

Sherman chuckled. "Yes, friends," he said, giving her such a loving smile it nearly made Joseph blush, and that wasn't something that happened too often.

"Well, there's no better place to be with friends," Joseph said, deciding now wasn't the time to push the new couple. They needed to come out in their own time. As people aged, there wasn't the hurry he saw in the younger generation. As long as they were together, that was good enough for him for now.

"I'm so glad Steve and Erin decided to have a second wedding in Fiji. Unbelievably, I've never been here before. But we've only been here two days and I already know we'll come back each year," Sherman said.

"I never traveled," Bobbie said. "So, this is beyond a treat for me. I was so glad to be included in this family event."

"Those boys work together and play together. When your Avery married to Carl, you became family as well," Joseph told Bobbie. The smile she gave him was sweet and appreciative.

"When you're on your own as long as Avery and I had been, it's sometimes difficult to feel like a family, but each day that passes in our new lives in Washington is another that makes me feel we're right where we belong."

"You've been here a while now. Will you stay?" Joseph asked her.

"Yes, I think we'll most certainly stay," Bobbie told him.

"There are many reasons you're wanted here," Sherman said. "I think this is an ideal location for a wedding and honeymoon. We might just have to come back real soon."

Bobbie's eyes widened at Sherman's words, and Joseph took another puff from his cigar and smiled as he looked out over the incredible ocean.

"I wouldn't mind attending a dozen weddings here," Joseph said. "Just let me know when."

Before Sherman could respond, Hendrick walked down the path, Mallory at his side, deep in an intense conversation. They stopped, Mallory blushing, and Hendrick looking quite pleased with himself.

"What are you up to on this fine day?" Hendrick asked as his arm wound around Mallory's waist. She squirmed for a moment before she sighed and snuggled in a little closer.

"We're just discussing how much we love this location for weddings and honeymoons," Joseph said. "Do you agree?"

Hendrick beamed. "I couldn't agree more. I was just saying the same thing to Mallory." The woman, who was normally so confident, blushed scarlet and looked at her sandals as if they were the most fascinating things she'd ever seen.

"How did you get Mallory here? The last I heard she was doing her best to avoid you," Joseph taunted.

Hendrick laughed, not at all affected by the teasing.

"I told her I was taking her on a date. Then I recruited her friend, who packed a bag for a tropical paradise, and whisked her off on the jet. She wanted to kill me at first, then decided since she hasn't had a vacation in three years, she'd earned one, and here we are."

"How did the FBI feel about you being kidnapped?" Joseph asked Mallory.

She glowered for a moment. Then she chuckled. "My boss told me it was about time someone kidnapped me. He said I talk so much smack to everyone he was surprised it hadn't happened sooner. Then he said I'd handled the senator's case to perfection, that I was getting a promotion, and to enjoy the next two weeks off. I think he might worship Hendrick a bit."

"Ah, it sounds like you have a pretty amazing boss. And he knows there's much more to come with the senator and the high-powered players who are beginning to go down. I'm glad you get to refresh in this paradise," Joseph said. Then he smiled as he gazed at Hendrick. "But more importantly, what is this about weddings you're speaking of?"

Hendrick looked like a kid in a candy store. "I've decided I'm going to marry this woman. But I don't want to scare her off, so I'm just throwing out little clues for now so she's prepared when I propose."

His words made all of them laugh. "*That* was a little hint?" Sherman asked.

"What?" Hendrick asked with an innocent act the man must've perfected in his thirty-two years of life because it was almost believable. "That wasn't a hint."

"If you say it's not a hint, then I'll take you at your word," Joseph said. "And I want an invite to the wedding. No more quickie weddings. The joining of two people should be celebrated and enjoyed for weeks not hours."

"I couldn't agree more. Plan on coming back to Fiji or somewhere else tropical in about three months," Hendrick said.

"Deal," Joseph said, beaming at Mallory who seemed as if she was accepting this new reality Hendrick had thrust upon her. They were falling in love, and it was quite beautiful to see they weren't fighting it.

They heard giggling and turned to see Carl and Avery running down the wooden dock in their swimsuits, grins on their faces as they clasped hands. They turned onto the next dock before they saw Joseph and the rest of their group, and then the two of them launched themselves from the end of the pier and dove into the ocean, breaking back out of the water and falling into one another's arm. The kiss they shared made the entire group turn away, not wanting to intrude on their intimate moment.

"I always hoped Avery would find a suitable husband. I'm so happy she got the love of her life instead," Bobbie said with a sigh. They heard splashing behind them, making all of their group giggle.

"Everyone deserves deep love," Sherman said as he again looked at Bobbie with so much love it was impossible not to be touched by it.

"I agree. Without Katherine life would have no meaning," Joseph said.

"My ears are burning," Katherine said as she walked down the pathway, light surrounding her in her flowing white sleeveless vest. She had a clip in her silver hair made of leaves and flowers that looked like a crown fit for a queen. Her lips were painted pink, matching her bare toes, and she was so stunning she literally took his breath away. She easily slid up to his side and wrapped her slender arm around her husband. He carefully pulled her close, knowing she was the most precious gift he'd ever been bestowed.

"You know I can't go five minutes without thinking of you, my love. Especially in this paradise. Let's come here next year on our anniversary and renew our vows."

She beamed up at him. "Oh, Joseph, that's a lovely idea. Let's spend a month here fishing, taking tours, and spending days at the spa."

He leaned down and kissed her. "I'll spend as much time as you like my love. There's nothing I won't do to see that smile on your face."

"That makes me love you even more," she said. "Those might be merely words to some men, but they are gospel to you."

He kissed her again, wondering how he'd ever gotten so lucky.

"A month here sounds like heaven," Sherman said. "Maybe we'll come and crash the party."

Bobbie beamed at him as if she loved the idea. "There's nothing that would please me more," Katherine said. "I want all of my loved ones at our side when we renew our vows."

"I can't imagine how wonderful it is to have a love like yours," Bobbie said. "It's transcended generations. You inspire me."

"My husband has always managed to find ways to make love happen when he's around. I think you might discover exactly how wonderful it is," Katherine said with a wink as she looked between Sherman and Bobbie.

"I believe our dinner is ready," Katherine told Joseph. "As much as I love our family, I'm very much looking forward to a private dinner at our villa overlooking the ocean."

"Then we're off," Joseph said as he took Katherine's hand. "I'll see you all in the morning.

The wedding will be spectacular." He led Katherine away.

He knew her trials weren't over, but he also knew they'd get through them together. With his wife, there wasn't anything he couldn't get through.

CHAPTER TWENTY-ONE

Erin had been in Fiji for three days and she was still having to pinch herself to accept the reality of her new life. She was enrolled in school, and she was thriving, loving her coursework, and loving her life.

She'd had a connection with Steve from the moment she'd met him, and though that had terrified her, it had also been one of the greatest blessings of her life. She reached down and rubbed her hand over her belly that only had the slightest bump on it. Awe still filled her when she thought that she was carrying their child within the safety of her womb.

They'd had a fun, crazy wedding in Las Vegas, but this day felt so much more real. This day they were surrounded by their crazy, adopted family, and it all felt magical and right. A person really could make their own family. She hadn't thought that possible when she'd lost her grandparents, but now she knew they'd sent Steve to her. He'd come when she'd needed him the most.

She was sitting in her gorgeous honeymoon suite at Namale's. Joseph had rented the entire compound, so only their people were there. She never minded strangers, enjoying meeting new people, but so many had shown up for their special event it was good he'd rented all nineteen units and the amenities that went with them.

They were in a private paradise of over five hundred acres, and everything had been set up for them. Namale's was the perfect host for any special event. It was secluded with world class chefs and accommodations. In the three days they'd been there, she'd felt like royalty. She was glad she'd bought a flowing dress for this event as she'd been eating for more than just two at this point. The food was delicious.

When she wasn't eating or exploring paradise, she was in the ten thousand square foot spa that overlooked the Koro Sea. Of course, their second night there, Steve had talked her into dancing all night along with the rest of their friends who truly had become family. Watching Smoke out on the dance floor was quite impressive.

Erin smiled when she thought about Katherine's neurologist Joseph had insisted come on this trip with them. The woman was absolutely drop-dead gorgeous. Erin had gotten to know her the past few days, and from the looks Smoke was sending the woman, she saw a romance blooming, not that Amira seemed to be looking at Smoke the same way — at least not when he was looking at her. Erin had seen a few hooded glances from the top-notch doctor.

She pouted a little as she looked at her image in the mirror. How did some women get blessed with all of the genes? Amira Ito was thirty years old with the naturally deeply tanned skin of a twenty-one-year-old. Her light brown complexion and incredible aquamarine eyes were enough to knock any man to his knees. And on top of that, she stood five foot, ten inches tall with sleek, toned legs that begged men to drop to their knees and worship at them.

Not only did Amira have the looks, but she was also a neurologist in such high demand she was hunted by hospitals all around the world. She'd only agreed to come with Joseph because she was speaking at a conference later that week about several of her cases. She kept up on all international studies and traveled the world. The man who captured her had better know what he was getting into, or she'd easily slip away.

Even with her charm, beauty, sophistication, and intelligence, Erin saw a shadow in Amira's eyes. They were becoming friends, so Erin was determined to find out what could possibly cause any distress in this woman's life. She knew everyone had a story, and it wasn't right to judge someone else for theirs.

"Are you ready?" a sweet voice asked from her doorway.

Erin turned to find Buck Melville standing there. He'd been her favorite customer at her diner and after years and years of him sitting with her between midnight and two in the morning, he'd become like a grandfather to her. With them both suffering great losses, they'd embraced one another.

"I don't know why I'm so nervous," she said with a laugh. "We're already married." She let out a little giggle. He moved closer, tears in his eyes.

"You're nervous because you said vows in a Vegas chapel, and while it mattered, this is before your friends and family and vowed to God," he told her. He clasped her hand in his wrinkled one, a lot of strength still left in his fingers. "And I've never been so pleased in my life as when you asked me to do the honor of walking with you."

"You were the only one I wanted to do it," she said as she stood, a tear running down her cheek. She embraced Mr. Melville. He'd insisted she call him by his first name, but she'd been taught respect long ago by her grandparents, and she respected this man as much as she had them.

"It's so beautiful here. I couldn't have chosen a better place," she said as she stepped up. He pulled out an old-fashioned hanky and handed it over.

"I agree with you there," he said as he laughed. "The private jet to get here wasn't too shabby either. I sure enjoy Joseph. He makes this old man laugh so much. I didn't think that was possible after losing my Martha. But I know beyond a shadow of a doubt, she's looking down and laughing with me. We promised each other we'd live our lives if the good Lord decided it was time for one of us to come home a little early. But we'll be together soon. I have no doubt about that."

"I don't doubt it either. That's why I left chairs open for my grandparents and your wife. I want all three of them with us," Erin said.

This time it was Mr. Melville who had a tear fall down his cheek. He turned as he swiped it away. "Now, none of that, little missy. Today is a beautiful, happy day. We aren't going to sit here shedding tears."

"Okay, I can agree to that. I love having my wedding at sunset. There's nothing about this day I don't love," she said.

"I agree."

The two of them stepped from her bungalow, and then walked to the lit path leading to the gazebo overlooking the peaceful ocean. They moved up the path with the ocean breeze gently rustling her cascading hair, while jeweled clips attempted to tame it. The tropical sun shone down on their faces as it fell from the sky in slow motion. She felt the air and sun, but she only had eyes for the man at the end of the aisle, looking so devastatingly handsome in his white island shirt and tan khaki pants. His bare feet made her smile. She held her foot up, wiggled her toes at him, and he laughed.

They had been doing things to please each other from the first moment they'd met. Steve absolutely felt naked going anywhere without shoes, but she'd asked him to keep this beautiful and casual and he hadn't hesitated. She knew there truly was nothing he wouldn't do for her, just as there was nothing she wouldn't do for him.

Their friends and family stood as she walked to her husband's side, and then they sat on the decorated chairs beneath a canopy of tropical flowers and greenery that she'd take the time to focus on when she looked back at the pictures. As they stood, it was hard to see anything other than her husband while they recited their vows for a second time, confirming their love.

His kiss at the end stole her breath just as it did every time she was in his arms, and then he led her down the aisle to the cheer of their loved ones.

They spent the night dancing beneath the stars that shined so much brighter in this paradise of low light, no city smog, and a cloudless sky. The incredible place truly was a pristine natural landscape that made a perfect backdrop and added a whole lot of magic to an already magical event.

They ate great food, including Macadamia nut crusted walu, coconut rice, and grilled sesame prawns. She blamed the baby for the extra appetite, but she could've just as easily blamed her love hormones. She was so happy, so in love, and so hormonal, she was sure her metabolism was running at a thousand percent.

Their cake from the resort's chefs and had three tiers with flowers and greenery from the island running over the sides like waterfalls. It was absolutely stunning and tasted even better than it looked.

The night was perfect in every way from the moment it began. But it became really interesting when it was time for the bouquet toss.

"Okay, all of the single ladies line up," Erin called. Only a few stood in front of her. She laughed. "Let me rephrase that. All of the ladies who *aren't* married, you *must* stand out front," she insisted.

Several of the women reluctantly took their place at the end of the pier as she turned her back to them. She looked over her shoulder straight at Erin's mother and sent her a wink. Bobbie's eyes widened before she sent a glare over to her daughter who sent an air kiss her way. Then Bobbie gave a warning glance at Erin who laughed. Bobbie sank to the back of the group of women and folded her arms across her chest.

Erin faced forward and brought her arms way down, wanting to toss the bouquet straight into Bobbie's arms as she'd promised Avery she'd try to do. They all wanted to attend Bobbie's wedding to

Mr. Sherman Armstrong. And the sooner the better. Avery had insisted that her mother had never been so happy, and she wanted to make sure she stayed that way for the rest of her life.

The bouquet went flying into the air, and Erin turned around as Steve moved to her side and wrapped his arm around her.

"Who will the lucky lady be?" he whispered in her ear, sending a shudder through her. It didn't matter how much they touched, how much they made love, and how much time they had together, it was never enough.

"I'm aiming for Avery's mother," she said. The bouquet seemed to hover in the air. But it didn't land where it was supposed to. It smacked right into the middle of Dr. Amira Ito's chest. Her eyes opened in horror as the bouquet hit her. But instead of trying to grab hold of it, she took a couple of steps back as if she was trying to escape the stunning bouquet.

And then her foot hit air and she fell off the end of the pier. Gasps sounded from the party as everyone . . . well, nearly everyone, stood stock-still, trying to figure out what had just happened.

There was a flash of motion, so quick they nearly missed it, and Tyrell dove into the water after the good doctor, who'd surfaced from below and was sputtering water. Smoke wrapped his arms around her and held on tight while she pushed the water she'd sucked into her open lungs back out. He patted her back, then slowly swam around the dock and straight to the shore, where he cradled her in his arms.

"Hmm, maybe the bouquet went where it was meant to after all," Avery said as she moved up next to Erin.

"I was thinking the same thing," Erin said. There'd been a lot of flirting the past few days, but Tyrell's absolute calm and need to save the doctor spoke of more than just lust.

"I saw what you were trying to do, little missy, and look at that, because of your shenanigans, the good doctor got doused," Bobbie said. Avery and Erin both laughed.

"I think it worked out for the doctor," Avery said. "It seems as if Tyrell's about to give her some mouth to mouth at any minute."

They all turned to watch Tyrell's head lower. They were nearly kissing when a voice rang out from above.

"You go, boy," Eyes called out.

Amira whipped her head around, her eyes widening in horror when she realized the entire wedding party was staring down at her and Smoke. Then she looked down and began scrambling away from Tyrell.

When she was up, Tyrell stood then glared daggers at Eyes, who laughed heartily. "Better luck next time," he called. Tyrell moved in a flash and now it was Eyes's turn to move. He took off running — and there was no chance of him getting away. No one moved as fast as Tyrell. That's why his nickname was Smoke.

He was up on the dock in seconds, and then Eyes went in the water. This time there was no one to save him . . . or was there? A woman none of them had seen there before stepped out onto the docks. How she'd gained access no one knew. She bent over the dock and laughed as she looked down at the man who was grinning as he pulled himself from the water.

"Totally worth it," he said, and then he stopped on the rungs of the ladder.

"Hello, Eyes, are you ready to finish our interview?" she asked, confidence and humor radiating off of her.

"I brought her here. When she said she'd been trying to get Jon to do a follow up interview with her for weeks now, I knew this was the perfect place to get her story," Erin heard Joseph say to the group around him.

Hmm, maybe there'd be more than a few weddings in the near future. From the sparks flying all over the place, it was a definite possibility.

CHAPTER TWENTY-TWO

Eyes didn't hear the murmurs scattering around the group of friends, and some he called family, when he stood on the rungs of the dock looking up at Courtney Tucker, a woman he hadn't seen in a few years.

She'd been attractive back then, a woman he definitely would've bedded in a heartbeat, but now, now Eyes had to catch his breath at how radiant she was. She'd become a full-blown temptress of a woman in a few short years, passing the phase between young adult and adult, obviously now understanding who she was. Confidence, humor, knowledge, and hunger for a story rested in her eyes — maybe even hunger for more.

"Get out of the water, you old bastard," Sleep yelled out, causing the crowd to laugh, which broke the spell Eyes was under. He swore he was going to make his friend take a long walk off a short pier for ruining the moment he'd been having with the incredibly mesmerizing reporter. Eyes normally hated reporters, but all he felt at that moment was pure lust.

He composed himself, smiled up at Courtney, and shook his head in disbelief at the craziness of the moment as he climbed the last few steps onto the pier.

"What are you doing here? How did you know I was here? Did you really want the interview that bad?" Eyes questioned rapidly.

"Let me see if this answers your questions before you ask more. I reached out to you multiple times, and even saw that you opened my emails — yes, I can see that — but you never replied. I sent another one two weeks ago, which wasn't opened. In the interim I found Carl's information and was able to not only get an email reply, but we also had a lovely phone call. He said he didn't have a phone number for you, but he knew where you'd be this week. Carl then took my information and told me to hold tight."

Eyes was going to kill Sleep. He didn't mind the reporter being there, but his buddy could've given him some warning. Then again, Eyes wouldn't have warned Sleep if the roles were reversed. Before he could say a word, Courtney kept talking.

"The next thing I know, I get a call from *the* one and only Joseph Anderson, telling me to pack a bag for Fiji because you'd be trapped here, and I'd finally get my interview. Do you know how many reporters dream of speaking to Joseph Anderson?" She gasped. "There was no way I was turning down this trip. Not only do I have you cornered, but he's agreed to a one-on-one as well. I might as well just place my Pulitzers on the wall now." She was giddy with joy.

"Yes, of course, who could turn down a twofer" Eyes asked with a slight laugh. Her pleasure was quite contagious.

"Exactly!" she gasped. "I barely had time to pack before I was picked up and driven to the airport. He bought me first class. I've never ridden in first class, and let me tell you, I've literally flown all around the world, and it sucks in the back of a plane for fifteen straight hours. I'd do it over and over again for a great interview though. I landed about two hours ago and I arrived here just in time to see you get chased around and thrown into the ocean," Courtney finished.

Laughter cut through the air and Eyes was damn glad Joseph had interfered. He was worried, but also quite pleased. He looked up and found their entire group staring at him and Courtney, and he sighed.

"Okay everybody, let's get back to the festivities and forget all the madness that just happened," Eyes said, waving his arm for everyone to move along.

Eyes had one goal at that moment, and it was to get the sexy Courtney Tucker to a private nook on the island and see if her lips tasted as good as they looked. If he thought that was going to happen he was sadly mistaken.

As soon as he spoke, his group surged around them, even a very soaked Amira, wanting to introduce themselves and welcome the newest member to their wedding party. If she was a reporter who was set on getting to her subject, they liked her immediately.

After dozens of questions were flung Courtney's way, she laughed heartily, the sound drifting over

Eyes like a warm tropical breeze. "Hold on, guys," she said through her giggles. "I'm a reporter and I'm used to doing the questioning, so if you want to ask things you'll have to slow it down and give me time to answer," she said.

The woman was wholly comfortable in this loud, large group. There was no shyness, no intimidation. Courtney was a woman who was comfortable in her own skin, and she obviously liked the group she was surrounded by. Eyes was impressed.

Eyes gave up trying to drag her away and made his way to the men. They were simply trying to keep up with the women in their lives.

He looked at Chad and Joseph. "Men, I have a plan, but I need to know how you want to handle this. I think it would be okay, but since you're the leaders of this group I'm asking for permission," he said while keeping his focus downrange at the beauty amassed on the pier.

"Let's hear it," Joseph said.

"When we started this, it was under the umbrella of family taking care of family and in that family taking care of community. Correct?" Eyes asked.

"Correct." Joseph looked over at the team leader, wondering where he was going with his question.

"With that, we're about to enter a new stage of this mission. There are still some drug leaders out there we're going to get, but there's a new world that hasn't been discussed yet, and one that I, nor any of these men, can take care of."

No one said anything, letting him continue with his thought process.

"My thought is to have the women take over bringing the sword to the neck of the dragon. Look at what we have in front of us. We have Courtney, a journalist who, as we know, we need to help control the media aspect. We have Avery, a lawyer who can handle a courtroom better that just about anyone on earth. We have Erin, a marketing guru who can work with the journalist in breaking this into a multi-media campaign. We have Mallory, the senator's assistant, or previous assistant now, who just so happens to work with the FBI, and will be able to give us more information than we know what to do with, and then we have Amira," Eyes stopped mid-sentence, looked down the line at Smoke, gave his goofball smile, and winked at his friend.

Smoke took his shirt off, wrung out the few remaining drops of water and said, "Keep going and I'll take you out to the deep end of the pool and see how far down I can push you."

All the men gave similar huffs of laughter.

"Anyway, before I was so rudely interrupted, I think they could make a formidable team that can help bring this all to a perfect ending," Eyes said.

Chad seemed shocked but intrigued by the idea. Staying secret wasn't so easy to do when they were all dropping like flies, falling in love. Wasn't it better to include the women and have no secrets? They weren't doing anything illegal and were actually cleaning up the city. They weren't using lethal force or bending laws — not exactly. They might enter some grey territory, but they were doing nothing that would get any of them thrown in jail. He'd love to have Bree on the team. She was brilliant.

"I like it," Chad said in only a few seconds.

"Eyes, your plan is excellent. I know your nickname is based on your last name but your ability to see things and put them together is amazing," Joseph said proudly. "And I see a great amount of strength in the women of this group, and in my granddaughter, who's dying to help."

"Thank you, sir, but it doesn't take much to see how perfect these women are," Eyes replied.

Heads nodded in unison and understanding. Before them were some beautiful women for sure, but even more important were how intelligent each of them was and how they used that intelligence to enhance their natural talents.

The men couldn't stand it any longer. Led by Joseph, they walked straight to the women they couldn't seem to function without.

Eyes walked up to Courtney, feeling a pull in his gut as her stunning eyes focused on him.

"Ready for your interview, big man?" she asked as she trailed a fingernail down his arm.

He laughed as he snaked that arm around her and pulled her tight. Her eyes widened for a moment as an electric current passed between the two of them, but she quickly composed herself.

"We'll interview tomorrow since you've come so far for your story. Tonight, we celebrate the wedding of good friends, we eat too much, and we drink way, way too much," he said. "Then maybe we sneak off somewhere and see what this electricity is all about."

He was trying to shock her, to see what she was made of, to see if she was a woman who wanted some mutual fun. Her confidence told him she was. But if he was himself from the start he didn't have to try to backtrack or give her the illusion they were going into anything other than a fun affair.

"Hmm, I'm definitely up for the party and lots of drinking. I like this crowd. As for you . . ." She paused as she pulled back and looked at him from head to toe before she winked. "I'm still deciding. Let's see how much you impress me, then maybe, just maybe I'll give you a little taste."

Eyes's mouth was left hanging open as she walked away from him, her round ass swaying in her short shorts as she moved to the open bar and ordered a Sex on the Beach. The damn bartender drooled as much as Eyes as she gave him her order with a husky voice that was every man's wet dream come to life.

Every hunter instinct in him wanted to stake his claim, but he wasn't going to make it that easy on her. He took his time walking to the bar and arrived just as she was handed her drink, one Eyes was sure had a few extra garnishments on it. She licked the rim of the glass before wrapping her lips around the straw and slowly sucking, making his shorts painfully tight. He was never more grateful for a stretched out wet shirt that was hiding what she was doing to him.

"Mmm," she purred. "Don't you just love a good Sex on the Beach?" The little minx batted her long, thick eyelashes at him, and he was close to throwing her over his shoulder and showing her how good real sex on the beach could be.

Eyes didn't get a chance to say a single word before she sauntered away. The party kept going, and no matter how he told himself to stop chasing her, he was a goner from the time she'd arrived. He was her damn puppet.

Once Joseph and the rest of the parental crowd went to bed, the party turned up about ten notches with music blaring, drinks continuously flowing, and laughter ringing out loud and clear. The team was hopeful, full of joy, and celebrating with the people they respected and liked the most in this world.

"Brothers! Listen to me," Eyes called out over the music that was possibly a hundred decibels too loud. He'd never admit it, but he was far past buzzed, something he never allowed himself when he was team leader and needed to be on constant alert. But they were on an island, had a crapload of security, and he knew how to sober himself quickly. If he was needed, he'd come back strong. For once he wanted to let go.

"I'm so thankful for all of you. Carl and Steve, I know I've said it before, but congratulations on finding women who could put up with your ugly butts."

"I love Steve's butt!" a woman's voice yelled out, laughs following the exclamation.

"Me too!" a man's voice replied, everyone knowing it was Sleep. He couldn't help himself, more laughs followed.

Eyes put up his hand asking for the crowd to listen. "I know I might be a bit tipsy, but I just want to say — I love you all." He then bowed, lost his balance for a step, fell forward, rolled, popped back up with his beer still in his hand, raised it, and started chugging.

Cheers went up in the air, drinks spilled from containers as they shot up faster than the cheers, and everyone gave hugs. The music became mesmerizing, drinks were passed around, dancing started, at first as a crowd but soon pairs parted off, sweat started to bead on foreheads, everyone felt the atmosphere and continued. Even the pregnant women, who were as sober as a summer day was long, kept cheering and dancing. Each song that brought back memories of youthful dancing was cheered and danced to.

At some point a slow song came on and the two pairs who weren't couples didn't hesitate joining together, and dancing along with everyone else. The cool sand was welcomed relief under hot feet.

Smoke and Amira looked as if they should be on the cover of every magazine gracing supermarket shelves. Their bodies were like Greek gods, making them seem more suitable on a Hollywood set than in the middle of nowhere. They were both laughing — heads back, mouths open, laughing.

The sexual energy between Eyes and Courtney was almost a living, breathing thing that made other couples around them hot and bothered. Eyes felt good, very good, and enjoyed the touch of this particular woman. He took control of her arms and placed them over his shoulders as he leaned into her neck. She obliged, but didn't pull him in closer like he wanted her to. She was having a hell of a time teasing him, and he was so entranced, he was letting her.

"Courtney Tucker," Eyes whispered.

"Jon Eisenhart," Courtney replied with a sexy smile.

They swayed together for a moment before Eyes stepped back, took one of her hands and twirled her around and then beneath his arm. When she came back around, he stopped, her back to his chest, his arms around her chest. The passion was so intense Eyes felt as if he couldn't breathe. Was this too much for him to enter an affair with her? Was he playing with fire? He'd desired women before, but never to this intensity.

Some franticly paced song stopped the sweet, romantic dancing as everyone instantly went back to hugging and laughing and kicking sand in a wild array of rhythmic movements. It was late enough to know it was late, but too early for anyone to feel like they needed to be in bed. The group had gotten two people smaller, but it wasn't noticed at first . . . then another duo disappeared . . . and then another. Soon there were only four people standing together. Smoke and Amira, and Eyes and Courtney. They turned the music down and started talking.

The music played in the background as they collapsed at a card table. Snacks were placed before them and they attempted to play some poker in their inebriated minds. They laughed more, talked a lot, and made it another hour before Amira's eyes began closing.

Smoke offered to walk her to her cabana.

That left Eyes alone with Courtney for the first time since she'd leaned over that pier looking at him with her mesmerizing eyes.

"One for the road?" Courtney asked Eyes as she rose, indicating she was going back to her sleeping quarters . . . alone.

"Let's do it," Eyes said, meaning more than one thing in that statement.

She leaned down and Eyes's body throbbed in anticipation. She whispered her lips across his so lightly he wondered if they'd touched at all. Then she stepped back.

"Not gonna happen, but thanks for the offer. Let's see if you impress me more tomorrow."

Eyes was so stunned by her words, he sat there as she walked away, a beer in her hand, her sweet ass swaying, and her laughter ringing back at him. He didn't turn until long after she'd disappeared.

And Eyes realized one thing in that moment. He didn't care how long it took, didn't care how much effort he had to put into it. That woman was going to be his.

CHAPTER TWENTY-THREE

Mallory leaned back in Hendrick's arms as gentle waves lapped the ocean shore, sliding over their toes, the warm water almost as soothing as the feel of Hendrick's arms around her. Sitting in paradise gave Mallory the illusion that the real world didn't exist.

"I don't ever want to leave here. I know when we get back to Washington there's going to be all sorts of BS raining down on us," Mallory told him.

"I know what you mean. Joseph insisted on a real wedding for Steve and Erin, and it really worked out for all of us. We need to refresh sometimes to do our jobs effectively. If a person is going to get a cleansing, a tropical island with no interruptions is the way to do it," Hendrick said.

"Well . . . there *have* been a few fun interruptions," she pointed out.

Hendrick laughed. "Damn, it was amazing watching Smoke dive in after the beautiful doctor who seems to have him all tongue-tied. And the fact that Joseph brought in the reporter who's chasing Eyes for a story makes me want a large bowl of popcorn so I can sit back and watch the show."

"Your names all fit you," Mallory said with a laugh. "Eyes certainly sees all except for cupid's arrow heading straight for him, and Smoke is the fastest man I've ever seen. For someone so large, that's crazy. Sleep is so relaxed and in love, and Brackish, well, Brackish I don't fully understand, but I'm sure there's a story there." She paused. "But why are you Green?"

Green laughed. "Because I've always been the youngest of the group, so they decided to call me Green as if I was a newbie," he said. "You've never shared your name. What is it?"

Mallory laughed. "I don't want to say," she said.

"Come on, you have mine. It's time you share," he said.

Mallory knew she was going to tell him, but she was a bit shy about talking about something so inane it didn't matter. How had this man made her lose all of her sense?

"Come on, Mallory, let it spill," he said.

She finally said it in a whisper. "I-Nee."

She watched as his brow furled as he ran the name through his head trying to figure out why in the world she'd be called I-Nee.

Finally, he smiled. "Ah, it's a play off the word hinny because your ass is so damn fine."

She grinned as she gave his great butt a squeeze.

"Hmm, you know what they say about flattery," she told him with a giggle. "But, no, I wish it was about my butt. The reality is I'm a book nerd – always have been, and always will be. So, my team found me reading a Harry Potter book when I was on the ship and began calling me Hermione. Eventually, it got simplified down to I-Nee."

Mallory had done so much in her short life from diving below the sea in a naval submarine to going through the extensive and often grueling training with the FBI, and the name she'd hold the rest of her life was I-Nee, a character from a book. On the good side, Hermione was one kickass character, her favorite of all time.

"I like it," he told her. "It's very fitting, and quite adorable, just as you are." Green paused and said in his nerdiest voice possible, "You've most certainly cast a spell over me. I knew you were secretly a witch." He gave her a wink.

"Okay, enough of my name. What do you think will happen with the senator? Will she get out of this mess she's in?" Mallory asked.

Hendrick seemed to be thinking hard on it. "There's always a chance of that happening. It amazes me when I see true criminals escaping the law because of technicalities. It makes me question our justice system."

"There are times I want to go back to the Wild West days. When you caught a man doing something wrong, he was tried right then and there and punished. It seems the more power people are given the more they abuse it. Why can't we all live by the same moral code?"

Hendrick laughed. "That's a really tough one because we all have different moral codes," he said.

"There are some things that should be basic. We don't lie, cheat, or break the law," she said.

"But whose law are we following?" he pointed out. "And if your child is hungry and you don't have bread, would you steal a loaf? Not everything is black and white. It took me a long time to figure that out."

"If people all lived by a decent moral code a child would never be hungry," Mallory said.

Hendrick hugged her tighter to him as he kissed the back of her neck. "I wish I had the answer you need to hear, but I think the more people try to impose their own vision on the rest of society the more they stray. If everyone simply lived their lives without judgement and fear the world would be a better place."

"I don't care what someone does in their own home. I just don't want them telling me what I can do in mine. How does anyone justify telling me how to live my life so it meets their vision?" Mallory asked.

"A lot of those people trying to tell you how to live truly believe they are helping. It's actually why I don't love cities. In the country where people aren't stacked on top of one another, they live freer with less stress and they live their own lives without the need to preach to others on how to live theirs. Maybe someday the world will take notice and go back to a simpler time."

"We can always dream," Mallory told him. Then she smiled big. "Didn't you tell me what seems like centuries ago to remind you to tell me the story of something on your ship?"

He laughed. She loved his laughter.

"Yes, I did. I forgot all about that," he said.

"Well, I didn't. Tell me."

"It was brilliant and painful afterward," he said.

"Go ahead then," she said.

"As you already know, shellback initiation dates back at least four hundred years in western seafaring. The ceremony entails a mariner's transformation from a slimy pollywog — to the layman, a seaman who hasn't crossed the equator — into a trusty shellback," he began.

"And once they're a trusty shellback they are also a son or daughter of Neptune," Mallory said. "It's a time-honored tradition for sailors to be tested for their seaworthiness."

"Ah, you might know a thing or two," he said with a laugh.

"I was *very* competitive during my time in the Navy. I know a lot," she said with a laugh.

"I think your competitive spirit is a huge turn-on," he said before kissing her neck long enough to fry her brain. She pulled away, feeling slightly dazed.

"Don't distract me. I want to hear the story," she said.

"Well, the day before we crossed the equator, my master chief told me I was to fall in with line with the rest of the puke polywogs and go through the entirety of the initiation process. As you know, a SEAL team would never allow non-SEALs to breach our ranks, especially with any type of hazing coming from someone who wasn't a SEAL. I knew better than to argue it, and also knew he'd already made his decision known to the rest of the team — so they didn't try to break any necks when they saw someone treating me like gum on the bottom of a shoe. So, that day, as you know, was the chance for all of us pollywogs to get some preemptive payback for the pain we were about to receive."

"Yep, the pollywog revolt. Most aren't brave enough to do much, knowing the punishment the next day will be too much to make it worth it," Mallory said.

"Yeah, I knew if I was going to be in it, I was going to dive in all the way. My mindset was that I made it through way worse training than anything these guys could throw at me, so I went all in," Green said with a laugh.

"But I bet you were pretty creative," she said.

"Yep. I joined about thirty other sailors standing at attention who were getting their orders for the day. The boatswain's chief petty officer told us we had a free day to revolt. But he also warned us of the payback coming the next day. He said it was our lives to gamble with. He also told us any revolt would have consequences."

"He can't tell you that you can't revolt," Mallory said, horrified.

"Nope, but he could scare the living hell out of all of them. I just laughed to myself. He stood six four and was well over two hundred pounds of solid muscle. No one dared mess with him — at least up until that point. I figured he didn't have much experience with guys like me."

"You messed with your boatswain's chief petty officer?" She gasped. The story was getting good.

"Ah, the good old days," Green said as he leaned back and looked at the stars. "After quarters I got with a couple of the shipmates and told him we had to get the sonofabitch. Out of six or seven guys I talked to, only one stepped up to the plate. His name was Ty. He wasn't too confident the plan would work but he had a fighter's spirit, and a few screws loose, and I liked it. Actually, him and I became pretty good friends after that day"

"Yeah, I can see why," Mallory said with smirk in her voice.

"I told him to go to engineering berthing and grab three or four feather pillows, cut them open, and dump the feathers into a bag. I headed to the mess-deck to steal a five-gallon bucket of maple syrup."

"You didn't?" Mallory gasped. "No way did you pull that off."

She could feel Green's smile grow wide. "That's pretty much what Ty said. He looked completely dumbfounded and asked if we were going to tar and feather the chief. I told him we were going to make him look like Big Bird."

Mallory was laughing so hard Green had to stop for a minute. He waited. "Please tell me you have a picture," she demanded.

"Let me finish the story," he said.

She was still giggling, but she zipped her lips and waited.

"I made it to the mess-deck and grabbed the five-gallon bucket, then had the cook tight on my ass as I ran through the ship. The only thought on my brain at that point was about how much damn trouble I was about to get into, but I'd come too far to turn back, so I ran forward. It was a good thing I was fast."

"Did you get away from the cook?" she asked.

"Yep, I reached the starboard weather deck, and Ty was there. We didn't give ourselves time to think. I ran up to the chief with a big smile on my face. He looked down and asked what I had in the bucket. I simply said, *you want to see what I have,* and then I emptied the entire bucket of syrup all over him. He was so dumbfounded, he didn't move. I quickly stepped back, and Ty rushed forward, opening his bag and letting the wind do the work. Man, you should've seen the number of feathers flying. And at least half the bag stuck to the chief."

"Holy cow," Mallory gasped.

"Yep, he did look a lot like Big Bird. I'm telling you, the man was huge," Green said.

"What did he do?" Mallory gasped.

"Well, nothing that day. He couldn't," Green said. "But before we ran away, I saw the light in his eyes and knew payback would be hell. I didn't care. It was well worth it," Green told her.

"I bet. You had to be celebrities on the ship after that."

"Hell yes, we were. I'm sure I'm still a legend . . . no, I know I am," Green said as he puffed out his chest.

"What happened on initiation day?" she said.

His grin fell. "Well, it was pure hell, but I took it like a man. My day began as I was rolled out of bed at 0400 hours by the chief himself. He took me down so hard I came up fighting, punching at the presence in front of me. It could have been ten men; I wasn't going to stop until I heard my master chief's voice tell me to stand down. The two of them had woken me from a dead sleep, what did they expect? As soon as I heard him, I came to attention."

"And then the pain began?" she asked.

"Yep, the berthing was a madhouse. All of us pollywogs had to dress inside out and backward, line up on our hands and knees, and crawl through a line of men who slapped the crap out of us with firehoses. The chief himself had a special hose for Ty and me, and I think my ass was red for a week."

"Still worth it?" Mallory asked.

"One thousand percent worth it," he said with a grin. "We crawled through gunk and were fed slop I wouldn't give an animal, though they'd probably like it since they think deer poop is gourmet dining."

"True," she said.

"Ty and I were put through a few more rounds than the others, but at the end of the day we were officially shellbacks, and the punishment was well worth the revolt."

"Was that the end of it?" Mallory asked.

"Yep, that was the end. After that the chief and I were friendly. It's easy to think everyone respects anyone who went through SEAL training but, I think, he had some respect for me as a person, which meant quite a bit to me back then. As a matter of fact, I even went on a date with his daughter."

"Oh really?" She raised her brow.

"Yeah, but I was nineteen and she was seventeen, so it didn't go anywhere." He pulled her tight to him. "And now I'm here with you and I couldn't be happier."

"Good save," she told him as she turned sideways, one of his legs over her lap, taking the kiss he was offering. He pulled back, a mysterious light in his eyes.

Then Green stood and held out his hand. "Do you want to do something crazy?" he asked, and she felt her belly clench.

"It depends," she said. She found, though, that with this man she wanted to do all sorts of things that were normally out of her comfort zone.

"You just have to agree, and I promise you won't regret it."

She reluctantly gave him her hand and stood. He reached behind her and undid the strap of her bikini, watching it fall to the ground. She immediately covered her breasts as she looked around.

"It's two in the morning and everyone's locked up inside. Let's skinny dip," he said. He stepped back and dropped his shorts, his impressive arousal standing at attention.

Mallory felt a surge of heat and humor at the same time. She only hesitated another brief moment before sliding her fingers into her bikini bottoms and pushing them down her legs. The desire in his eyes was her reward.

"You need some cooling off," she assured him before she held her chest and ran to the water, diving in only a millisecond before Hendrick joined her.

They stopped trying to solve the world's problems as they splashed and played in the water for nearly an hour, doing lots of touching and kissing as they played catch and release.

Finally, Hendrick scooped her up in his arms and swiftly walked back to their blanket where he carefully laid her down and covered her body with his own.

"It seems most of you confirmed bachelors have fallen. Who do you think will go down next?" she asked with a laugh, her arms wrapped around him as they lay beneath the moonlight, water beaded on their skin.

"I don't know, but I do know there's no way I want to talk about any of the men on my team when I'm about to slide inside of you," Hendrick said as he nudged her thighs apart.

"Mmm, good thinking," she said, the laughter ebbing as she looked into his passionate eyes.

He leaned down and kissed her, and then they stopped talking as he showed her again how much passion the two of them shared. This might be the beginning of their journey, but she had no more doubts that they were going to finish the adventure together.

The real world would step back in when they returned to Washington, but this fairy tale she'd found with Hendrick was going to end with a happily ever after, and she was the mermaid princess for the first time in her life.

EPILOGUE

It was the Fourth of July, and Smoke had been serenading his team with Christmas music, making them all moan and groan as they performed security for a large Anderson family gathering. Joseph hadn't been happy with how easily his home had been breached, and Brackish was in heaven revamping the entire system. It was a process that took a lot of time, though, with a place the size of Joseph's estate.

Two weeks had passed since they'd returned from Fiji. Their lives had changed in the past few months, making the days feel like years instead of a short period of time. They'd accomplished so much in their work and personal lives, so it was easy to see how time could stop having any meaning.

Three out of five of their team members had fallen in love, and now, all eyes were on Smoke and Eyes, the last two bachelor's of the group. Though, from the sparks that had flown in Fiji, it didn't appear as if they'd be single much longer.

"Sleigh bells ring, are you listening . . ." Smoke began singing yet another Christmas song. Then the air shifted.

"Hold up," Green said, all humor dropping from his voice. The team was instantly on alert. No one asked questions, no one said a word. They waited. They knew that tone, and they knew the recon had gotten serious . . .

Green put his hand over the team comm system, only speaking to Smoke.

"It's hard to tell right now, but can you confirm what I think I'm seeing?" Green asked.

Smoke quietly lifted his own binoculars and took in the view.

They were up in the hills, staring down at the private beach the entire Anderson family was currently on. The sun was beginning to set, casting a stunning sunset over the water, painting the skies vivid colors of pinks, purples, and blues that seemed to just be for the Andersons. The other members of their team were down there with the family, eating, drinking, and laughing while remaining on alert.

"At the second bend, just before going out of sight, it looks like a boat with a person looking through binoculars at the Anderson party. Look through the trees. It won't show up easily," Green said as Smoke found the location.

Smoke smoothly transitioned his point of focus to the area. The sun was playfully bouncing off the small ripples in the otherwise smooth water that lapped against the shore of Joseph and Katherine's property. The beach had been carefully crafted, sand brought in, and a large oasis for fun-in-the-sun had been built many years ago.

"Yep, I see it. Your young eyes aren't tricking you," Smoke said. "I see the reflection in the binoculars. What has them so interested in the family? Do you think it's reporters?"

"Could be nothing more than tourists wanting to get some pictures of the Andersons, but I don't like it," Green said.

"Are your Spidey senses tingling?" Smoke asked. He was joking, but they were both taking it seriously. Someone studying a family they were protecting was a serious matter.

"Call it in," Smoke said.

"We have a boat coming down the river, hugging the bank approximately nine hundred yards to the beach," Green said to the team. "Binoculars can be seen. We don't know how many are on board."

The Andersons loved the Fourth of July, enjoying their time each year celebrating the freedoms that had allowed them to not only prosper themselves, but to give tens of thousands of people jobs, lifting those employees and contractors up with wages and benefits better than any other company in Seattle and her surrounding cities.

The Andersons also knew the sacrifices that had been made over the hundreds of years their beloved country had been forming and growing. Those sacrifices had allowed them to be in the position they were currently in. That was why they'd created the veterans center and why they gave so much money and time to Wounded Warriors. It was the men and women who answered the call that allowed the Andersons to be in the position they were in. Because of that, the Fourth of July was their second biggest celebration of the year. Katherine's birthday was number one because Joseph insisted none of his success would be worth it or possible without his wife at his side, and her birth deserved to be a national holiday.

"I hope this is nothing. The family has had a great day so far," Green said.

"Yeah, I'm not usually into the family party thing, but I've been a little bummed to miss out on their different events," Smoke told him.

"I know. Did you see the kids' faces at that parade?" Green asked, his eyes never straying from the boat inching closer to the shoreline.

"Yeah, those kids are far outnumbering the adults. They looked like ducks scattering on a pond as people throw bread. I was half expecting them to drop to their knees and start pecking at the candy being thrown from the floats," Smoke said in a deep chuckle.

"I laughed so hard I about peed when Mark Anderson joined in with the kids and came up with two handfuls of candy," Green said.

"He was like a madman, running around while the kids tugged on his shirt and jumped up at him, trying to get his candy," Smoke said.

"Mark is most definitely an overgrown child," Green said.

"Like we aren't?" Smoke asked. "If we were down there, we'd have been grabbing and running, then bribing the kids with the candy."

"Very true," Green said. "Who needs money when you have candy to bargain with?"

"But when that VFW float came into view with men and women in their uniforms — young and old, walking along, their shoulders back, their chins held high — all of the horseplay stopped," Smoke said with respect.

"Yeah, and they were playing the Star-Spangled Banner, not blasting Christmas carols," Green pointed out. "My respect grew deeper for Mark when he stopped, and he and the kids all stood at attention to give respect to the servicemen and women. I was very impressed, looking down the line of the family and seeing them all showing the same respect."

"Jasmine's still my favorite," Smoke said. "When the parade paused right then, she took one of the younger girls, walked to the float, and handed one of the older men a small flag. His face lit up when Jasmine and the younger Anderson thanked him for his service."

"Yep, if I was a softer man I might've teared up over that one," Green said.

"Ha, I'm sure you did," Smoke teased. But there was no doubt they'd both choked a bit at that one.

Green and Smoke had moved positions after the parade and had been watching the Anderson property ever since, while the family played games, barbequed, and set fireworks off amidst music, talking, and laughing a heck of a lot.

They'd just started to settle down to get ready for the fireworks display in the sky when the boat came back into view, making Green and Smoke nervous.

As was the tradition for the past twenty years, except one year when they were utterly rained out, Joseph and Katherine set off the first firework for their family. Then a hired company put on a show that rivaled the shows most towns put on across the country. Outside of Christmas, Joseph spent more on the Fourth than any other holiday.

"Sleep, how's it going down there?" Green asked.

"We have our eyes on the boat. But Joseph's getting ready to speak so we're standing back and watching without upsetting the family," Sleep replied.

"I agree. I don't want to jump the gun," Green said. "But my gut's telling me something's off."

"Mine too. We're watching. Eyes is in position near the water, and Brackish is close to Joseph. I'm in between."

"Sounds good," Green said.

Joseph started talking, and they all remained silent. "My beautiful family and friends, thank you for being here today," Joseph started. He didn't need the microphone, his booming voice easily carrying across the beach. Katherine laughed as he began speaking and stepped back from him so her eardrums wouldn't get rattled. She smiled lovingly up at him from about a dozen yards away. "My lovely Katherine and I are going to light the first firework in just a few minutes, but I wanted to remind us all again why we're here."

"Because we're free to be here," someone called out.

"Exactly!" Joseph said with a proud smile. "We live in the greatest country in the world, and while we celebrate our freedoms, we also appreciate all of our diversity and opportunities. We appreciate the men and women who have served our nation, and we celebrate new beginnings. Happy Fourth of July to all of us. Let's continue to celebrate and appreciate all we have."

There was a round of applause as Joseph stepped aside and began moving toward his wife.

"Eyes, the boat is creeping along the shoreline now. He isn't out for a leisurely float on the river. He's just moved around the bend and is staying way too close to the shore," Green conveyed to the team, the stress in his voice unmistakable.

Eyes was well on his way to the area Green had mentioned, but the urgency in Green's voice got

Sleep and Brackish moving faster to the same area, trying not to cause a scene and startle any of those in attendance.

"A person from the boat exited next to the bank, coming toward the beach," Green informed the team.

Smoke started canvassing the area around the river, looking for any additional contacts, or anything out of the ordinary. The shadows made each flicker of a leaf seem like someone was walking through the woods. He knew not to let his imagination get the best of him but something, other than the person walking through the water, was wrong — he could feel it.

"We need to get everyone out of here," Smoke calmly said.

"Agreed," Green replied.

"Sleep and Brackish, get back to the group and clear them from the beach. I'm getting Joseph," Eyes said sharply. This single message sent the men into motion.

Green hated the thought of being in this position and not having a long gun. Information was good, but not being able to put lead downrange if needed was making Green sick to his stomach.

"Thirty yards," Green informed, sharing how far the contact was from the beach.

Sleep and Brackish were jogging to the large group of people. Eyes was running hard toward Joseph and Katherine. People were starting to notice the commotion. The Anderson sons took note of the energy of the special ops men they'd come to know and knew action was needed. Not waiting for direction, Lucas, Mark, and Alex got up, started gathering their family members, and getting farther away from the beach. Those same sons turned to their parents, wanting to make sure they also moved away from the beach.

"Twenty yards," Green said.

Eyes was now in a full sprint. His hip, injured long ago, was feeling the strain placed on it, but that pain wasn't going to stop him from getting to those he'd promised to protect.

"Eyes! He's armed. Confirmed weapon in his hand," Green called out. The glint of silver and black reflected from the last remaining sunlight.

The sand sucked at Eyes's feet as he hit the beach. He yelled for Joseph and Katherine to get away.

It was too late.

He saw the man bring up his arm and aim directly toward Joseph and Katherine. Eyes's legs churned harder, sand spraying beneath him, no feeling coming through his body, just pushing as hard as he could. He refused to feel anything. His brain worked through scenario after scenario of how to end the threat of violence.

Joseph caught Eyes's movement and noted he was headed toward the water. He turned his head, seeing the silhouette of a man standing in the water only a foot from the beach. What was he holding? Who was this person? Then his brain brought all of the information to instant recognition.

It was the man his wife had dropped all charges against, the man who'd viciously attacked Katherine. Questions started forming in his brain, but he never got a single one out.

The man was pointing his gun at Katherine — he didn't even seem to see Joseph standing there. His eyes were glossy, bloodshot, and wild. The gun shook in his hand. Hell, his entire body seemed to be shaking. His finger was on the trigger.

Then it happened. The moment Joseph recognized the man was going to shoot. The man gave a huge inhale, opened his eyes wide, slammed them back shut, then pulled the trigger.

Joseph screamed as he tackled his wife, shielding her as they flew up in the air, then landed hard on the cool sand. Their eyes locked, speaking volumes without words.

Joseph pushed back from Katherine, looking at her for injuries from head to toe. He touched her head, shoulders, arms, torso, hips, and legs.

"I'm sorry, Darling. I'm so sorry. But there was a man with a gun. He was going to shoot. I had to block you," he said as he continued running his hands over her.

"I'm fine, Joseph, I'm fine," Katherine said.

"I took you down hard," Joseph said. "I'm so sorry. Let me just make sure his bullet didn't reach you. Let me make sure I didn't hurt you," he said, his adrenaline running five hundred percent.

"I'm okay, Joseph. I'm okay," she assured him, grasping his hand and cradling it close. "Please, let's just lie here for a moment. My heart's thundering," she told him.

There were shouts echoing all around them, but the two of them might as well have been in their own little bubble. Joseph would die for his wife. There was no doubt about it. If he caused her any pain, he'd still die a little.

"Stay down," Eyes yelled. "He's coming closer."

Joseph whipped his head around in time to see the shooter trying to get off another shot. Then there was a blur in his peripheral vision. The man turned toward the blur, firing off a shot before he was slammed to the ground.

Joseph watched as Eyes took the man down hard in the water. He held him under for a moment before dragging him back up and pulling him onto the beach where he quickly secured him, his hands tied behind his back as Eyes literally sat on him.

Chaos had erupted all around them as the Andersons circled each other, making sure the kids were safe while trying to get to Joseph and Katherine. Joseph felt weak. He turned as Sleep and Brackish made it to Eyes.

"Get 911 on the line. This guy's seizing. It isn't from anything I did. He stinks to high heaven, a burnt smell; I think he's higher than a kite," Eyes said calmly as he knelt down to assist the man.

"Eyes . . ." Sleep said calmly as he placed his hand on the shoulder of his friend.

"Did you call?" Eyes snapped.

"Eyes . . ." Sleep said again. This time he pulled his brother away from the man, put him into a sitting position, then grabbed Eyes's leg and inspected it, the same leg that Sleep had shot years earlier. It was bleeding.

A few inches above the knee, blood was streaming out of a small hole. No exit wound was found, meaning the bullet was still in his leg. The warmth started slowly, then fire caught life and radiated up through his entire body. He looked over at the man who'd shot him. Brackish was performing CPR on him.

The shooter began choking, a wail coming from his chest. They weren't sure if it was from physical pain or from having just returned from where he was going to spend his eternity after this life — a sneak peek into what awaited him because of his life of crime and misery to others.

"I didn't want to," he said. "I had no choice."

"What do you mean you worthless piece of shit?" Eyes snapped. "You *accidently* shot me?"

The man's eyes rolled back in his head, and then he wasn't going to talk to anyone ever again.

"What in the hell just happened?" Green gasped over the comms.

"I don't know," Eyes said. It was clear he was losing too much blood, and they needed to get him to the hospital.

"This is a clusterfuck, that's what happened," Sleep snarled.

Before they could say more, a woman's scream broke through the air. The men turned to see it was Katherine yelling. Was there another attacker?

"Green, talk to me," Eyes demanded, but he was growing weaker.

"I don't see any other threats," Green said. He was scanning everywhere. "Dammit! He's been hit."

Brackish and Sleep were done wrapping Eyes's leg before they turned and looked where Joseph's family surrounded him. Joseph's head was resting in Katherine's lap and there was a visible trail of blood dripping from his mouth.

The only sound after that was a helicopter in the distance — way too far away.

"Nooooo . . ." Katherine's anguished cry rippled through the air . . .

Printed in Great Britain
by Amazon